A SECRET KISS

"Soph. I want to be with you. Trust me, I know. I've had my whole life to figure it out. Nothing worth having is ever easy. We'll manage."

She moved the tiniest bit closer to him. "I was so mad at you after you kissed me in the kitchen that night. But being mad and not talking to you for weeks, *hurt*. Now I'm glad you kissed me and caused us to fight, and everything else. Otherwise, we wouldn't be here."

"Wasn't easy, but worth it." He tapped his glass against hers.

With a quick glance around, she counted five Chamber members still loitering upstairs and her entire family gone downstairs, where the music had already started.

She faced Wright, and the knowing look in his eyes unfurled a ribbon of heat that tickled her core.

"Come here and let me kiss you," he whispered.

Sophie went to him, eager for the day they could do this whenever and wherever. There would soon be a day when she was able to say, out loud, that she and Wright were together and know, in her heart, that he'd never leave her.

Wright kissed her, soft and seeking, gentle pulls at her lips as he slid his arm around her waist.

They kissed until there was no space between them, heating up until she shivered . . .

Books by Heather McGovern

A MOMENT OF BLISS

A DATE WITH DESIRE

A TASTE OF TEMPTATION

Published by Kensington Publishing Corporation

A Taste of Temptation

Heather McGovern

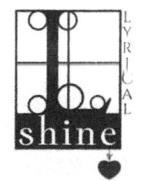

LYRICAL SHINE
Kensington Publishing Corp.
www.kensingtonbooks.com

LYRICAL SHINE BOOKS are published by

Kensington Publishing Corp.
119 West 40th Street
New York, NY 10018

All Kensington titles, imprints, and distributed lines are available at special quantity discounts for bulk purchases for sales promotion, premiums, fund-raising, educational, or institutional use.

Special book excerpts or customized printings can also be created to fit specific needs. For details, write or phone the office of the Kensington Sales Manager: Kensington Publishing Corp., 119 West 40th Street, New York, NY 10018. Attn. Sales Department. Phone: 1-800-221-2647.

Lyrical Shine and Lyrical Shine logo Reg. U.S. Pat. & TM Off.

First Electronic Edition: April 2017
eISBN-13: 978-1-60183-840-7
eISBN-10: 1-60183-840-9

First Print Edition: April 2017
ISBN-13: 978-1-60183-841-4
ISBN-10: 1-60183-841-7

Printed in the United States of America

To You. For reminding me, every day, what true love and forgiveness means.

This book would not be possible without the support and guidance of so many people. Thank you to my family, for their love and understanding. And thank you to my executive committee: Jeanette Grey, Elizabeth Michels, and Laura Trentham. Their friendship, wisdom, and willingness to respond to my random messages with equal or greater randomness make this journey worth taking.

Chapter 1

"What's that smell? Is something on fire?"

Sophie cut her eyes at Devlin. "Do you mind? I'm mid-order here." She needed their bartender's wish list so she could place a call to the vendor tomorrow. Then at least one thing would be off her to-do list. "I don't smell anything."

She went back to leaning on the bar, writing down what Steve wanted. At the end, she added a few extras, just in case.

One could never have enough swizzle sticks.

"You seriously don't smell that?" Her brother got up from his usual spot at a nearby table.

Like her, Dev preferred doing all of his paperwork after hours, in Honeywilde's restaurant. He claimed it was the only time he could work without interruption. Yet here he was, doing a fantastic job of interrupting her.

He walked past the bar, scowling and sniffing as he went.

She and Steve shared a look.

All summer long, Dev had been slightly left of center. Dev lived left of center, but this summer, even more so. In the weeks since he'd met and fallen in love with Anna, he swung back and forth between being completely distracted by love or totally fixated on random things. To the point that nothing could derail him.

Like right now, and his insistence he smelled smoke.

"I'm telling you, something is on fire." Dev headed toward the kitchen.

He'd always had a flair for the dramatic as well, but Sophie eased off her stool to follow him anyway.

Even on her tippy-toes, she could barely see through the swinging doors' small windows into the restaurant's kitchen, but there were no flames or smoke that she could tell. Only Devlin being Devlin.

She rolled her eyes as he pushed open the double doors that led to the back. "You're imagining things. The kitchen is not—Holy shit, the kitchen is on fire!"

Sophie bolted through the doors. She pushed past her brother to find the stove engulfed in smoke and white clouds, Wright standing in the midst of it as he doused the open oven with a fire extinguisher.

Her heart jackhammered against her ribs. She opened her mouth to say his name, fear choking off any sound.

Steve rushed in and skidded to a stop beside her.

"I'm okay." Wright turned toward them, answering her unasked question. "Kitchen is okay. I saw the flames in time." He cursed and sprayed the oven with the fire extinguisher one more time, though it did appear any fire was completely out. "That damn thing catching my oven on fire is all." He jabbed his finger toward the racks of the oven.

Sophie couldn't make out what damn thing he meant because the inside of the oven was all foamy white.

Dev moved closer and glanced inside. "What is it?"

Wright took a step back and slammed the extinguisher down on the prep table. "It *was* a pie. Jesus. About gave me a heart attack."

Him?

Her chest aching, Sophie braced her hands on the other side of the prep table, trying to catch her breath. Her mind hadn't had time to fully comprehend the scene before her. All she knew was Wright and fire, deadly flames, thoughts of him being injured, or worse.

She'd had enough loss for one lifetime. She couldn't handle losing anyone else.

With a steadying breath, she loosened her grip on the table.

Now was not the time or the place to crack up. Wright was fine. A little kitchen mishap.

For almost two months now, they hadn't spoken more than a few words to each other, and even then, only if it was necessary for their jobs. She'd frozen him out, with good reason, but the idea of him getting hurt . . .

No. Just *no.*

"Are you all right?" Dev grabbed Wright's shoulder, looking him over.

There was a time Sophie would've done the same. Without a trace of self-consciousness, she would've put her hands on Wright, reassuring herself he was unharmed, still there for her, unwavering and steady. Her Wright.

But those days were gone.

"I'm fine. Adrenaline kicked in, damn heart is racing and I'm pissed off, but fine."

She managed to make her way to the shelves of glassware, plucked a short tumbler from its spot and, with shaking hands, got water, straight from the tap. Mouth dry, if she spoke now, her shakiness and concern would be obvious.

Wright couldn't know how rattled she was. Their friendship embargo was her choice and her doing. Falling apart in front of him, all because she thought he was hurt, would demolish the walls she'd put up.

Those walls were there to protect her. They had to stay.

But she had to do or say something. Dev had already given her the inquisition about her and Wright not speaking. If she remained silent after a kitchen fire, he'd be all over her again, wanting to know why.

She refilled the glass again. With a nod, she placed it on the prep table, near Wright.

He stared at her as Dev kept talking, but she was not going to make eye contact.

"What were you baking?" Steve asked.

"The goal was bourbon-soaked cherry pie."

Dev clapped him on the back. "Man, if you're soaking shit in bourbon, you might be asking for a few flames."

Before, Sophie would've given Wright hell about causing a fire too—or taken any chance to tease or pick at him, as he would with her. She'd have done so out of reflex and never thought twice.

Now she overthought every interaction, and there'd be no way she could tease him. The loss twisted the empty spot inside her into a knot.

Too much had happened; too many things said between them. Hurtful, angry words that couldn't be taken back. They couldn't return to the role of buddies who joked around, nothing heavy, no real weight, between them.

And instead of saying the sight of his kitchen, thick with smoke, filled her with fear and panic, she said nothing. Her hands on her ribs like her heart might suddenly break through, she simply stood there. Silent.

Wright lightly shoved Dev, muttering a curse. "It wasn't the bourbon. The butter dripped out of the pan and hit the coils. I made one without any issues, so I wasn't hawk-eyeing the second one."

Dev turned to the unsinged pie, cooling on the counter. "I vote you keep trying. I'm willing to be the guinea pig if you need one."

"I'll keep at it. Minus the flambé." Wright glared at the stove, his jaw tight, hands curled into fists.

He was clearly shaken and more than a little angry at himself, no matter how much he joked about flambés. He always joked more when something bothered him, and right now he was rattled.

Whether she was mad at him or not, it was her unofficial job in the family, and at Honeywilde, to soothe raw nerves. If she didn't calm the waters, no one would.

She clicked into operations manager mode. "Dev, Steve? We don't want to use the good kitchen towels to clean up once everything cools. Why don't you grab some of the housekeeping towels in storage downstairs." If she could send Steve and her brother on a task, it'd give Wright a few minutes to bounce back.

"Good idea. You sure you're okay?" Dev checked on his best friend one last time.

"Yeah, man. I'm great. Irritated, but great."

With a laugh and another pat, Dev left, with Steve right behind him.

A moment passed before Wright turned to her, yet didn't meet her gaze. "Thanks for that."

Suddenly, the privacy of the moment was unmistakable. She was alone with Wright, in the kitchen.

A million times they'd been in here, chatting or commiserating, nothing new or unnerving—except for the one time it was.

Lifting her gaze, she studied the top of Wright's bent head.

He was turning the fire extinguisher around, probably berating himself for what he believed was some great failure.

Wright took his work very seriously, and no one was a harsher critic.

"It's a pie. No one got hurt." She pointed out the facts that they both needed to hear.

Wright jerked his chin up, their gazes colliding. "I know. But they could've. I'm a better chef than that. I wasn't paying attention because . . ."

Because of things like what'd happened between them in this very kitchen, over a month ago? Or things like breaking up with his girlfriend immediately after?

"So stupid. I've made dozens of pies."

She hated feeling sympathy for Wright, especially after all that'd happened, but she did.

It wasn't stupid for him to have a lot on his mind after the breakup, and toss in how much his parents probably flipped out about it . . .

Holy wow, they were hard on Wright. She could imagine the hell he caught for not making things work with a girl as perfect as Katherine Hurst.

No, woman. Katherine was not a girl. She probably hadn't been a girl since she was ten years old.

Sophie didn't want to ask. *Shouldn't* ask, but the ugliest part of her—the dark place where she carefully hid her jealousy and resentment, any bitterness or other unattractive feelings—had to know.

"Were you thinking about her?"

"No." His answer came quickly and Wright chuffed, startling her. "I have more important things to worry about besides all that."

More important things?

Wright's breakup with Kate had come fast and hard. Not a friendly parting of ways or even a consolatory "Let's still be friends." Their relationship got nuked in one day, and it'd stunned everyone.

The consensus around town, and the inn, was Kate might be *the one* for Wright. Pretty, sweet, wealthy family to keep his parents happy. Then Wright straight up dumped her.

Some tiny, nonenvious part of her actually felt bad for Kate.

Wright had his flaws, and he'd been a complete asshole to Sophie last month, but her family excluded, he was still ten times better than every other guy she knew—which might not be saying much, now that she thought about it. Most of the guys in Windamere were dicks.

"Kate and I are old news." Wright jerked his gaze away before picking up the extinguisher and placing it back on the wall. "You don't need to worry about me."

"I'm not worried about you." She crossed her arms as she lied.

Of course she was worried about him. She worried about everyone under this roof, but this was Wright.

They'd known each other since the Bradleys adopted her. He was one of her closest friends, and they'd hardly spoken all summer.

But he was so aggravating. And talking to him again jumbled her nerves, tilting her off balance. The silent treatment had sucked, but not talking at all was still easier than this.

Before, they could talk about anything. Dates, guys, girls, sports, food, her brother Dev. Nothing was off-limits and nothing was uncomfortable.

Until Wright went and ruined it all.

During the planning of the Blueberry Festival, when Dev was completely consumed and distracted by all things Anna, and everyone was busy planning, she and Wright had taken a sharp left turn into terrain neither of them could navigate.

Now here they were. Wandering. Lost, and off track. And it was all Wright's fault.

Two months earlier

Sophie swung her feet, her heels bumping the cabinets under the kitchen's side counter. "Matt might win worst date ever. He didn't get my humor, I could tell he wasn't into me, but he still tried to kiss me. *No.*"

Wright hopped up next to her, ready to run color commentary on her ill-fated love life, same as they always did. "This is your third date. He must be a little into you."

"How do you know it's our third date?"

With a pop of his eyebrows, he shrugged. "I . . . I don't know. Probably because you complained about the other two as well."

And there was the tone; the judgment in Wright's voice when it came to her dating life and her awful track record.

He wasn't wrong. She had a long list of failed second dates, and a guy would have to be nuts to want to be with her, but still, Wright could've dialed it back a smidge.

"Matt isn't into me. He's into getting laid. There's a difference."

"Then screw him." Wright bumped his arm against hers. "I mean figuratively, not literally. If he's that big an asshole, you're better off finding that out now."

They sat close enough together that their arms kept bumping, even when Wright didn't do it intentionally. She could easily rest her head on his shoulder, if she considered doing such.

Which was only every other day.

With a heavy sigh, she admitted the truth. "He wanted me to be someone I'm not."

"Why would he want you to be someone else? That doesn't make sense."

She asked herself the very same question all the time, but digging for the answer would be too painful to bear.

"I don't know." She tried playing it off. "I could just tell. He wanted a certain kind of girl, and I'm not it."

"What kind of girl are you?"

The kind no one really wants.

"I don't know." She bristled at his concern. Wright had his own girl. A perfect paragon of charm and sophistication, who probably had sex with him every night without a single hang-up or ounce of neurosis.

Kate was everything she wasn't, but Sophie wasn't jealous. Their happiness gnawed at her insides, but that wasn't jealousy.

"You don't know?" His question dripped with sarcasm.

"Forget I said anything."

"I thought you wanted to talk about it."

"It's just . . . I don't know. I'm burned out. I'm better off alone anyway. I have my family to worry about. That's enough to deal with."

His arm brushed her again. "You're not better off alone. Everybody needs someone."

"I wouldn't mind being alone." Now that her brothers had someones of their own, she might get a little lonely, but she'd survive.

"Hey." Wright leaned in before turning toward her. He waited quietly until she met his gaze. "You won't be alone unless you want to be. You're great. Matt is the one with the problem."

She had no response. Not only because she vehemently disagreed, but because he was so close. Looking at her like he sometimes did, soulful brown eyes, seeing something special in her. She forgot how to speak.

Her brothers loved her, but as far as romantic relationships, she was terminally solo. A few dates followed by long stretches of a singular existence. Her solitude was her choice. It had never bothered her until this year. The rest of her family was moving on, finding love and happiness.

Sometimes she wanted someone in her life. More and more, she found herself longing to be with someone. And that's what scared her.

Being with someone meant letting them in. Too often, letting them in meant losing them.

In the silence, Wright eased closer, putting his arm around her, trying to comfort. "Soph, I mean it. You aren't meant to be alone. Don't say that."

"I'm fine. Probably hormones or something. I don't know."

"Maybe because it's summertime? July fourth isn't so far away."

She turned to him. "How did you—"

"Come on." His gaze was tender, eyes soft with sympathy. "We've lived in the same small town our whole lives. I remember when the accident happened. Everyone remembers."

Her parents' car accident. *Her* accident. Except she was still here, and they were long gone.

"Every year about this time, you're a little off. Not really yourself. It's understandable."

Except this *was* herself. She was always *a little off*. Beneath the managerial efficiency and enthusiasm, she was uncertain and unsure. She might be able to run an inn and wrangle her family, but when it came to handling a personal life, she hadn't a clue.

"I was so little when they died." When she'd loved and lost them. "I don't know why this time of year still messes with me. It's stupid."

He tightened his arm around her, tucking her close. A comforting hold that soothed her ragged nerves. "No, it is not. They were your parents."

She pressed in close, refusing to cry. The anniversary of their death was coming up on twenty-two years. What the hell was wrong with her that this time of year still made her nuts?

Wright's warmth and closeness were both things she desperately needed but would never ask for.

With him, she didn't feel alone.

Theirs wasn't the kind of togetherness she had with her brothers. Never had been. There were times she'd dreamt of them being more than friends. When she was a teenager, again in college, then most recently before he started dating Kate.

Then reality would kick in.

They could never be more than friends. Her family would be shocked, and his family would have a conniption. Toss in that, to Wright, she was first and foremost the Bradley brat sister—romance was never going to happen.

Her consolation was Wright *chose* to be her friend; he didn't have to be. He chose to be with her late at night, fixing the world's problems, and she chose him. It was nice to know that somebody, somewhere liked her for her, and they could be together without fear of everything falling apart.

He rubbed her shoulder, his touch light against the top of her head as he brushed over her hair. "You're going to be okay. You're having a bad run of dates and it's a shit time of year, that's all. And you insist on going out with these losers."

A puff of laughter escaped her, jostling both of them. Didn't he see these losers were the only ones interested?

"Sorry, but it's true. You could do so much better." He kept his arm around her, touching her.

"No, I can't."

"Hey." He leaned away, making her look up. "Yes, you can. I don't want to hear that kind of stuff from you. Got it?"

Then she wouldn't say more. Didn't mean she wasn't still thinking it.

Wright tucked her back against him, his hand warm on her shoulder. "I'll find you someone. I know some decent guys . . . I think. Who aren't your brothers."

As they sat there, Wright trying to think of someone for her to date, the energy between them began to shift.

The change was so slow, so subtle, that she didn't recognize the difference until it was already upon her.

Wright moved his hand to her hair, threading his fingers through the waves to the ends, caressing her back. And she didn't stop him.

His touch was nice. Gentle.

No, it was more than nice. Her skin tingled, warmth spreading from her scalp, down her neck, and over her limbs. She craved touch. *His* touch, and their closeness, even as she knew this wasn't what friends did.

She didn't stop him.

As a matter of fact, her thirteen-year-old self was jumping for joy.

What if?

What if she and Wright could be more than friends?

As foolhardy as the thought was . . . what if?

But Wright had been dating Kate for months now. In Windamere, that was grounds to be called a potential fiancé. The women who Wright dated were always sophisticated, stylish.

Sophie felt more like a girl than a woman. Half tomboy, half spastic kid sister. For god's sake, she had freckles and only owned one pair of heels.

Wright didn't want someone like her. His track record proved it.

She risked a glance up. He was so close, gaze hooded and his face even more handsome than usual.

She wasn't oblivious to Wright's good looks. Since she'd come home from college, she'd been even more aware of how truly attractive Wright was.

Good-natured, even-tempered, always steady Wright. Capable of being as goofy as always, but he'd grown into a man. With a rough baritone voice and more rugged features to match, the lanky boy she once knew was gone.

In the four years she'd been consumed with college, Wright had been consumed with culinary arts—and catching a severe case of hotness.

Yet he was still Wright. Like a brother to her, and her brother's best friend. Thinking of him in any way other than platonic . . . it knotted her up inside.

But not necessarily in a bad way.

A thrill rippled through her body.

He touched her hair again, weaving his fingers through the thick waves. He cupped the back of her head, his palm warm and wide against her skull. Then, so gently she almost missed it, he scratched his nails near the nape of her neck.

A shiver shot across her skin and she bit down on her bottom lip.

She wanted to lean into the contact, let him touch her that way everywhere. Softly drag his nails down her back.

Oh god, she *was* leaning into his touch. Leaning into him.

His hand drifted lower, to the small of her back, as he leaned slightly toward her.

She wanted him to kiss her.

For years, she'd wondered about Wright's kiss. How would it feel? How would he taste?

As he leaned in, she was frozen by her longstanding curiosity, held in place by her desire to have a guy like Wright as her own, but knowing she could never actually have *him*.

Wright brushed his lips against hers, tentative at first. Her pulse thumped, her heart doing back flips within her chest. When she didn't stop his gentle exploration, he covered her mouth with his, and she whimpered.

He was as warm and sweetly solid as she'd dreamed. Her little noise of need spurred him on, and as he deepened the kiss, all she could manage was to hang on.

She opened to him and Wright swept his tongue inside her mouth, brushing against hers. He sucked at her bottom lip before dipping in again, and Sophie was like putty.

Pressed against him, she gave herself over to the kiss.

This was really happening. It wasn't a daydream or something she conjured up. Wright was kissing her.

He touched her face, fingers dancing across her cheek, then down her neck. He brushed past the buttons of her Honeywilde polo and cupped her breast.

Her begrudgingly small breast.

But he moaned against her lips. A greedy, carnal noise of appreciation, and heat coiled between her legs.

Wright wanted her.

He wanted *her*.

Eagerness and need bolted through her, followed quickly by fear. And guilt.

Wright wasn't hers. He was with someone else. He had a girlfriend. A decent girl. And Sophie was the other woman. She was screwing things up; behaving like some kind of home-wrecker.

Her muscles went stiff as she jerked away. "What—What are you doing?"

Wright flinched, taking his hands off her like he'd been burned. In a blur of movement, he was off the counter and on the other side of one of the prep tables. "I don't . . . I wanted to make sure you were okay. I didn't—I didn't mean to do that. I don't know what happened."

"You don't know?"

Wright had a serious girlfriend. He was not that kind of guy, and Sophie wasn't that kind of girl. He was one of the good ones. In her mind, he would *never*.

But he'd kissed her.

Since when did Wright McAdams kiss *her*?

Sophie slid from the counter and followed. "That was . . . what were we *doing*?"

"Nothing." Both of his hands went up. "I wasn't doing anything."

"You were doing something."

His face drained of color, his eyes going wide before he blinked. A lot. "No, I didn't."

A honker of a lie if she'd ever heard one, and her brain zigzagged between excitement and disgust, elation and devastation.

If Wright wanted to kiss her, she couldn't be a total loss. He dated these perfect women and he was pretty close to perfect himself.

Except . . . if he wanted to kiss her, then really, he was far from perfect. Guys with girlfriends didn't kiss other girls. They especially didn't kiss their best friend's little sister.

There was no winning ticket here, no matter how she looked at it. Either he hadn't planned on kissing her and she did it, and she was slowly losing her mind, or he'd kissed her and was destroying the pedestal she'd put him on.

Sophie's stomach dropped. "You kissed me. I know you kissed m—"

"No." Wright gave her a hard look. "I would never kiss you."

"I got the towels." Dev hurried back into the kitchen, dragging Sophie into the present, a knot in her throat from the memory.

Same kitchen, a totally different night, but her friendship with Wright was still in tatters.

She *had* to let go of that night and the look he'd given her. Really, she needed to let go of all of it.

The warmth of his arms, the solid caress of his touch. They'd kissed for maybe a minute, and even that was a stretch, but everything was different now.

"Thanks, Dev." Wright took some towels and headed to the sink.

For weeks and weeks, she'd nurtured the hurt and betrayal, and feeding it had only made the bitterness grow. Since she'd been crystal clear how was furious she was with him, Wright barely spoke to her, leaving a gaping hole where his presence should be.

She didn't like living this way. This version of who they were now, stilted and awkward, withdrawn from each other's lives, hurt as much as him saying he would never kiss her.

The solution was simple. She could stop turning that moment over and over in her mind and try to forget. Rehashing did no one any good anyway.

If she forgot about the kiss, then they might be able to move forward.

She could help him clean up the kitchen, fix the mess from his fire, do her best to keep things casual and light from now on, and maybe things would be okay between them again. Somehow.

The two of them would never be more than friends, but they could at least stop being enemies.

Chapter 2

Wright went to work immediately, grabbing a bunch of towels and filling the mop bucket with water.

He was determined to clean up the lion's share of the mess.

The mess was his making, after all.

Actually, the cherry pie was his making; the mess was a result of him not paying attention to what the hell he was doing. Distracted by his undecided future, confounded by his current situation, and too busy dissecting a silly comment Sophie had made in passing earlier in the day, he was screwing up perfectly good pies and catching shit on fire.

And Sophie hadn't even made the comment to him. She'd said it to Dev.

"Between you and Wright, there's enough scruff to line a coat. We're running a nice place here. Either grow a decent beard or shave. Y'all look homeless."

Dev had shrugged her off, while Sophie's words clung to Wright's brain.

Noticing things about him, and being a smart-ass about it, was something the old Sophie would've done. Months ago. Before that night.

Fair enough—he was getting too scruffy. But shaving had slipped his mind right along with keeping an eye on his pie.

But that wasn't because of the break-up with Kate.

He was in what folks called, "a quandary."

Today, he'd gotten another call from a completely different restaurant group. Since early spring, he'd gotten calls about job opportunities from restaurants as far away as Los Angeles to as close as Asheville. As much as he wanted to do something more, any opportunity he pursued had to be the right one. He wasn't going to leave the Bradleys and Honeywilde for anything less than a dream job.

He lifted the full mop bucket from the sink, and his gaze found the back of Sophie's head, red hair piled high in a sloppy ponytail, slender neck, petite frame, and a big pile of wet towels at her feet.

When he was with Kate, she'd constantly insisted he kiss this place goodbye.

Instead, he'd kissed Sophie.

With a groan, he lowered the rolling bucket to the floor and imagined smacking himself upside the head. He'd kissed Sophie while he had a girlfriend.

What the hell?

A testament to how badly he needed to get on with his life and get out of here. Stop wishing and start doing. Do something for himself that didn't rely on or involve the Bradley family.

He was so interwoven with them, the prospect of life without Bradley support was terrifying. But he had to prove, to himself and everyone else, that he was capable of success without Honeywilde.

Kate knew that, same as his parents, but she pushed and pushed. In the end, it wasn't her insistence and his procrastination that put the nail in their coffin. No, he'd done that all by himself.

By kissing his best friend's sister and unleashing a need that refused to go away.

Wright slapped one of the wet towels on the door of the oven with too much force.

Sophie looked up, her gaze colliding with his. "The fire was an accident. Don't beat yourself up."

Easier said than done. He beat himself up because that's what he did.

He knelt and began wiping the oven as she took the last of the towels from Dev and set them aside. "I think Wright and I can handle the cleanup if you want to turn in."

She walked past him to get the mop from the storage room, and Wright froze mid-wipe, fighting to keep his mouth from gaping open.

Offering to help him, alone, made no sense. Sophie had made sure she was never alone with him for weeks now, and hell would've frozen over before she spoke to him, much less helped him clean up.

Now all of a sudden she was willing to push a mop and be in the kitchen with him?

"You sure?" Even Dev looked suspicious.

The three of them were close enough that the wall of ice she'd put between her and Wright was obvious. Dev had even asked him about it, to which Wright played dumb.

Hell would freeze over *twice* before he confessed to kissing Dev's little sister.

"I think two people can manage," Sophie reassured him.

"All right then." Dev scrubbed a hand through his hair. "I guess I'll call Anna and turn in for the night. No more fires, okay?"

Wright shared a look with his friend, but as soon as Dev left, the reality of him and Sophie, alone, in the kitchen, punched home.

For his entire adult life, Sophie had been there to help. Even when they were kids, she was around, though sometimes far from helpful, but lately . . .

Lately was a major problem.

They hardly spoke at all, and if they did, he couldn't say more than two words to her without recriminating himself.

All because of one stupid mistake.

A huge mistake that was his fault, like with this damn cherry pie.

He took his frustration out on the side of the oven, scrubbing and rinsing, anger-cleaning, fighting the memory of the night he'd been dumb enough to kiss Sophie.

Yes, he'd kissed her that night. No, he hadn't owned up to it.

In chivalrous male fashion, he'd freaked out and tried to act like nothing happened.

He had no business making a move on Sophie. She wasn't just his best friend's sister, she was *his* friend. She trusted him, and though they sometimes flirted, they weren't like that.

Not to mention he was dating someone at the time. He wasn't that guy. The guy who messed around on the side. He *hated* that guy.

But Sophie felt so good in his arms.

Kissing her was spectacular. More amazing than he could've imagined—and damn his soul, he'd allowed himself to imagine it a few times—but he always hated himself after.

That night, he couldn't have gotten away from her any faster if his ass was on fire.

He'd bolted from the spot next to her on the counter, running from a five-foot-two-inch woman like she was a copperhead snake.

Whether he was scared of her or scared of himself for what he'd done, he couldn't figure out. She'd hopped off the counter and come after him. So like Sophie to chase down a problem and try to make it right.

Gaze sharp, her delicate features hard.

"I would never kiss you."

The truth was he swore he never would, not that he didn't want to.

"Are you trying to act like you weren't just kissing me?" She'd been right on his heels that night.

"This is crazy."

"Oh, so now I'm crazy?"

"No, not—" She wasn't crazy. He was. This was *Sophie*. "Let's drop it."

"Same way you dropped interrogating me about my date?"

"I wasn't interrogating you."

Her mouth had fallen open, hazel eyes bigger than serving platters.

"You offered to tell me about your date with Matt. I wasn't prying. You wanted to talk and I had to listen."

"Had to listen?"

"Yes, had to." He wanted to be there for her, but the knots of jealousy he felt—every time some piece-of-shit guy got to go out with her, got her time and her humor, her intelligence and beautiful smile, and then didn't appreciate her—kept getting bigger with each guy. They were eating him up inside. Hearing about Matt made him want to slam the asshole through the wall, or some other caveman response.

His reaction wasn't normal for him. It wasn't healthy, and he was disgusted at feeling this way.

He'd tried to leave the kitchen that night, unsure where to go, but he had to get away from her.

Before he could reach the swinging doors that led to his freedom, she'd stepped in front of him, one hand out like she was stopping traffic. "Why did you kiss me when you're dating Kate?"

Because he finally realized Kate wasn't who he wanted. "Please let it go."

"No. I need an answer."

He still didn't know why he'd said it. Every night, for weeks, he'd played the moment over and over in his head, and each time, his dumb ass spoke out of frustration, saying the same stupid thing. "I don't know why I kissed you. Okay? Temporary insanity. It won't ever happen again."

He'd never in his life laid a hand on a woman, and he never would, but the look Sophie had given him that night—he might as well have.

Sophie had recoiled, stricken.

Wright knew how insecure she was; about her background, her appearance, her worth. Everything. He'd never understood why, but he knew. And he'd gone and said the worst thing possible.

Matt wasn't the biggest jackass of the night; he was.

"Soph, I didn't mean—"

With her hands in little fists and her chin up, she'd given him a look that would burn through steel and turned her back on him.

"Soph. I didn't mean it like that."

But she was already gone. She'd stormed out of the kitchen that night and left him far behind.

He should've gone after her. Chased her down and made her listen. Told her how he thought she was the most incredible person he knew. Not only the funniest or smartest or prettiest girl he knew, but an amazing person.

But he hadn't.

And now she was on her hands and knees next to him, scrubbing the oven he'd almost destroyed, helping, and he didn't deserve her. He'd yet to apologize, but here she was, helping him.

This was her family's oven. The family he worked for—his friends and employers. Not only was he entertaining offers to leave them, but he'd tried to make a move on their baby sister, and then he'd insulted her.

He was the lowest of the low.

And who even contemplated shit like how Sophie was the most incredible person in the world?

That was lovestruck teenager goo. He was a grown man with a promising career ahead of him, and the chance to build a life of his own.

"Wright."

"What?" He looked up from scrubbing to find Sophie inches from his face.

"I said, is anything in the fire extinguisher toxic? Is soap and water all we need to clean this up or should I get something else?"

Right. The oven fire.

Focus on the problem at hand, and worry about the Sophie problem later. But the fiery point of Sophie's stare burned a hole right between his eyes.

"Nothing toxic." He couldn't maintain eye contact.

"Are you okay?"

No, he was not okay. He was alone with her at the scene of the crime.

Wright gave the inside of the oven one last wipe with a clean towel. "I'm fine. Not thrilled to be cleaning an oven at almost midnight, but other than that I'm good."

A handful of seconds ticked by before she blew out a breath, but thankfully stopped staring.

"If you say so." She left her towel on the floor and began mopping.

Now that she wasn't so close, he could breathe again.

Once finished, she dragged the bucket and mop to the industrial sink and, with a grunt, lifted the bucket to the edge.

Sophie was no waif, but she had one of their thirty-five-quart mop buckets and didn't know the water could be drained from the bottom.

"Here, let me get that." Wright rushed to take the bucket before it could slip off the lip and send water splashing across the kitchen floor.

He wheeled it to the floor drain and let the water out.

"Oh." Sophie watched as the water flowed out the bottom.

All he could see was the top of her head and part of her forehead. A forehead peppered with just the right number of freckles. Not too many, not too few.

She bemoaned them, especially during the summer, but they'd always fascinated him.

She probably had them everywhere.

How much time would it take to find each one, memorize the patterns and map out the private places they hid? He'd press his lips to each one and compliment them until none of her insecurities remained.

Wright shook off the thought.

In what parallel universe would Sophie ever let him near her freckles? She could barely stand speaking to him anymore.

She didn't think of him that way, but when they kissed, had she wondered?

His initiating the kiss had led to her participation, and it'd seemed like she wanted the same thing, but . . .

He could never ask. Not now.

They were finally able to be in the same room together, alone, without nuclear fallout. Pushing for an answer would destroy what little progress they'd made tonight.

When the bucket was empty, Sophie grabbed the mop handle, and began dragging everything to the cleaning supply closet.

"Thanks." She tossed the word over her shoulder.

Wright cleared his throat. "You're welcome," he said, even though she was already gone.

After he finished putting all of the dirty towels away, he found Sophie back at the prep table, staring at the lone surviving cherry pie.

"I washed my hands." She put her hands up in defense, knowing how much of a stickler he was for hygiene.

He washed his hands and watched her as she watched the pie.

She tucked her hair back, away from her face, her gaze dancing between him and the dessert. "Are you . . . is there a plan for this one? Since it didn't burn."

Sophie wanted to try a bite of his pie.

He didn't have to ask to know. She had a sweet tooth to rival anyone, and she loved cherries and bourbon.

"No plans. Just giving a new recipe a test run before serving it to patrons."

"Thank goodness. Could you imagine if this had happened during open hours?"

Wright's mouth fell open. He hadn't thought about that. He would've been mortified.

"Stop looking like that." She nudged his arm with her fist. "It didn't happen. I said *if.* I shouldn't have said anything."

With a shake of his head, he tried to get rid of the image and focus on the first, briefest bit of contact from Sophie in weeks.

It was a simple nudge, but they'd gone from always being fairly physical to her keeping about a hundred feet back like he was a fire truck.

Wright turned the surviving pie around for inspection. "I guess we could try some. See how it turned out."

"Okay." In a heartbeat she had two forks, one held out for him and another already sunk right into the center of the pie.

A smile toyed with his lips. Maybe this much hadn't changed.

She lifted a sticky sweet bite to her lips. Once she tried it, Sophie made a perfect O with her pink lips and fanned her mouth. "How much bourbon did you put in this?"

"The exact right amount." He slid the pan away from her and had a taste.

The cherries danced a tart tango on his tongue. Sweetness followed, and the bourbon seeped in, warm with a delightful, though strong, afterburn.

"Or a little too much." He scooped up a second bite.

The bourbon packed a punch, but it was bearable; cherries were a touch too tart, but the crust was buttery and crisp, almost ideal in flavor. He'd try again tomorrow, with a little more sugar and a little less booze.

One imperfect pie wouldn't kill him; that he'd scorched the second one so completely might.

Sophie stuck her fork in again and took another bite. "You're beating yourself up over the other pie, aren't you?"

Sometimes he forgot how well they knew each other. "A little."

"Well, stop. Accidents happen. And this pie happens to be delicious."

Sophie trying to allay any bad feelings wasn't new. Always the one to talk her brothers down off their ledges; she liked harmony, and disliked discord.

But just last week she would've let Wright twist on a spit, not tried to make him feel better.

They kept eating, and as he chewed, he considered the mangled mess they were making of his creation.

Forget cutting slices or being civilized. Before, the two of them always ate straight from the pan, late at night, scraping the dish clean and telling no one.

Heathens ate pie this way, and he loved it. This was one of their things—back before he'd ruined it.

"Oh." Sophie covered her mouth. "Should I get plates?"

"No." The answer came out a little louder than necessary. Plates meant doing things differently than before, regressing further into formality. If they couldn't go back to the full friendship they once had, maybe they could still have this. "No, I like eating this way." He dug in again.

A few bites later, Sophie finally spoke. "Me too."

Her gaze met his and fire lit his veins.

Day after day she'd barely looked at him, and now that she did, he felt the full weight of how much he missed her.

"I can fix you something to eat if you're hungry," he offered. Because that's what he did. He fed people. And when he wanted to apologize, his skill in the kitchen spoke with more eloquence than his words ever could.

Sophie covered her mouth and laughed.

The sound was magic. He hadn't heard it in two months. Never mind that she was laughing *at him.*

"I've had what amounts to two or three slices of pie now, if we bothered to cut slices. I'm not hungry, but thanks."

He checked the progress they'd made in the pan. Almost half of it was gone, and most of that half was because of Sophie.

They often split dishes and drinks, and she had a tendency to help herself to his share. There was even a time she'd steal comfy articles of clothing he left behind when staying over with Dev. Her favorites were his sweatshirts. He'd lost at least half a dozen hoodies to her thieving little hands, yet he kept leaving them behind.

It never meant anything, until it did. Until the very moment he could no longer deny how he felt.

Then he thought he'd gone and lost her forever.

He would not make that same mistake again.

They stood in the kitchen, leaning against the prep table, a pitiful-looking pie between them, and somehow Wright found the courage to say what he should've said months ago. "I'm so sorry about what I said to you. That night. In here."

Her gaze flicked up, apprehension forming fine lines by her eyes.

"You know, about temporary insanity and "

"I know what you're talking about."

Of course she knew. They'd walked on eggshells around each other since then. "I'm sorry. I don't know why I said that."

Not entirely true. He'd said it because he was aggravated. Frustrated that he couldn't tell her how much he despised the guy she'd gone out with, how much better she could do, or how jealous he was. That he loved being her friend, but he'd started wishing he were out with her instead of Kate. That the time they spent together were his favorite times. And when he kissed her, the truth of what he really wanted hit him like a bomb. But because they were friends, and he was Dev's friend, he wasn't free to blurt out everything he felt.

Sophie tilted her head to the side. "Maybe you said it because you were being a jerk?"

He laughed. "Sounds about right."

Then she shocked the hell out of him. "You weren't the only jerk that night. I was pissed off at Matt, and you, and the world, and . . . I was a jerk too. And I'm sorry."

He had no idea how to respond.

They were apologizing to each other. This was progress.

It seemed they weren't going to talk about the kiss, and he wasn't about to bring up something that could sink what was barely afloat.

He needed to forget about that night.

She crossed her arms. "Does this mean we can try to be friends again? At least talk to each other again?"

"I never stopped you from talking to me."

She couldn't hold his gaze. "I know. That was . . . that one's on me, but you know what I mean."

Unfortunately, he did. "I deserved the silent treatment, but I want us to talk again. I've missed you, Soph."

Her smile warmed and broke his heart at the same time.

"We could even grab a couple of beers together, make it official, if you want?"

Her smile remained. She knew the significance of reconciliation beers.

It was tradition. They'd done it plenty of times before, at the end of many bouts of bickering.

One year, after a particularly prickly month of college basketball tournaments, she and Wright and Dev had been so annoyed with one another, the friendly competition bled into thinly veiled animosity. They all ended up with teams in the Final Four bracket, and they'd goaded and smack-talked for weeks. In the end, they'd all lost, but learned they shouldn't take the tournament quite so seriously.

They made up over beers and wings at the Tavern—with Dev drinking water, but eating twice as many wings as the two of them—and promised not to be assholes to each other anymore.

Reconciliation beers were a must. Given the reconciling he needed to do, he might be buying a few rounds, for a few weeks.

But it was worth it.

He wanted to make amends, put what he'd said behind them and get back to being the Sophie and Wright he'd taken for granted. They could at least go back to the old them, even if he wanted to be a hell of a lot more than Sophie's friend.

Chapter 3

The next morning she spent a little bit longer fixing her hair and makeup, even applying eyeliner and lip gloss.

Then she scrubbed it all off and put her hair in a ponytail.

She never fixed herself up too much for a day of work at the resort. If she left her room today looking freshly coiffed and glossy, not only would it be obvious she was making an effort, but Dev would give her crap about it.

He'd already pulled her aside once, right after the Blueberry Festival, with twenty-one questions about why she'd been "so bitter" lately. Then he pressed her on what was going on between her and Wright.

To her credit, she'd played the whole thing off well.

When she reached the great room, Roark was already up—naturally—sipping his coffee, Beau at his feet. Dev and Trevor joined them a few minutes later and they moved from the comfort of the couches to Roark's office.

"You need a bigger office so we can get a sofa in here." Dev took the chair by the wall, saying exactly what she was thinking.

"Or we could go back to having meetings by the fireplace out there." Trevor half sat, half leaned by the window seat.

Sophie took the chair near him. "We have too many guests now, and plenty of them wake up early enough we can't risk putting our operational business on display. They're here to relax. They don't want to hear our boring morning meetings."

"Thanks, Sis." Roark's mouth quirked as he sat at his desk.

Their daily meeting went on as usual—or at least as usual for nowadays. There was a lot less bickering between them and more productive contributions. Even Trevor had the occasional reasonable idea, and he volunteered to help without flaking out on everyone.

Sophie loved the change. For the most part.

The only problem was, now that everyone wasn't on the frayed edge of coming apart at the seams, she didn't know what to do with herself.

She wasn't born into the Bradley family, but tragedy made them her brothers. At four years old, her parents dead and her world a disaster, she was left with her godparents, Suzanne and Robert Bradley. Dropped at the Honeywilde doorstep, making it the only home she knew.

As a little girl, she remembered laughter and her older brothers' taunting, but as they all got older, she mostly remembered strife: her adoptive parents' anger and arguing, Roark's frustration, Dev's resentment, and Trevor's silence.

They'd managed to keep the family together, even after their parents split, but just barely.

Now things were ... better.

They talked more and raised their voices less. Roark and Devlin both had amazing women in their lives. She admired Madison and Anna while she envied them. They'd found someone who understood them. She envied her brothers. They'd managed to find love outside their family.

"That covers all of the key items." Roark set his phone down from where he'd been checking off a list that Sophie hadn't paid a lick of attention to. "But the Chamber of Commerce chose Honeywilde as their venue since the college had the water line bust. I want each of you to give thought to a theme for the event. They'd like our help since the theme for their original location won't work at the inn."

Trevor wrinkled his brow. "Why? What was the theme for the original location?"

"Some circus or fair theme, I don't know."

Devlin and Trevor both groaned.

"It was going to be more casual but they've scrapped that."

Great. What the heck had she missed?

With a dramatic lean, Dev propped his elbow on the arm of the chair. "Help sounds like code for we need to come up with the whole thing on our own."

"We're getting paid a lot of money to emergency host their annual fund-raiser," Roark pointed out.

"It's going to take a lot of work in a short period of time."

Roark scrolled through his phone. "We've got almost two whole weeks."

"Oh, then *plenty* of time." Dev smirked.

"We've pulled off a lot more with less."

One thing hadn't changed in their family. Dev still baited Roark, and Roark nibbled every time.

Sophie grabbed what little bit of information she'd managed to pick up. "In what way do they want us to help with the theme?"

Roark avoided looking at Dev. "They want us to suggest theme ideas and create an event space that suits the theme and new location, along with providing the staff to work the event."

She drummed her fingers against her lips. "Mmm, I'd ask Anna and Madison for suggestions on themes. That seems like it'd be right up their alley. Find out how many people the Chamber expects now and I can get you a number on staff we'd need that night."

"See?" Dev smirked. "Do everything."

Roark still didn't look at Dev, but he fought not to grin at his snark.

A big change from years past.

"I'm meeting with the Chamber's board this week and, Dev, I think you should come with me, since you're so in tune with predicting what they want."

Dev made a show of slumping back, but everyone in the room knew he loved being included.

"Now, unless anyone has anything else."

No one spoke up and Roark stood, signaling the end of the meeting.

The remainder of her day swept past in a rush of phone calls, a meeting with their maintenance guy and Trevor, and putting out a fire—figurative this time, not literal—for one of the housekeeping staff when they accidentally washed a guest's headphones in a bundle of bedsheets.

Actually, for a Monday, her day was going astonishingly smooth. Right up until the moment she ran into Wright.

Literally, not figuratively.

She rushed around the corner of the laundry area and struck a solid six-foot-two-inch man-wall.

The air whooshed from her lungs as she ricocheted off Wright's chest. With a hand out, she caught herself, grabbing the door frame as he snagged a hand around her waist.

"I've got you."

"Where'd you come from?"

As soon as she had her footing, he jerked his hands away like she was boiling water. "I was down here grabbing a clean chef's jacket."

She glanced down at his empty hands.

"But I can't find one. What are you doing down here?"

"I told Vivian I'd see if we had some sort of linen table cover for a side table in reception."

Easily the most inane conversation she'd ever had with Wright, except for the time they debated, for almost an hour, which was better, Sun Drop or Mountain Dew.

Still, it was better than not conversing at all.

"I know we have more jackets for you down here somewhere." She stepped around him.

"And I saw something that'd probably work to cover a side table." He joined her in searching the shelves and baskets.

As they searched through layer after layer of cotton in cream, ivory, and stark white, she snuck a glance his way.

He was less tense than last night, his expression not quite as strained.

She'd never say it, but stress wasn't such a good look for Wright, and he'd seemed pretty stressed lately.

Every other look was fine on him.

Better than fine. Even when he got really pissed off, that was still a hot look, but tension and fretting made him squint and he scrunched his nose up.

Okay, so stress wasn't a horrible look on him either, but it wasn't his best.

Last night he'd insisted they get a beer together soon, making official the fact they were speaking again.

And apparently they'd made some silent agreement never to discuss their kiss, ever again.

Seriously. They weren't going to talk about kissing each other? How did you not talk about lip locking your best friend?

Guess she'd find out.

Wright hadn't mentioned when this beer would be. Weekends were out. They both worked late hours on weekends.

This was assuming they'd actually go out at all. He could've just said that to be nice. A metaphorical "let's grab reconciliation beers" and stop acting weirder than a cross-eyed cat around each other.

No. They were going to have beers together, dammit. And she wasn't going to overanalyze her motivations or insistence. She missed Wright too, plain and simple. Missed him a lot.

She wanted to hear his goofy laugh and be the cause of it. She longed to listen to him be a smart-ass about Dev and watch him finish half a pint in one long swallow, then try not to burp or at least hide it because he tried so hard to be a gentleman . . . except when she got him to eat dessert straight from the pan.

Only she could get him to break out of that mold.

With her, he'd still be chewing one bite while spooning out more, cherry glaze staining his lips as he unabashedly tried to outeat her.

She missed being around Wright because together they could be themselves. He was the one person who made her feel good in her skin.

"You find it?" Wright turned and his gaze clashed with hers.

She'd been too busy staring at him to look for whatever it was she was supposed to be looking for. "I . . . um . . . I can't find anything."

He shrugged and tugged on a bundle of linen. "Don't worry about it. I may have an extra chef's jacket in my locker."

Mmm. His chef's jacket.

She had an odd, probably slightly twisted, thing for him in that jacket.

He had double-breasted white ones, with black buttons and cuffed sleeves. In the summer, the white was a crisp contrast to his tan skin and muscular forearms.

Wright had great arms. Even as a friend she could admit that.

Though her thoughts on his arms couldn't really be classified as friendly.

"I did find some tablecloths." Arms outstretched, he held them toward her. She closed the distance and tried to take the bundle from him, her tugging meeting resistance.

Wright wasn't letting go.

"I . . ." He lowered his gaze.

His pause made her stomach somersault.

What was he going to say that made him hesitate? They'd never hesitated when speaking to one another before.

Was he finally going to bring up kissing her? They were alone, in a quiet room, free from interruption.

And she was terrified.

She wanted him to broach the topic of their kiss, and she prayed he didn't. What would she say? There was no correct response. If he apologized for the kiss, it meant he was sorry, and she didn't want him to be sorry. Sorry for his timing, sorry for being an ass afterward, sure. But now that they were free agents, no boyfriends or girlfriends between them, and he'd apologized for what he'd said . . .

"Remember what I said about grabbing a beer?"

Of course she freaking remembered. "Yes."

"What about tomorrow? Tuesdays aren't too busy at the restaurant. I can get out of here at a decent time. Want to grab beers tomorrow night?"

"That sounds . . ." Perfect. "That should work."

Wright's grin was a knee-melter. Brilliant teeth, eyes all puppy-like and pleased.

Damn him.

She hadn't crushed hard on him since high school. She'd outgrown all of that ages ago, and sure, there was that momentary lapse of reason when she'd first moved back home from college and ogled him more than she should, but she'd moved past it.

She wanted them to be friends again, but she couldn't get that kiss out of her mind. How were they supposed to go back to being the way they were BK? Before Kiss.

Wright released his hold on the table linens, and she had half a mind to bury her face in creamy cotton and scream.

Why couldn't she stop thinking about that night? Stop thinking about him in that way?

She'd been doing fine for years, until he came along, touching her the way he'd touched her that night, saying all the words she longed to hear and then kissing her like no one else ever had.

Damn him.

She shouldn't think of him in those terms. Kissing terms and touching terms, and how good he looked in his chef's jacket . . . or how good he'd look with no shirt on.

In the weeks after their kiss, she'd lie in bed, reconsidering dozens of their interactions, holding them up against this reality where Wright McAdams was someone who would kiss her. Might actually be interested.

She imagined their exchanges going in totally different directions.

Like the time he'd helped her chase down Beau when the dog bolted out of the lobby.

In reality, he'd bumped against her good-naturedly, telling her to keep a grip on the crazy dog.

What would've happened if, instead of simply taking the leash from Wright, she'd let their fingers brush? Let her hand linger on his skin. Then Wright would keep hold of the leash in one hand and grab Sophie with the other. He'd pull her into his arms and they'd make out like something from a movie.

She'd fall asleep with her legs squeezed together against the tingling, and wake up wondering if she was slowly going insane.

"Soph?" Wright waved a hand in front of her face.

"I'll see you tomorrow night." She turned and all but ran from the laundry area. Her pulse pumped, her breath coming in quick pants.

Constantly thinking about his kiss, how solid and smooth he'd felt under her fingertips, was torture. And the kiss was a fluke. They were moving on.

No more thinking about Wright in those ways.

He was a guy and her friend. Period.

By the time she reached the reception area, she'd worked up a sweat and was breathing heavy.

"Are you okay?" Vivian, their newest employee and front desk attendant, took the tablecloths from her. "I told you I would fetch these. You've got enough to do around here."

Sophie stared, only hearing every other word over the rushing in her ears.

Had she just run up a flight of stairs in about ten seconds?

"Here. Have some water. You look a little pale." Vivian guided her to one of the chairs behind the reception desk.

"I don't mean it in a bad way." Vivian tried to backtrack. "But you look like you're going to pass out."

Sophie took a sip of water from the glass she offered, scrubbed her hands over her face, and stood. She had no time for dramatics, and that's all this was.

So what if she'd occasionally daydreamed about Wright? It made sense that the kiss and arguing had her rattled. She hadn't thought clearly for weeks, with good reason. But things would go back to normal now.

No more daydreams about his eyes or the chiseled cut of his arms, or the breadth of his back as he bent over a mixing bowl. They would go back to being who they were before, and she'd get on with her life.

"I'm fine now."

"You sure?"

"Positive. I have to get back to work." Hands on her hips, she turned to Vivian.

Vivian mirrored her posture. "Me too."

Sophie headed toward Roark's office, more certain than ever that the past month's events were an anomaly. Nothing between her and Wright had really changed.

Chapter 4

Everything had changed.

Wright stared at the large pan of dinner rolls, still hot and steaming from the oven. He'd forgotten to melt the butter to brush over the top before serving, *and* he'd forgotten to make the marinade for tonight's chicken dish.

He never forgot to melt butter or make marinade. He'd gone from exceptional chef to a bumbling amateur, all because tonight, he was taking Sophie out for drinks.

Drinks. That was all.

They'd had drinks together a million times.

His well-run life was crumbling like dry cake. First he tried to burn out an oven, baking half-ass pies, now he had no melted butter.

"What the—?" He threw his hands up as he rushed around, putting butter on to melt.

He'd always been a messier—though he preferred the word "passionate"—chef, but he was competent.

If he weren't, he couldn't have pulled off the meals for Honeywilde's rock-star wedding. He couldn't pull off the weekend rush at the inn, and he sure as shit wouldn't be pulling in offers from New York.

Wright let out a rough sigh.

New York City.

His problem wasn't only Sophie, though she took up more than her fair share of his attention.

In a million years he would've never believed it, except today he'd talked to the man himself.

Evidently, word traveled fast when you got featured in national magazines and celebrities with a lot of pull went around bragging about your food.

Recently he'd heard from Charleston and Asheville, but today, he got the call from the Big Apple.

A city known for its dining and some of the greatest chefs in the world, and an investor wanted Wright. They made him an offer and agreed to let him think things over.

They understood it was a big move.

Working at Honeywilde made him happy enough, but every chef in their right mind dreamt of an opportunity like this. He'd been with the Bradleys for years now and started to wonder if he was even capable of anything else. Maybe all he could manage was being a chef at an inn.

Then Madison and her wedding happened, and the world unfurled before him.

Shit, he had a lot of thinking to do. And he needed to get his act together. Quick.

He needed to concentrate on what he was doing in the here and now, not get distracted by thoughts of New York, or of *her*.

They were only having beers. This wasn't a date.

"You need a hand, boss?" Marco, his new sous chef, handed him a brush for the butter.

"Yes. Please. If you'll go ahead and plate the salads, we'll get this order out."

Thank God for Marco. It'd taken some convincing to get Roark to hire him, but at the rate Honeywilde was growing, he was desperately needed.

Luckily, during the remainder of dinner, Roark didn't burn anything, nothing fell apart, and all of the food went out perfectly. It wasn't until they were cleaning up that tonight's plans rose again and slapped him across the face.

He *had* to play it cool with Sophie.

Be normal. No awkward pauses or lingering gazes. That was weird between friends.

He was a grown man and she was a grown woman; he had no reason to act like a silly teenager.

With drinks, he hoped to reclaim more of their casual chemistry. Just two pals being pals. Friends who could talk about whatever. All of the temptations that'd started dancing through his mind had no place with them tonight.

Tonight was a fresh start, and he wasn't going to let his wayward thoughts get in the way.

"Hey." Sophie stood in the kitchen doorway, holding it open with her hip.

Arms crossed, she still looked inviting. She'd changed into jeans and a fitted shirt in deep green, enhancing her coloring and shape. Her hair was down, her eyes bright.

"You ready?"

"Almost." He looked away. "I brought some clothes to change into. Give me ten minutes?" So he wouldn't smell like the kitchen.

"I'll wait for you at the bar."

Unlike the Bradley siblings, he didn't live at the main inn. All of his belongings weren't right here under one roof. He had an apartment in town that allowed him to get away from work and served the double purpose of driving his parents insane.

If you insist on staying in Windamere for the foreseeable future, selling yourself short at that inn, you could at least invest in a house.

They were both proponents of his big-city opportunities and cared very little about hearing Wright debate the matter.

You have the chance to move on to bigger and better things. Take it.

His father repeatedly badgered him about seizing the opportunity. Particularly if opportunity meant getting away from Honeywilde— and the Bradleys.

His family's dislike of Devlin, and therefore the entire Bradley family, was no secret.

They were convinced Dev was a bad influence on him growing up and even now, never guessing their sweet little Wright was equally mischievous, but better at hiding it.

Wright washed up, tugged on some jeans and a T-shirt, and thanked his lucky stars that Roark Bradley, whose family his parents loved to look down on, saw fit to employee him years ago.

Right out of culinary school, Roark gave him a job. Kept him on, even when times were so tight they barely made payroll.

Honeywilde was home. His insides twisted as he stuffed his dirty clothes in his backpack. Leaving here wouldn't be easy.

But he didn't want to think about that now. *Now* he had to deal with Sophie.

He hurried to find her at the bar. Steve, the restaurant's bartender, was already gone, as was everyone, since it was after ten o'clock on a Tuesday night.

"You ready?" He'd already lifted his hand to rub or pat her shoulder, but withdrew at the last second.

Were they doing that again? Maybe he should stay hands off for a while. They were touchy-feely before, but dammit if he didn't second-guess every single action now.

If he squeezed her shoulder, would she think he was going in for a kiss again?

The self-scrutiny was going to drive him insane.

Sophie turned on her stool. "Ready if you are. You driving or shall I?"

"I'll drive so I can drop you off afterward."

Without another word, she followed him to his Jeep and crawled up into the passenger side.

"The Tavern okay with you?" The Tavern was Windamere's best watering hole, by far. Open every night but Sundays, it wasn't pretentious or overpriced, even during tourist season. The food was simple and fresh, and they had the best local brews on tap, including a delicious Belgian-inspired white.

"You know I love the Tavern. I could go for something to eat too. You?"

"Always."

He had the metabolism of a racehorse and a deep love of food. Trying new foods and recipes, and eating, were at the top of his hobby list. Lucky for him, working out was a close second.

"What about the nachos at the Tavern?" She angled her body toward him in the Jeep. "Mmm. Or their Welsh rarebit."

"Done. I love their rarebit, and they make a phenomenal corned beef sandwich. That's what we're getting."

The Tavern's interior was dark wood floors and wainscoting, brightened up by warm lighting and walls painted a creamy yellow. He and Sophie grabbed one of the high tops near the bar and ordered as soon as they sat down. Once their beers arrived, he held up his pint glass, determined to go ahead and get this part out of the way.

"Here's to putting the last couple of months behind us and speaking to one another again."

Sophie raised her glass. "Hear, hear."

He clinked his glass against hers.

They kept the topic of conversation light until their food arrived, discussing the newest employees, how to keep the momentum going on Honeywilde's recent success, the startling realization that Devlin, of all people, was settling down with a nice girl and likely to be the first Bradley to get hitched.

"I never would've guessed, but I think he might beat Roark to the altar." Sophie sipped at the stout she ordered, a little mustache of foam decorating her upper lip before she licked it clean.

Wright coughed and stared into his beer. "Yeah. Crazy. You'll be the first to know."

"Doubtful. He'll come to you first for guy advice; how to pop the question, buying rings and stuff."

"You'd know more about rings than I do."

She cocked an eyebrow at him.

Sophie didn't wear rings or much jewelry at all. Tiny gold ball earrings and occasionally a gold chain with a horseshoe pendant. The necklace was her biological mother's, the earrings a gift from Mr. and Mrs. Bradley, before they separated.

Did anyone else notice that Sophie wore the earrings almost every day, but the necklace only came out a few times a year?

Why those few times? What was the significance of when she chose to wear it? He never asked, but always wondered.

"Maybe. But you'll be the best man and I'll be . . ." Her gaze drifted to the bar, a shadow of sadness briefly drifting over her before she shrugged it off. "I don't know what I'll be. Flower girl?"

He took a sip of his beer and shook his head. "Dev can be pretty untraditional. Maybe you'll be the best man."

Her laugh brought a smile to his face, like the first warm day of spring.

"Besides, I think you've outgrown flower girl eligibility."

"I've outgrown a lot of things." She met his gaze, unwavering.

See? What was that supposed to mean? She'd outgrown her connection to him? Or had she outgrown being just friends with him?

He'd sworn he wouldn't overanalyze or try to guess at offhand comments, but noticing every little thing Sophie did was in his blood. His bones were dense with years spent as her confidant.

He knew all of her little quirks, her telltale signs, and what he didn't know made him wonder, longing to learn more. And yes, he even knew about her teenage crush on him.

He was running around with Devlin in high school, raising hell at the age of sixteen and seventeen, and little freshman Sophie had looked at him like he was a god.

He'd hated and loved it. She was his best friend's baby sister, the one who told on them *all the time* and relentlessly picked at his ego—which in fairness, at sixteen, probably needed the picking. But she was funny and cute and didn't intimidate the shit out of him like everyone else of the opposite sex.

Now she was still funny, more hot than cute, and sometimes she intimidated him. But he liked it.

"Hot plates. Here's y'all's rarebit and corned beef." The waitress slid their orders onto the table and Sophie finally looked away.

"This smells delicious." Wright thanked the waitress and waited on the dish to cool.

"You're not digging in?"

"Ladies first."

Sophie rolled her eyes but gave him a small smile. She cut off a corner of the rarebit and popped it in her mouth, immediately trying to blow and chew the hot bread and cheese.

"'S hot." She puffed the words and fanned her mouth.

"The waitress did warn us."

"Smart ass." She kept fanning and laughed.

After that, the meal went smoothly; no more resolute stares, no proclamations about outgrowing things that confused the hell out of him. Just the two of them, some rich food and beer, and he couldn't be happier.

He considered telling her about his job offers. The chances to work nearby at a flagship in Asheville or move hours away, to try and make it big in New York City, but as much as he wanted that level of confidentiality back between them, Sophie was still a Bradley.

Honeywilde was her family business, and as chef, he was employee first, friend second.

"Did you hear about the Chamber booking an event at the inn?" Sophie asked. "And they want us to pick the theme."

"What kind of event?" He bit into his half of their sandwich.

"I'm not one hundred percent sure, because I wasn't paying attention—"

"You sound like Dev." He laughed.

"No, that'd be old Dev. New Dev pays attention. But apparently they want to host their fund-raiser at Honeywilde last minute because a common area at the college is now a swamp. I'm guessing we'll provide a chunk of the labor and have to work under their direction, again, because it's the Chamber and they can do what they want."

"That could be a good thing. Their fundraiser brings in Windamere's finest, and that helps Honeywilde via word of mouth."

She picked up her half of the sandwich. "True. But I'm worried about what theme they'll want us to go with. Their original theme was some kind of circus or farm days thing. I don't want to wind up with a farm on our property. Goats are cute, but not when they're running around, chewing up my flowers and pooping everywhere. The operational side would be a nightmare. Plus, poop."

Wright laughed, choking on his sip of beer.

Sophie reached over and slapped him on the back a few times.

"I don't think they'll do anything circus related at Honeywilde. They should make it a swanky event. No goats or things you bounce up and down on."

This time, she had to put her sandwich down to laugh. "The *what*?"

"The bouncy things. You know; the blow-up things." Wright patted her back to return the favor, the cotton of her shirt soft and thin enough that the heat from her body warmed his palm.

"Is there something you need to tell me, Wright?" Her eyes sparkled. "What have you been bouncing up and down on in your spare time?"

She was teasing him.

Eons had passed since he'd seen that look in her eyes or the taunting curl of her lips, but there they were.

His heart kicked. He'd begun to wonder if he'd ever see that expression on her face again.

"As you know, I don't have any spare time." He hurried to respond, determined to hold on to the moment. "But if I did, my bouncing would be my business."

When he moved his hand away from her back, she pushed against his shoulder with the tips of her fingers. "No, it wouldn't. You know how things go at Honeywilde. First it'd be Dev's business, then it would be my business, then Trevor's, and then everyone else's."

"Sad how true that is. Except Devlin was . . . bouncing with Anna for a while before any of us knew."

"Oh come on." Sophie tossed her head back, the Tavern's lighting catching the gold in her red hair. "I knew they were bouncing."

"When he asked us to help him with their picnic dinner?"

"Before then."

"You did not."

"I did too."

"Sure you did. Easy to claim, now that everyone knows." He was pressing his point just to pick on her. He knew she'd known.

"I will call Dev right now and he can tell you I was on to him before anybody else."

"You like to be a know-it-all. Go ahead and call him."

She reached for her purse, but Wright grabbed it off the back of her chair.

"Real mature. Give me my bag."

He might as well be ten years old again, playing keep away from Sophie, but he couldn't help himself.

Sophie glared playfully as he held her bag out of reach. "Don't make me hurt you."

How could he stop now? He'd enjoyed teasing her more today than he did ten years ago.

If the spark in her eyes and the smile on her lips were any indication, she enjoyed it too. He wasn't going to put the brakes on something that made them both happy.

And as he turned this way and that, his height and long arms giving him the advantage of keeping her bag well out of her reach, she got closer and closer. She stretched and made grabs, stopping short of climbing on him to get her bag back. He twisted to prevent her until she wound up standing between his legs, swatting at his arms, both of them laughing like little kids.

But the heat spreading through his body was far from innocent.

"Hey, guys." A male voice startled them.

Sophie dropped her outstretched arms, her hands landing on his thighs, before she snatched them away.

Two of his acquaintances, Caleb and Shane, had walked in without him noticing.

Wright lowered his arms and she tugged her purse free, hurrying back to her chair.

"Hey." He made himself smile at Caleb and Shane.

He wasn't overly fond of either. They both partied too much and talked too much about their supposed "conquests," and they leered at women, including Sophie.

"Surprised to see you out in the real world, man," Shane teased. "Thought you said you worked all the time."

"He does." Sophie gave them a tight smile.

Wright didn't think she had much history with them, but he could be wrong. Being single in a small town meant the dating pool was that much smaller. She could've gone out with either or both guys at some point.

A sharp bite of annoyance made him shift in his seat.

Sophie was too good for the likes of them, and the idea of either guy having their hands on her—"You should go ahead and order if you're here for food." Wright jumped onto something to get rid of them. "Kitchen closes in a bit."

"Nah, we're just here to drink." Caleb pulled out one of the other chairs at their table.

Neither guy acted like he needed more to drink—this was probably their last stop of the night—or bothered asking if they could join them.

He and Sophie shared a look.

Hell yes he minded, but making that point was tricky. He wasn't here on a date with Soph. They were pals, and to indicate otherwise would start Caleb and Shane running their mouths again, and the gossip mill would start churning. Still, he didn't want to share their time together with these guys.

He opened his mouth, prepared to tell them they were discussing Honeywilde business, so maybe they could shove off, when Sophie spoke, her voice dripping in sarcasm. "Go ahead and sit down, why don't you?"

She was being a grade-A smart-ass, but neither of them was intelligent enough to pick up on it.

"What's new up at the lodge?" Caleb asked, pulling his chair close to Sophie's.

"It's not a lodge." Wright corrected him. "And lots of things are new. We hired on some new staff and, as a matter of fact, we were in the middle of talking business, so—"

"Yeah? Any girls? Any of them hot?" Now he had Shane's full attention.

They ordered beers and another half an hour went on like this, Wright getting more annoyed with each inane comment and topic.

Eventually, Sophie met his gaze, and a silent agreement was reached.

The two of them were getting the hell out of there.

"I'm going to the restroom before we leave." Sophie slid off her stool, taking her purse with her, and as soon as she was out of earshot, Caleb and Shane were on Wright like leeches.

"So what's up with you and the ice princess being all over each other when we got here?" Shane asked.

The hairs on the back of Wright's neck stood on end. "We weren't all over each other. What do you mean *Ice Princess*?"

Caleb laughed, slapping the table. "You didn't know that's her nickname? Ever since she turned Shane down cold when he asked her out, and Matt told us he drew back a nub when he put the moves on her."

Wright glared. "She only went out with Matt three times."

"Exactly! They hung out for a couple of weeks and he got nothing. No kiss, nothing."

"You know . . ." Shane tapped his chin, and the smarmy look on his face made Wright want to break it. "Now that I think about it, maybe the reason she shut me down, and Matt wasn't getting any, was because Princess and Wright have something going on."

Caleb slapped him across the back like he ought to be congratulated.

"You can shut up now." Wright bristled and Caleb pulled his hand away as both men snickered.

"Tell the truth, Wright. How long have y'all been hooking up?"

"We aren't hooking up."

Caleb wasn't going to let it go though. "Not for a lack of trying, I bet."

Wright glared and Shane howled with laughter. "You should see your face, man. You *are* trying to hit that."

"Sophie and I are friends and you're an asshole."

"Whatever, man. Y'all sure looked cozy when we got here. If you're not already tapping that ass, you're at least trying to."

God almighty he wanted to hit them. Beating their ass might not do any good, but it'd certainly make him feel better. Back in the day, he would've, but he wasn't a stupid kid anymore. He needed his hands, unbroken or busted up, in order to do his job, and he wasn't keen on getting banned from the Tavern for these two losers. "You know what, you've both had too much to drink and—"

"She could've kept sitting in your lap, we wouldn't have cared."

"No wonder we never see you out anymore."

"That's because I'm working."

"Yeah, working." Shane made little air quotes. Wright was going to punch him anyway, hands be damned. "I'd be working with her too. I'd work all the damn time."

"Me too." Caleb laughed. "I bet she's a spitfire in bed. Redheads usually are."

"Tell the truth, how many times have you screwed her in that kitchen?"

Wright shoved his chair back and stood, ready to grab Shane by the neck. Then his gaze met Sophie's.

She stood in the doorway by the bar, eyes wide, her expression frozen in horror.

Caleb and Shane both buried their faces in their beers.

Sophie blinked, right before she turned and ran.

"Soph." Wright took off after her, the sound of Caleb's snickering called to him, making him want to go back and kick both their asses. But Sophie was what mattered.

How much had she heard? *What* had she heard?

"Sophie, stop."

"No." She spun on him. "You stop. Stop pretending you're my friend."

She stalked off again and Wright went after her. "What are you talking about? I am your friend."

She turned again. "A friend wouldn't let them say that about me."

"I wasn't *letting them* say anything. I was about to beat the shit out of both of them when I saw you."

This time, she had no response, but she still took off again.

With his height, it was easy to catch her. Wright moved in her way, blocking her path. "Will you stop for a second and listen to me?"

"How can they talk about me like I'm loose? They know perfectly well I'm not. They've both tried to get in my pants and both got my foot in their ass for their efforts."

"They've hit on you?"

"Of course they have. They're jerks, right? That's who I attract. But for them to sit there and say that about me . . ."

"No one thinks you're loose, Soph."

"Then why were they saying all of that?"

"To get a rise out of me."

"That doesn't even make sense."

"Yes, it does."

She tossed her hands up, letting them fall at her sides. "No. It doesn't."

"They know I'm protective of you, okay? I always have been. Everybody knows that. The damn bag boys at the grocery store know it. Shane and Caleb *know* I'm not hooking up with you, but they're messing with me because—" Wright clamped his lips shut.

Shit.

Shit fire. He shouldn't have said so much.

"Because why?" Sophie's gaze homed in, a tiny crease forming between her brows.

Wright walked past her to get to his Jeep, and she was right behind him.

"Because why, Wright?"

Not this again. He couldn't go through this a second time. They'd finally gotten somewhere near back to normal.

"Wright." Sophie grabbed his arm, yanking hard to make him stop and turn around.

In her eyes he saw suspicion and confusion. But more than that, he saw the vulnerability, the same yawning empty space and need that everyone else seemed to overlook. How could they miss the delicate side of her? She rarely showed her insecurities, but when she let her guard down, it clawed at his heart.

He hated that emptiness. Hated that Sophie didn't feel whole and wonderful, because to him, she was.

He was tired of dancing around his desire for her. Tired of acting like he only saw her as a good buddy who he didn't find insanely attractive. Most of all, he was tired of lying to her.

"Why were they saying that about us hooking up?"

"Because I wish we were," Wright blurted.

Sophie straightened, frozen.

They stared at each other in that empty parking lot for what felt like eternity, until finally, she took a step back. "Wh . . . *What*?"

"Not just hooking up," he added. "It's not about that, but . . . you know."

"No. I don't know."

Wright bit back a rumble of frustration. She had to know. There was no way she didn't feel their chemistry, understand the history between them. "They know . . ." He couldn't believe he was saying this, but he was done fighting the truth. "They can tell I like you. Guys know. They know I have a thing for you, and they're giving me hell for it. It's immature bullshit and that's what guys like them do. They use it. I was going to defend you because they shouldn't be saying that shit, but they don't actually think any of it, I promise. They did it to mess with me."

Sophie stared, again unmoving. "You have a thing for me?"

Of course she was calling him out on the truth. This was Sophie. She wasn't about to let him slide. And knowing that, he'd still fessed up.

"I kissed you, remember? You had to realize then that I was into you."

"So now we *are* going to talk about the kiss? Because I thought we were pretending nothing happened."

"Oh, come on!" His raised his voice. "You weren't bringing it up either. I'm following your lead. I pissed you off something awful once; I'm not trying to do it again."

"That night you insisted *you* didn't kiss *me*."

He threw his hands up.

"You did, and you got all defensive and yelled at me."

"I know I did, and I'm sorry. You wouldn't believe how sorry. But I was mad. Not at you, but at myself."

"Why did you kiss me? After all this time, why now?"

Good question. He'd asked himself the same thing, over and over, for the last two months. "Because . . . I don't know." Not good enough. Even he knew that was a bullshit answer. "Because I couldn't fight it anymore. You kept going out with these dumb-ass guys and I kept hating it. Every time, I hated it a little more. I was with Kate, but I kept thinking I couldn't wait to get to work the next day to hang out with you. That's not how it's supposed to be. I couldn't stop thinking about you, but I wasn't supposed to be into you like that. I got mad because I'm sure as hell not supposed to kiss you. You're my friend. You're Dev's little sister, and I had a girlfriend. I was mad about all of it."

She didn't say anything. Instead she just kept looking up at him with this wounded confusion.

Holy shit, what had he done?

Selfishly, he'd wanted her to know. Why? What did he expect? That she'd confess she had a thing for him too, and damn all the complications and reasons they shouldn't be together, she'd leap into his arms?

Sophie wasn't an idiot like him.

Attempting to kiss her had screwed things up so badly they hadn't spoken all summer, and now he did this.

Instead of spilling his guts, he should've kept his mouth shut. Then he wouldn't be here, his insides in knots, sweating like he faced a firing squad, Sophie looking like she was either going to run again or be sick.

She could at least say something. Tell him to go to hell. Anything other than her wretched silence.

"Please don't stand there not talking to me."

She blinked, shaking her head so slightly he almost missed it, her lips together in a flat line.

She never let anything go, and tonight, of all nights, she was clamming up. Perfect. No words of condemnation and definitely none of reassurance. Only him, swinging in the breeze, praying the earth would open up and swallow him whole.

He deserved as much. That's what he got for betraying her faith in him. Even if he was telling her the truth, he was supposed to be the guy she could rely on. The one who treated her right without expecting anything in return.

"Fine." His feet kicked into gear. "You know what? It's probably best we don't talk about this anymore. I shouldn't have said anything. Let's forget I did." He reached past her to open the door to the Jeep, but Sophie moved.

In a blur of movement, she was in his way and in his arms. Then she kissed him.

Chapter 5

Sophie kissed Wright.

After what he'd confessed, there was nothing else she could do.

Plenty of times she'd imagined kissing him. Not like what'd happened in the kitchen. This was *her* kissing *him*.

Wright rocked backward with the force as her lips met his.

She pinched her eyes closed. She didn't want to see the fallout if he shoved her away, somehow changed his mind about what he wanted.

Then, as quickly as he'd moved back, he surged forward, his arms around her, pulling her closer. He was over a foot taller than her, and she clung to his arms until he bent down. His lips were smooth, his kiss solid and seeking. He sucked at her lips, his hand on her cheek, cupping her jaw. When she opened, the first sweep of his tongue against hers shot a surge of heat down her body.

His arm around her waist was an iron bar, the hand splayed at her back a sure sign at least one of them didn't have any doubts.

"Wright." She panted against his lips. They were really doing this. Again.

"I know."

He moved until her back bumped against the Jeep door, slanting their mouths together as her breath caught in her chest.

Her arms around his neck, she held on as he lifted her up. Only the balls of her feet remained on the ground, but she was flying.

No longer earthbound, she soared.

She was kissing Wright, and her desire should feel wrong. This was her friend of countless years, her brother's closest friend, and a man she worked with and relied upon every day. The two of them kissing was a horrible idea, which didn't explain why she felt so amazing.

Wright liked her. Was into her. For how long?

As long as she'd had a thing for him? Longer?

No way was it longer. Her crush dated back to their teen years, and even though it'd died a fiery death a few times, the embers had always remained.

Her feelings had scattered, evolved, and then changed again, to the point even she didn't understand them. All she knew was that in this moment, she had to kiss him. And now that she had, she didn't want to stop.

He sucked her bottom lip between his teeth, making her gasp. The warm brush of his hand against her waist focused the heat in her body, sending it slithering to her core. He slid his hand up farther, caressing her bare skin, his thumb brushing over her ribs.

She pressed into him, their bodies flush, his opinion on the matter evident in the hard line poking against her abdomen.

"Oh god." She might pass out.

She was making out with Wright. He was turned on. What the hell was happening? They'd lost their minds. Wonderful, and terrifying.

He leaned away, only inches, his breath came in short bursts. "You okay?"

She didn't know what she was. "Are you?"

Wright's chuckle warmed her face. His cheeks flushed and the familiar grin melted her insides. "Do I look okay?"

His hair was ruffled, his gaze hooded. In the dimly lit parking lot, his eyes shined, dark and hungry.

Never in her entire life had she seen Wright like this. Thank goodness for the Jeep behind her or she'd collapse from the weight of his stare.

"We . . . um . . ." She glanced around. "We're in a parking lot."

He moved to withdraw his hand, the tips of his fingers brushing past the sensitive skin at her waist.

She tensed against the wave of fresh desire that followed his touch.

Her feet began to find the ground, gravel and sand. Behind the Tavern, in their hometown. Where they knew everyone and literally anyone could see them, and know.

"We shouldn't do this here," he said.

They shouldn't do this at all. But when she opened her mouth to tell him so, no words came out.

"Just . . ." He glanced around the lot before fumbling with the passenger door. "Here. Get in the car."

She climbed in and he rounded the front of the Jeep, dragging a hand through his hair, looking as rattled as she felt.

Holy shit, she'd kissed Wright. More than kissed.

This went further than any brief sweep of lips in the kitchen, followed by fleeing. This was . . . this . . . He'd had his hand up her shirt. And she *wanted* it there.

He had a hard-on. This was Wright McAdams.

What'd gotten into her? Why would she—well, she knew why. For years there'd been reason enough to want to kiss him, but ten times as many reasons not to. Clearly, they'd both lost their minds.

Wright started the Jeep and jerked the gearshift into drive. Kicking up gravel, he sped out of the parking lot.

They made it a whole half a mile in silence before she couldn't take it anymore. Shifting in her seat, she faced him. "Are you mad at me for kissing you?"

He ground the gears, missing fifth. "*What?* No, I'm not—did any of that seem like I was mad?"

"No, but I did jump down your throat for kissing me in the kitchen and now here I am, kissing you, and you're flying like a bat out of hell. Could you please slow down before we die?"

With a rough exhale, Wright eased off the gas. "Sorry. Kind of flustered, that's all."

"Tell me about it."

"Sophie—" He stopped himself from whatever he was about to say and let go of the gear, gripping the wheel with both hands, tight enough to make mountains and valleys out of his knuckles. "I thought you didn't . . . I don't know what I thought."

Suddenly, her petite frame, the body she'd bemoaned since puberty for its insistence upon staying as prepubescent as possible, weighed half a ton. She sank into the bucket seat, her shoulders and arms like lead. "I think it's safe to say, for two people who run their mouths a lot, we both suck at communicating."

His gaze jerked to hers, his mouth agape. "*Both?* Not ten minutes ago I admitted I have a thing for you. That's some damn good communicating."

Indignant, she opened her mouth to match his. "Yeah, after swearing you would *never* kiss me. That's pretty piss-poor communicating, if you ask me."

Eyes narrowed, he refocused on the road. "At least I finally said something."

There was no way in hell she was telling him how long she'd wanted to kiss him. There was the all-consuming high school crush that lasted her freshman year and even some of sophomore, again when she was twenty-two, lasting a few months, and finally, this summer—when Wright had decimated all of her hard getting-over-him work by going for the lip-lock and making her think about him every damn day since.

"I didn't say anything or do anything because you have a girlfriend."

"*Had.* Did you want to kiss me the whole time I was going out with Kate?"

Ah, hell's bells. "No."

He went from studying the road to studying her.

The biggest problem with Wright was he knew her. He knew her too well and saw too much.

"Holy shit, you did want to kiss me then. At least a little." He went back to watching the road. "I had no idea."

If Wright was the one looking, her feelings were too transparent. Sometimes she didn't mind; most of the time it annoyed her. Sometimes she hated his insight so much she'd pick a fight with him.

At the next red light he glanced over. "Were you thinking about kissing me too, that night in the kitchen?"

Yes. "No."

He shook his head. "I think you're lying. You wanted to, but I was with someone so you didn't act on it. You're a better person than me, and that's why you got angry."

"You really think I'm a better person than you?"

He gave her one last glance, his expression pure puzzlement, as the light turned green. "I don't think. I know."

The revelation washed over her, surprise numbing her senses, making her eyes go wide.

"And I know you're trying to change the subject." He focused on the road. "You wanted to kiss me as much as I want to kiss you."

All true. As true as the very harsh reality that Wright wasn't some guy she could kiss, or even hook up with, and get away unscathed.

There were too many complications: the mess of being Dev's best friend, the dilemma of being coworkers, and the certain disapproval of his family. Talk about rocking the boat—their being together would capsize all of Honeywilde, at least for some period of time, at a time when everything was finally smooth sailing.

She couldn't be responsible for that. Sophie was the solution, not the problem.

And he was her closest friend. For them, going down the path of kissing and making out didn't lead to some casual fling.

And she couldn't do more than casual. Simple. Unmessy.

She didn't know how.

She could barely bring herself to see a guy more than three times or date more than a few weeks. Wright was there all the time. She saw him every day.

They spent the final two miles in silence, every question and concern churning inside her. She should say something. How had they gone from delicious, desperate kisses to her fretting?

That's right, because this was her life and that's how she rolled.

And yet, she wanted to kiss him again.

She wanted to kiss him without thought, with no repercussions, even though, with him, impact was unavoidable.

As they climbed the mountain, Wright reached for her hand. A reassuring squeeze, her fingers dwarfed within his.

Over a year had passed since she'd let anyone touch her. Maybe more. Even then she was tense, 50 percent nervousness, the other 50 reluctant.

But Wright . . . She often wondered about him, about what intimacy would be like with him. Right before she scolded herself not to.

If she could relax enough to be with anyone, it was Wright.

She didn't dislike sex, but she couldn't say she'd ever had any that made her desperate for more.

Wright's thumb brushing ever so softly over the back of her hand, the tips of his other fingers gently pressed into her palm, made her desperate.

That simple movement alone was better foreplay than she'd experienced in years.

His hands were almost big enough to span her waist, cover her ribs, fit each cheek of her—Holy smokes, she was horny.

Aroused by her imagination and alarmed at the reality, she didn't know what to do. She wanted the impossible, and Wright and his sexy hands weren't helping matters.

"We're here." He parked his Jeep in the side parking for employees.

She jumped out, ready to beat a retreat into the inn and hide— maybe for a day or five—until she figured out what the hell was happening and how to gain even the tiniest bit of control over her life and libido.

"Wait." Wright was suddenly in her way again.

Curse him and his height and long legs.

Not really.

Sometimes she wanted to climb him like a tree.

"Are you trying to walk back in like nothing happened? Like it's any other night? What the hell, Sophie?"

She craned her neck to look up at him, ready to stomp her foot like a petulant child. "I . . . I don't know what the hell, okay? I don't know what I'm doing. I'm annoyed and aroused. There. Happy? Because that's all the communicating I can manage right now."

His gaze went from aggravated to amused to completely understanding, all in two seconds, and she was helpless when he looked at her like that.

"I'm sorry." And as suddenly and without warning as she'd done earlier, he grabbed her and kissed her.

Rougher this time, their frustration poured into the kiss, trying to sort through what they couldn't handle with words.

Her heartbeat raced and she clung to him. Rising onto the balls of her feet again, she wrapped her arms around his neck. She wanted to throttle him and melt into him, all at once.

Wright kissed with skill, the kind of skill that made her mind turn to mush. And it shouldn't surprise her. Being a great kisser was probably what happened when one had a string of long-term girlfriends for most of one's life.

He'd always had a girlfriend, for as long as she could remember.

Jealousy rose up, belligerently poking into the moment. Sophie swatted it back and brushed her tongue along the seam of his lips, dragging a gruff sound from his throat.

He broke away, only to press hot kisses along her jaw, toward her ear. "I'm sorry," he whispered.

"What—" Her breath caught as he kissed a particularly sensitive spot. "What do you keep apologizing for?"

"Because I know you. You're nervous and a little *what the hell* right now, but I can't stop kissing you." He straightened up, his familiar face so different when they were mid-kiss.

"It's aggravating that you know all of that." She smiled despite herself.

"You? Aggravated at me? No." His smile was playful, a reminder that the two of them got aggravated with each other on a weekly basis.

Reality crowded back in, stealing her smile.

"Aw, come on." Wright bent lower, his teeth perfect. "Let me see that smile again. Just think, we ran out of the Tavern tonight and stuck Caleb and Shane with our bill."

Her mouth fell open before shifting into another smile. "Holy crap, we did!"

"That's better. Those two deserve getting stiffed with the check."

"I wish we'd run up a bigger tab."

He laughed along with her until her face hurt. Then he cupped her jaw, his hand warm and sure against her skin. "I shouldn't have kissed you last month. My timing was shitty and I'm sorry. But I am *not* sorry for tonight."

She opened her mouth, and closed it. She wasn't sorry either.

Freaking out about the whole thing, but not sorry.

For his part, Wright seemed way too calm and self-assured for her comfort. Did he not realize what they were doing? Was he not wise enough to know this was unwise?

He glanced around again, a lost expression, possibly not that self-assured after all, "I know this is a lot to process. For me too."

Thank goodness.

"But it's all going to be fine. I should probably get you back inside now."

Yes, he probably should.

If Wright was another guy, and she was this attracted to him, she might ask him in. But there was no way. If anyone saw him coming inside with her this late, guilt tattooed all over their faces, tongues would start wagging. The more they wagged, the more tawdry the story would get, because that's how things worked in a small town.

She couldn't risk her brothers hearing secondhand, and God help her if they saw her and Wright right now.

"We'll . . ." Wright scrubbed a hand over his jaw. "We'll talk to-morrow?"

Talking seemed like a really bad idea. As a matter of fact, all of this was awful. And amazing. "Okay."

They stood toe to toe as the seconds ticked by. Was she supposed to hug him good night? Kiss him again? The handbook on How to End the Evening after Making Out with Your Friend didn't exist, and it was a damn shame.

"I . . ." Wright took the smallest stutter step forward. "I'll walk you to the door."

"No." Wow, that'd come out way too forceful. "Sorry. I mean, no, that'd be—someone could see us. I'll go by myself."

"Right. Good thinking."

She should leave now, except she couldn't get by him. She was trapped between his big body and the Jeep.

A whimper built in her throat at the images that created.

"Oh, sorry." He seemed to realize the issue and stepped aside.

With slow steps at first, Sophie eased by him. If she lingered too long, chances were they'd end up kissing again. Each kiss grew deeper, went on a little longer, their hands wandering a little farther. A third time and they would end up on second base.

Or was that third?

Sophie quickened her pace. Going from zero to her tongue in Wright's mouth was enough for one night. No way could she handle his hand down her pants, brushing his fingers against her—*"Dammit."* She tripped going up the front steps of the inn.

Yeah, she'd had all she could handle for one night.

Chapter 6

The next morning, Wright woke to find himself sprawled horizontally across his bed, the sheets wrapped around him like a burrito. As he attempted to untangle himself, the memory of the night before flooded back.

"Ah hell." He flopped back on the bed.

No wonder his bedding was like a rat's nest. Now he remembered. All night last night he'd gone back and forth between carnal dreams and horrible nightmares.

He and Sophie all over each other. Naked in his bed, on the floor, standing up, sitting down, and yes, even in the kitchen, and one particularly kinky dream involving the floating dock.

Then the relentless nightmare. Her looks of betrayal, rejection.

He was telling her about leaving Honeywilde for a new job—the locations changing from Charleston to Chicago to Asheville to LA—where he would never go.

He was pretty sure she dream-slapped him at one point.

Then there were the dreams about the other Bradleys. The big Bradleys, who could kick his ass, and *would* kick his ass if they thought he was fooling around with their sister.

Best friend or not, Devlin would have no qualms about tearing him a new one if he hurt Sophie.

But he would never hurt her. The sky would fall before he'd allow it.

With a groan, he rolled farther into his sheets until they engulfed him.

Technically, he'd already hurt her once before. Now . . . well, now he didn't know where they stood, but he wasn't going to hurt her again.

Sophie wanted him as much as he wanted her.

Last night, his blood had turned to fire, burning in his veins with the need to touch her and hold her and bring her the kind of pleasure that'd ruin her for all others. Mark her and keep her and make her his, make sure the world knew she wasn't looking for anyone else—and *none* of these prehistoric reactions could be normal.

They sure as hell weren't rational.

He banged the back of his head against the bed. He needed a harder surface, because something was seriously wrong with him.

Who thought these things? He was a modern guy, in a very forward-thinking career, and he'd been in plenty of relationships. Not once had he ever wanted to suck kisses into a woman's skin, hard enough to see the result the next day and mark Sophie in a way they would both know.

Or even better, have Sophie do the same to him.

He shifted against his thickening cock, happily on board with the idea.

"Holy shit, you have got to get it together." Wright unrolled from his bed burrito and slapped his face with both hands.

His body battled with his brain, and his body was leading the charge.

He'd been with Sophie through the few boyfriends she'd had. Unless he was mistaken, she probably didn't have a ton of experience. But after last night, the way she clung to his kisses, her slender frame pressed against him, small curves making him want to whine like a stray dog, any notions of "little Soph" were gone.

He knew the woman Sophie had become. Complicated and sexy, and stronger than she realized.

Feet planted on the floor, he leaned forward with his elbows digging into his thighs. He had to talk to her, ensure every moment from last night was real and they were still on the same page.

And he needed to kiss her again. As soon as possible.

He didn't see her all morning.

Normally, she stopped into the kitchen once or twice during or after breakfast. But not today.

He wasn't going to let that bother him, but when lunch came and went, he was officially bothered. His job chained him to the kitchen most days, and she knew that. That was why she typically visited him. Sophie had the freedom to wander the resort.

His longest break in the day was between lunch and Honeywilde's coffee and cookies hour, and that was the time he usually tried to get away from the place; take a walk around the lake or, on particularly busy days, sit in a quiet spot and stare off into oblivion for a few seconds.

Today he had enough time for a walk, and he used it to go in search of Sophie.

In the blazing afternoon sun, he found her arranging chairs and lounges at the lakeside with Trevor.

She had on a navy tank top and khaki shorts. Simple enough, but damn, she looked good. An enormous navy-and-white striped beach hat sheltered her fair skin from the harsh rays, big sunglasses covering her face. Trevor, on the other hand, was a tawny brown, with only a ball cap and maybe some SPF 30 for protection.

"You guys need a hand?"

Sophie straightened at the sound of his voice, turning toward him.

"Yeah, man." Trevor was hauling two umbrellas from the tiny building where they kept the beach furniture. "Grab a few more of those umbrellas and we should be set."

As soon as the umbrellas were up and Sophie had the plastic Adirondacks positioned exactly the way she wanted them, Trevor got fidgety.

"You need a hand with anything else here, sis? I've got something I'm working on that'd I'd like to get back to."

"What are you working on?" Wright asked.

"No, you can go." Sophie kept him from answering. "Thanks for the hand."

With that, Trevor was nothing but a blur, leaving the beach.

"Am I not allowed to know what he's working on? I didn't know Trev worked independently."

She fussed with one of the chairs again. "I don't know what he's working on either, but I didn't want you encouraging him to stay."

"You're going to talk to me now instead of avoiding me like you have all morning."

"I haven't been avoiding you."

He stood, silent, and cocked an eyebrow at her.

Eventually, she glanced over. "Fine, I've been avoiding you. But we can't do this here."

Voice pitched low, he leaned forward. "What'd you have in mind?"

"Oh my god." She held her hat and checked the area around them to see if anyone could hear.

They couldn't.

"You can't say things like that."

"We say stuff like that all the time."

"Not . . ." Another check. "Not now we can't."

"What do you mean, we can't *now*?"

With those huge sunglasses, he couldn't tell if she was looking at him or through him, couldn't read her expression or even fathom a guess as to what she was trying to say.

"Come on." He took her hand and started walking.

"Where are we going? You can't hold my hand like that."

"No one out here cares. We're only going right here." He led her inside the small storage building.

A stack of plastic chairs and extra umbrellas still filled one side of the building. Inside was dark and stuffy, the only light coming from the open door, but he needed a place where he could talk to her. Immediately.

"You've been avoiding me all day."

"No, I haven't."

He gave her a blank-faced stare. "Before we fought, I'd see you two or three times a morning."

"I've been busy today."

"You're busy every day. You're the busiest person at Honeywilde, and you'd still manage to pop into the kitchen. I thought you would again since—"

"We kissed."

"Exactly."

"No, I mean *we kissed*, Wright. You and I. Twice. I . . ." She jerked the sunglasses off her face and looked around the cramped building. "I don't know what to do with that."

He knew exactly what to do. Kiss again, and again and again. "It felt like a lot more than a kiss."

Her hand went to her forehead, knocking her hat off balance as she rubbed. "I know, and that's why . . ."

"Why what? I'm not dating anyone anymore. You're not dating that shit heel either. Why shouldn't we kiss?"

Even in the dark, he could make out her eyes going bigger and rounder than soup bowls, her voice shrill and a little manic. "*Why not?* Are you freaking kidding me?"

"Easy." He moved her away from the door. "You're going to have guests running in here to save a dying cat."

She grabbed his arm. "Be serious. You know exactly why, whether we're dating other people or not. We can't just start dating or hooking up."

Okay, so they *weren't* on the same page.

"My family is finally getting along. Business is going well and my brothers aren't at each other's throats. Things are copacetic. Peaceful. Do you realize we've had zero drama—I mean, besides you and me not speaking—almost all summer? That's an entire season. That's a huge deal in this family."

"I know, but—"

"And the last Honeywilde drama was when I wasn't speaking to you and Dev held an inquisition after the Blueberry Festival as to why."

"What did you tell him?"

"I made something up. Doesn't matter. What matters is, if Dev found out his best friend and baby sister were fooling around, at best, he'd be disturbed. At worst, he'd be furious. He's finally happy. Our Devlin. Happy."

Shit. If anyone knew how hard Dev had to fight for happiness, it was Wright. "But what if the two of us being together made him happy?"

Sophie snorted. "You didn't invite me to cotillion, Wright. Knowing we made out in the kitchen and the parking lot of a bar isn't going to make any of my brothers happy."

"Shit." She had a point. "Then I could ask you out proper. Do this the right way."

"And the two of us will date under the scrutiny of my entire family? Every day, my brothers watching you like hawks? Three big, annoyed hawks? Wondering how long you've had your eye on me? What you're up to and whether or not you're going to dump me like you did Kate?"

Wright's mouth fell open. "You know I wouldn't do that. I dumped her because . . ."

Sophie gazed up at him, her hat askew, lightly freckled shoulders on display in the tank top. Damn, he loved those freckles, especially with her skin flushed from the heat and exertion of working by the lake.

"I dumped her because I kissed you."

Her expression softened. "I know. But do you want to explain to Dev about how you kissed me when you had a girlfriend? Because I don't."

Wright bit back another curse. "No."

Nothing could stop his desire to kiss her again. Take her into his arms and feel the gentle give of her lips, the small curves of her body.

"So what do we do? Never touch each other again, when that's all I can think about?" He took a step closer, and her eyebrows rose, her expression shifting away from the wry look to something expectant.

"Kissing you. Kissing you other places. Everywhere."

With her lips pinched together, she glanced away. "Wright."

"No one can hear me. Stop worrying. Last night was wonderful."

"I know, but . . ."

"But what?"

"But if we do that again, and it leads to . . ." She gave him a pointed look.

Everything within him screamed *Yes!* He wanted their kissing to lead exactly there. Sex and more sex and Sophie being his. If she didn't want to rock the apple cart now that Honeywilde and the Bradley family were finally a balanced bunch, fine. He could live with not bumping up against her brothers for the time being.

"Who says your brothers have to know what we do?" The question was out of his mouth before he could catch it.

Sophie gasped and his mouth fell open too. He was equally shocked he'd suggested it.

"Are you suggesting we hide this from my family?"

"Technically, what we do isn't their business unless you want it to be. Dev didn't tell us he was with Anna. So this is your call. If you want to tell them, I'm in. I'll deal with the scrutiny. I'll go tell your brothers right now."

"No!" Sophie pinched her lips together again.

"Then we don't have to say a word to them."

"But . . . it feels wrong to lie. Doesn't that mean we're wrong?"

He could see where this was going. Sophie was a soft heart. Always had been. The last thing she'd ever want was to hurt or disappoint anyone. She was a pleaser, going above and beyond to make her family happy, even if it meant putting herself last.

And they were treading into what many thought was questionable territory: attraction and sexual interest for someone who was once a platonic friend.

Especially when that friend was his best friend's sister.

Now that he'd accepted his desire for Sophie, there were plenty of times in the past when he should've known.

Two years ago, during a long, hot summer like this one, he and Dev had taken a day off. Dev had already stopped drinking by then and gone on to bed, but Wright didn't want to go home. He'd pilfered the bar for beer and sat on the verandah.

Sophie had flopped down next to him and taken his beer. She gave it back after a sip or two, but it tasted like beer and citrus-flavored ChapStick.

He should've been disgusted at the fruit flavor disrupting his perfectly good beer. Instead, he'd shifted in his seat, his dick twitching in interest about what she'd taste like if he kissed her. But because sometimes he was a horny guy, like anybody else, he'd written it off.

Then he'd damned himself for having impure thoughts about the Bradley baby sister, and drunk half his beer to put out the fire and brimstone.

Sophie had lingered, griping about something or other with the staff. A cool breeze blew across the verandah and he'd tried not to notice, but her nipples pebbled against the cotton of her shirt, just enough to see.

He'd jerked his gaze away and told himself boobs were boobs and they were all attractive. He was a hot-blooded, heterosexual male. How could he not notice?

She kept talking and making him laugh with her impressions of her brothers, and he didn't want to leave. Two more beers borrowed from the bar, and he got her to stay. Together, they complained about almost every single person they worked with, and a few of the folks in town, laughing until his sides hurt.

When she did finally leave, he craved her company. He saw her every day, talked to her all the time, and still he wanted more.

He didn't *want* Sophie. He liked her. At least, that's what he'd told himself at the time.

Now he was done fighting his desire. He liked her and he wanted her.

Sophie fiddled with the sunglasses in her hand and shrugged. "I don't know, but if I feel this guilty about last night, then maybe we shouldn't do it." Her statement was a plea, her gaze longing for answers.

He only had one answer, and it wasn't going to change.

Even as she questioned everything they were doing, she took a step toward him, not away. "We should stop, right?"

He closed the gap between them in one step. "Wrong."

Chapter 7

Wright cupped her face with both hands and kissed her. With more pressure and purpose than ever before, like he was making a statement, he molded their lips together and she fell in.

Headfirst, she fell into kissing him, grabbing his bent arms, sliding her hands up until the tips of her fingers went underneath the short sleeves of his shirt. His skin was hot from the sun and smooth. She'd seen Wright's arms a million times, at least half of those times with some kind of pervy thought, but now she'd never be able to look at them with any other kind of thought.

Hard muscle, the rise and fall making a perfect arc, and even though it was a little more than her hands could hold on to, trying to get a good grip was half the fun.

Wright deepened the kiss and she opened to him, all her talk about why they shouldn't do this, *couldn't* do this, falling away and rolling across the sandy lakeside. He swept his tongue against hers, gentle sucking pulls against her lips before he rained kisses along her jaw, his hands smoothing down her neck to her collarbone.

They were making out in a freaking shed at the lakeside of her family's resort, and she was doing nothing to resist. She didn't want to. She wanted this with Wright as much as he did.

Her concerns about why they couldn't do this were valid, but deep down, the only thing that ever stopped her was fear.

Fear of losing everything. Her family, Wright, her own tenuous grasp on happiness.

Her whole life she'd worried about what came next. The what-ifs.

That's what happened when your entire life changed in the five seconds it took for a car to skid on water. Then changed again in the time it took for one person to say, "I'm leaving."

But if no one knew what she and Wright were up to, then no one would be affected. There'd be no what-ifs to worry about.

Since she'd become a Bradley, it felt like most of her life was spent trying like hell to keep the peace. When had she ever done anything for herself? When was the last time she selfishly went for something she wanted, not what was best for everyone else?

Never. That's when.

She'd always gone through phases of lusting after Wright. She'd stomp it down and they'd move on, only for it to rear back up again.

What if she could simply let go and let this happen?

She slid her hands farther up Wright's arms and wrapped her arms around his neck, pressing her body firmly against his.

With an appreciative hum that rumbled like a growl near the end, he put his arms around her too, hoisting her up, taking her lips again, kissing her like he was starving. She sucked hard at his bottom lip, earning another delicious noise from his throat. Then he started moving.

It took a moment before she realized her feet no longer touched the ground.

Wright walked until her bottom hit something—the stack of plastic chairs.

He set her down, never breaking the kiss, not so much as a pause as he went back to kissing her cheek, her throat. She threaded fingers through his hair, holding him closer as he licked and nibbled her neck.

Testing his reaction, she gave his hair a gentle tug, wanting him to take her lips again.

Wright met her gaze, his skin as flushed as hers felt, a sensual grin on his face, his eyes shining.

He leaned in, kissing her again, his hands smoothing up the back of her bare calves.

All of her nerve endings fired to life, her skin prickling, hairs standing on end.

She had on shorts, and Wright wasn't shy.

He dragged his hands up and up, to the back of her knees, tugging them wider and dragging her toward the edge of the chairs. His hands were strong, deft. An artist's hands that she'd watched create delicacies and beauty. Those hands slid up her thighs, to the edge of her shorts, shooting a bolt of need straight to her core.

Her muscles clenched and she tightened her legs together, around

Wright. He sucked hard against the skin of her neck, murmuring words of approval.

"Go on. You won't hurt me," he said.

Having a man between her legs? Not that common an occurrence. A man like Wright? Never.

She squeezed tighter against the swell of need but forced herself to let go of his hair, touching his neck, finding his skin even hotter than before, the feel of his throat, the vibrations as he spoke sexier than she ever thought possible.

Inside, her nerves sang, a pulsing between her legs that she recognized but couldn't believe.

Wright tugged at the strap of her tank top, her bra sliding with it. He pulled and yanked, dragging his lips over every inch of skin as it was revealed.

He murmured something she couldn't make out against her skin. Something about her freckles. Then the air hit her, warm and humid, but his mouth was hotter, wet, and when he closed his lips around her nipple, she pinched her lips together to keep from crying out.

She didn't war with the sensations he wrung from her, or that it was Wright doing it. Right now, she didn't care. She'd never felt this way. A dancing flame on the edge of wildfire.

And when he grasped her hips and jerked her even farther forward, the hard line of his erection rubbed against her, and she knew.

She and Wright were going to have sex.

Maybe not right now, maybe not tonight. But they were eventually going to have sex—and it would be amazing. If everything so far was any indication, it'd be the most amazing sex of her life.

And she couldn't wait.

She couldn't wait to make him clamp down against his cry of pleasure the way she had. To see him naked and satisfy the dozens of curiosities she'd had for years. She couldn't wait to make him come and then see him again later, both of them knowing what they'd done, what she'd done to him.

Sophie moved her hand from her mouth and grasped Wright's shoulders, keeping her lips pinched tight as he rocked into her. His hard-on rubbed against her just right, the friction making her blood sing. The cleft of her sex went full, sensitive, and she knew, if he kept going, what would happen.

"God, you're amazing," Wright murmured against her skin, brushing his thumb over her nipple. He pressed himself harder against her, rubbing just right. "I knew it'd be like this with you. I *knew*."

As he pinched her nipple, Sophie pinched her eyes closed, and stars danced on the backs of her eyelids. She gasped, one long tremor taking over her body.

Wright straightened to his full height, eyes wide, his beautiful square jaw slack. "Did you just—"

She kissed him to shut him up.

Yes, of course she came. Her body was highly sensitive when treated right. Thanks to no guy, she had to find that out for herself after college. But Wright knew what the hell he was doing.

A minute later she leaned back, Wright's expression still one of awe.

"Why are you looking at me like that?" She let her head fall back against the top of the chair. "Was that not the intention with all that rubbing and sucking?"

He grinned, catching his bottom lip between his teeth. Then his laugh washed over her, full and rich, making her smile right along with him. "You're so awesome. Why weren't we doing this sooner?"

"Soph?" Her brother Dev's voice boomed across the beach as he called her name.

"Shit." She slapped her hand over Wright's mouth, his eyes wide over the top of her fingers. "Move. I have to get down." Once she hopped off the stack of chairs, she righted her top, fluffed her hair, and put her hat back on. "How do I look?" she whispered.

Wright's voice was a low-pitched, promising drawl. "Delicious. Like you've been debauched."

She swatted him on the arm. "Don't just stand there. Help."

He tried smoothing her hair down, fixing her clothes, but in the end, him touching her wasn't helping matters and she had to shoo his hands away.

"Fine." He stepped back. "You can pass for being overheated. But I can't."

She checked him over again. He was gorgeous. Even better looking than yesterday, but there was no missing the tent he was currently pitching.

"You can't go out there like that."

"No shit."

"Don't . . ." She let out a huff of frustration. "Stay in here and don't come out until the coast is clear." She shoved on her sunglasses and headed to the door, which was still slightly open.

"Don't lock me in here," he hissed.

Flapping her hand behind her she walked out into the sunlight, putting on her brightest, sweet sister smile, and closed the door behind her. "Dev. You looking for me?"

Dev tossed his hands up and stalked through the sand. "Yes, I'm looking for you. Where have you been? We were going to go over the numbers for the catfish dinner at the Butler reunion."

The Butler reunion hadn't occurred to her once today. "I know. But I had to make sure the lakeside was all set for this afternoon."

Dev took the time to check out the small beach, admiring her work. Which gave her an extra second to catch her breath and try to recalibrate after going from climax to catfish in less than sixty seconds.

"Looks nice. Good work, Sis. I like the different colors of chairs. Festive." He smiled, and while the sight was less rare nowadays, she remained as grateful every time.

For all they'd been through, the times he'd broken her heart and made her want to cry with frustration for him to *try* not to be so angry, Dev was undeniably her favorite brother.

He knew it. Everyone knew it. You weren't supposed to have favorites within your family, but she and Dev broke that rule.

The rough road that took Dev from wayward resentful son to one of Honeywilde's greatest assets, and the town's favorite Bradley, had only brought them closer. Of all her brothers, he was the one she could always talk to.

And his best friend had just made her orgasm.

"When did we get the umbrellas? They're Honeywilde themed." He held his hand over his eyes, looking at the signature apricot-and-white striped umbrellas dotting the beach.

"A month ago. Madison helped me pick them out."

He hmmed. "I hadn't noticed."

"You wouldn't have. You've been blind to everything except a Blueberry Festival and your girlfriend. Or is she your fiancée yet?"

Without looking at her, he said, "Don't start."

She had to start because she needed to think about something besides what she'd done. "Don't avoid the question."

"She is not my fiancée, but I promise, you will be the first to know when she is. Satisfied?"

Sophie rocked onto the balls of her feet and back again. "Very." She adored Anna. Dev had never been more at ease, happy, or more positive about life's possibilities. Anyone who could do that for him was a keeper in her book.

"Come on then, let's go inside or at least in the shade and talk about this reunion. I'm roasting out here."

And Wright was currently having a sauna in the storage building. They needed to leave the lakeside so he could escape. "How about inside? I need something to drink."

She led the way off the beach as quickly as she could. Only when they reached the crest of the slope leading up to the inn did she risk glancing back to see the storage room door ease open.

Chapter 8

Wright sucked in lungs full of fresh air, cursing the summer heat. Luckily, the few lakeside guests around were too caught up with their books or sunbathing to notice him stumbling from the storage shed, pouring sweat.

It wasn't as bad earlier, with the door cracked open and Sophie arching into him, but alone in the stuffy dark, in what had to be ninety degrees, he was about to die. Particularly when he heard Dev's voice outside the door, chatting with Sophie, the way they always did.

His best friend and the woman who seconds before was writhing in his arms, the most intoxicating look on her face as she reached climax.

Damn, he could get addicted to that look and the high he got putting it there.

Wright dragged a hand through his hair, damp at the temples, and fanned open the hem of his T-shirt. He had to go back inside without looking like he'd hiked a few miles in the middle of the afternoon.

Taking his time, he went the long way, circling the inn and going in the front. Maybe by then he wouldn't look like he'd been in a sauna.

Vivian cocked her head to the side as he walked in the front door. "Did you go for a run with Roark?"

"No, just a walk. Hot one out there today."

Her eyebrows pinched together.

It wasn't *that* hot—unless you exerted yourself by getting it on in an oven.

Rather than stick around and try to explain his sweaty state, he hightailed it to the kitchen. In the back room was his backpack, and in his backpack he always kept a change of clothes. If you worked in a kitchen, you quickly learned to pack extra clothes.

Once he pulled a clean shirt out of his bag, he tugged the damp one over his head and used it to pat himself dry. Probably not good enough, though.

"Where is it?" He dug around in his bag. There was deodorant in there somewhere.

"Ahem." The intent yet delicate sound of a woman clearing her throat, and he didn't have to turn around to know it was Sophie.

He turned anyway, to find her leaning back against the door frame, her hands tucked behind her.

"Why do you have your shirt off?" Her gaze swept over him, the greedy way she took him in rippling goose flesh across his skin.

"Because I was soaking wet. Thanks for closing me up in a million-degree wooden box, by the way."

She strode toward him. "I had to close the door. Dev was standing right there. Besides, you weren't complaining about the heat before."

He stared down at her. The hat and sunglasses were gone, but if anyone really paid attention, they could see the how the skin of her neck was a littler pinker, her hair a little messier than normal. "That was different. You were in there with me."

She slanted her gaze down, over his chest, to where he held the clean shirt in his fist.

"Stop looking at me like that," he warned her.

"Like what?" Her gaze flitted up.

"Like you want to eat me."

The corners of her lips quirked up. "That's not *exactly* the scenario I was envisioning, but close."

A sound escaped his lips, a punched-out noise like she'd knocked the air from his lungs. Because she had.

Imagining her laid out before him, legs spread, with him on his knees between them—

"What the hell has gotten into you? Are you trying to kill me?"

"No." She tugged at the shirt in his grip. "I'm trying to collect you. I was meeting with Dev, and Roark barged in. He wants to talk to us. All of us. And you know precisely what's gotten into me."

His mouth fell open as she turned the shirt in her hands, gathering the cotton until she held the shirt open at the neck. "You can't be serious. I have to meet with Roark? Right now?"

She lifted her arms, jerking her chin until he bent down so she could shove the shirt over his head. "Yes, unfortunately I'm being dead serious. He interrupted me and Dev—which was just as well; I couldn't focus worth a darn—and said we all had to meet in his office immediately."

Wright stuffed his arms through the short sleeves, being careful not to knock into Sophie within the close confines. "So you come in here, looking at me like that, and now we have to go to a meeting with your brothers and talk about work?"

"Basically."

"You're evil."

"It's not my fault. You were the one in here topless."

"I was topless because you shut me up in that damn hot box and I was dripping sweat into my—Ah, to hell with it." There was no point arguing with her, so he grabbed her up and kissed her instead.

She clung to his shirt, fisting the material in her hands, holding him closer while also trying to push him away. "Don't start this. We have to go to the meeting."

"I know, I know." He cupped her jaw. "I'm done now. Let's go talk about whatever it is Roark wants to talk about. I'm sure I'll be able to focus, *no* problem."

Sophie led the way from the kitchen, her slim hips swaying with each step, her tight little body on display in the simple khaki shorts and tank. How did he ever get any work done around her before? A switch had been flipped and he couldn't go back. Everything about her captivated him.

The way her hair was long enough to brush her shoulders, how her eyes weren't exactly green, but a hazel mix of gold and brown, depending on what color she wore. And that every time she'd teased him—relentlessly—over the last few years, she'd given him that same little smile, but now it wasn't simply mischievous. Her smile was thick with promise, secretly seductive, making him reevaluate every smile he could remember.

And, as a point of fact, since it was currently right in front of him, she had a *phenomenal* ass. He'd been remiss about noticing how great it was.

"Stop it." Sophie pulled up short, forcing him to slam on the brakes.

"Stop what?"

"Stop looking at me like that. You're being super obvious."

"You mean the same way you were looking at me about a minute ago."

"Yes, but now we're going to be around other people. You look at me like that in the middle of Roark's meeting and they're all going to know. Dial it back a notch."

He could try, but it would take a monumental strength of will. "Okay, but don't sit near me."

"Fine." She started walking again, her legs shapely and strong. They'd felt particularly long when wrapped around him, squeezing him tight.

"And don't cross your legs."

Her pace slowed and he took the opportunity to walk beside her. Behind her wasn't doing him any favors.

"Why can't I cross my legs?"

"Trust me on this one. I'll stand off to the side and you take the seat by the wall, and I won't look at you. At all. We should be fine."

Sophie rolled her eyes, but when they reached Roark's office, she sat in the chair nearest the wall, and he took up his position by the window.

Devlin was already in the other chair and Trevor soon joined them, leaning against the wall near Wright.

"Thanks guys, for dropping what you were doing so we could meet." Roark closed the door on his way in and sat in the old leather chair at his desk. "I know this is last minute, but the Chamber wants our theme suggestions tomorrow morning, so we need to decide."

Dev angled himself toward Sophie. "Everything is booked and official. Now all that's left is executing the event."

Her delicate brows drew together. "All that's left? That's easy enough for you to say when I'm the one stuck with most of the executing. On top of everything else I do."

Both Roark and Dev spoke at the same time, claiming that wasn't true, but everyone knew Sophie worked harder than anyone. Whether from lack of help or because she didn't trust anyone else to handle things properly, Sophie tended to end up with more on her plate than anyone.

"I'm here too," Dev argued. "And I'm of actual use now, so that ought to make a huge difference."

"I know." She reached over and patted his arm. "I wasn't imply-
ing otherwise. I . . . I don't know."

Wright knew.

Sophie was hoping for the occasional moment of free time, same
as him, because now they had an excellent use for it.

Trevor bounced his weight off the wall. "You know whatever
work you get stuck with, I'll help. I've been helping more too."

Before Sophie could respond, the words were out of Wright's
mouth. "And I can help."

Her gaze clashed with his.

Offering to help her wasn't completely out of the ordinary, but it
wasn't common either.

Wright's job at the resort was more streamlined than anyone's.
They weren't going to let their chef take on the job of setting up
chairs and tables or calling up a DJ or band to perform at an event.

He was food. He was always food, and if Honeywilde had something going on, he would be cooking.

There'd be no way for him to help Sophie, that was why he rarely
offered, and what made his offer now so out of place.

"It's funny you say that, Wright." Roark tapped a white index
card against the ink blotter on his desk, studying Wright, jaw set like
he was about to lay down the law.

Uh-oh. Sophie's oldest brother knew about them. How in the hell
could Roark already know? He couldn't know. Wright was screwed.
He was going to be fired and get his ass kicked and lose his best
friend, lose everything, including Sophie.

His heart kicked in his chest, heat spreading across his back, making him sweat. The sensation was only slightly worse than if he were
locked in a lake shed in the summer heat.

"The Chamber's board sent us their list of theme ideas, and they're
horrible and boring. At Sophie's suggestion, I put Madison and Anna
on it and they gave us a few options."

Roark tapped the card again. "The ideas are all conducive to a
semiformal environment. Guests will be in dinner jackets and cock-
tail dresses. The theme is really more about the décor and menu,
which is why I'd prefer we pick our poison and get the Chamber to
go along."

"Enough with the dramatics already." Dev snatched the card from his brother as Wright's heart tried to skip back into rhythm, leaving him breathless.

"Carnival," Dev read.

"No." Wright and Sophie axed the idea in syncopation and she glared at him again.

"It's overdone and can get tacky," she explained.

Dev tilted his head. "Agreed. We want something classy, but unique. Something out of the ordinary." He scanned the list, shaking his head at one or two more. "*Ooh*, I like this one. A Midsummer Night. Nice."

"Of course you like that one, it was Anna's idea."

"What can I say, she has great taste."

Sophie took the card away from Dev. "I like it too. An enchanted evening feel. Magical atmosphere."

"I could come up with a menu that suits." Wright nodded to himself. "Lots of rich food, but small plate items, European fusion style fare, plenty of drinks, people giving away their money. A fund raising *gala* sounds about right."

Roark leaned forward. "I like it. We could wait until six for cocktails, dinner at seven, so it'll only be hot for the first hour or so. But we'll need food stations versus a lot of wait staff. Lots of food stations." He looked at Wright. "Which is why I'm glad you want to help. They want a completely unique menu from what we normally serve. What you already have in mind sounds perfect. I want you to get with Steve on some signature drinks to complement the dishes. They're paying us a lot of money to host this. Pull out all the stops so they get a good return from donations."

In other words, fill them up on high-end food and beverage to make their wallets loose.

Wright didn't have to look to know Sophie was staring. Her gaze buzzed against his skin as Roark kept talking and making notes in his phone. "To keep Sophie from doing too much and telling us all to taking a flying leap, Dev, I'd like you to head up the event. Sophie and Wright can take lead on operations and food, respectively. Trevor, you'll be Soph's right hand. Everybody okay with this?"

They'd all be working on another big event together, spending even more time with each other than usual, this time with him and Sophie teamed up to create a magical night for a bunch of strangers.

Great. All of them together, all the time. How could any of this possibly be a problem?

When Sophie gave him a warning glare, he realized he'd been staring at her. He jerked his gaze away. "Sounds like a good plan to me."

Sophie began typing on her phone, likely making a list of things they'd need to do. She'd picked up the habit from Roark, but she held the phone, slender fingers dancing across the screen in a way Roark's never could.

Wright had to tear his gaze away again. "Do you want me to create a few different menus and let you guys decide?"

Roark shared a look with Dev and smiled. "I think I speak for everyone when I say you have more knowledge and skill about designing a menu than any of us. Pick whatever you'd like. You make the executive decision. Something that fits with the night and can feed approximately one hundred people. We trust you."

A knot formed in his gut.

They trusted him.

Only because they didn't know he'd entertained offers from their competitors, talked to people who'd hire him away, move him hundreds of miles from here, and pay him twice what he was making now. Maybe more.

They trusted him because they didn't know the way he felt about their sister. The way he saw her, the things he imagined.

Whether or not the latter should matter, he still felt the weight of guilt.

He and Sophie were adults, capable of making their own decisions, and it was no one else's business, not even her brothers.

Still, his loyalty to the Bradleys ran deep. They were as much a second family to him as they were to Sophie.

She'd lost her parents but the Bradleys had filled that loss.

Her brothers' approval mattered, to both of them. No matter how much Wright might insist their opinions didn't count, they did. And if Dev knew about earlier today, in the lake shed, his head would spin around.

Sophie glanced up and caught him watching her. She gave him another pointed look, but amusement sparkled in her eyes as she shook her head.

Wright's chest swelled, his limbs going warm and gooey at one little look, and he knew. Head spinning or not, he wasn't going to stop this thing with her. If Sophie wanted him, he would never throw on the brakes. It wouldn't be him to say no and walk away; it'd have to be her.

With a history of doing exactly that, she probably would, and he'd be left to clean up the mess. But even the thought of losing her someday wasn't enough to deter him.

He'd deal with heartache and fallout if they came. Better to only be with Sophie for a little while than to never be with her at all.

"Good." Roark slapped his hands together, and Wright jumped. "I'll email the board and let them know we're in. I'll give them the theme idea and you guys can run with it. Keep me informed and I'll keep the board informed."

Dev glanced around at each of them and laughed.

"What?" Roark frowned.

"Oh, nothing. But you letting us run this whole show, while you play messenger? It's—"

"Awesome," Trevor filled in.

Everyone chuckled but Wright.

"I'm working on delegating more, lording less." Roark rose from his chair.

Sophie tucked her phone into the pocket of her shorts. "We approve."

The meeting was over and Wright needed to get back to the kitchen or there'd be no cookies or dinner for anyone, but he lingered. With steps much slower than his normal hauling-ass speed, he loitered outside Roark's office until it became obvious he was lurking.

He'd turned away, giving up, when Sophie finally emerged. She fell into step beside him, silent as they walked toward the kitchen. Her destination would be one of the tables in the restaurant where she often did paperwork before and after dinner service.

Almost every day, Wright saw her in the restaurant working, but today was unlike any of the others.

Next to him, Sophie laughed softly, shaking her head and checking behind them. "Nice work on the gala spin."

"Thanks."

"But you were so bad at everything else. Even with all of your experience."

"Bad at what? What experience?"

She paused, turning toward him, her voice quiet. "Oh, come on. You've dated how many women?"

"Several."

She stared, blank-faced.

"A lot. But I treated all of them well."

"Yet you are *horrible* at playing it cool. You kept staring at me during the meeting, with this look."

She began walking again and he waited until they reached the restaurant before taking her hand and tugging her into the kitchen. The dry pantry was the first door on the left. He dragged her inside. "What look?"

"That look." She pointed at his face, but her smile dazzled, even in the poor light.

"I'll try to do better next time, but it's not my fault. You look so good and I keep thinking about earlier."

"Then stop thinking." Her gaze danced away. "But me too."

He stepped closer. "I have to start making cookies."

"I know."

"Then I have to start dinner. I won't have any free time until after we close, and tonight will be late." He wanted one last kiss. Something to hold them over until . . . until who knew when.

Her fingers laced with his, she pulled him to bend down. "I know. But seeing as how we work together, I imagine we'll run into one another very soon."

That was one of the perks of their situation. No matter how late he finished tonight, he'd definitely see her tomorrow.

"Plus, I know where to find you if I need you." Her smile clenched his heart as she rose and pressed her lips to his.

The kiss wasn't one of desperate need, like before. Gentle and unhurried, it soothed a wave of anxiety that he didn't understand. He brushed their lips together and wanted to say he'd always be right here, but he couldn't make that promise anymore.

For now, though, he wasn't going anywhere.

Sophie leaned away. "And I promise not to hide this time."

"Doesn't matter." He gave her hand a squeeze before finally letting go. "I'll always find you."

Chapter 9

The next morning, Sophie popped her head into the kitchen to say hey to Wright and was immediately swept up into a housekeeping emergency.

They were short-staffed on housekeeping already, and one of her employees called in sick. After cleaning some of the guest rooms herself, she sat down to complete the online posting to find a new housekeeper *today*. Hiding at the bar after the lunch rush, she typed furiously, determined to knock that off her list.

Then Devlin parked it on the stool next to her.

"Hey." He was a little breathless. "What are you doing?"

"Working." She kept typing. "What are you doing?"

"I need you to run an errand with me. Real quick."

He got the side eye for that one. "Right now?"

"Yes. It won't take long, I promise."

"Can't Trevor help you?"

"Absolutely not. I need your help."

She grumbled and moaned at his insistence, even though she'd never tell Dev no.

"I mean it, Soph. I need you."

Slowly, realization began to dawn. Dev wouldn't demand her help, and only her help, unless it was something private. He trusted her the most, and the only private thing he had going on nowadays was Anna.

"Wait, are you—"

"Don't ask questions. Say you'll go with me." His blue eyes practically glowed with excitement. "Come on. Close the laptop and put it away. We won't be gone half an hour."

Her voice conspiratorially low, she leaned close. "Where are we going? Nothing around here takes less than half an hour. It takes ten minutes just to get off the mountain."

His smirk was classic Dev. Unruffled with a whiff of brotherly judgment. "Would you stop fretting and move your butt already? We won't be gone long. I promise."

Twenty minutes later, they were inside Larkin's Jewelers, staring at two of the prettiest engagement rings she'd ever seen.

"I can't decide which one to get Anna."

She tried blinking away the burn in her eyes. "Awww, Dev." She wasn't going to cry; she was *not* going to cry.

Both diamonds were set in in platinum, one a classic Tiffany-style solitaire, the other a vintage style with the round-cut diamond surrounded in a halo of tiny diamonds.

"They're both gorgeous." Sophie turned the vintage style in the light, making it sparkle.

"Thanks. I have a favorite, but I need you to weigh in. I want to be sure I make the right choice."

Sophie considered both rings. He really couldn't go wrong either way, but which one would Anna love most? "I don't know. You know her best, which one do you think?"

"Nuh-uh." He shook his head. "That's cheating. I want you to give me your honest opinion."

Anna was classic and stylish, like the clean-lined solitaire. But since she'd met Dev, she was a little bolder and free. She was still classic, but Anna was far from ordinary. A ring like anyone else's would never do, and it certainly wouldn't do for Dev.

"This one." Sophie held up the vintage halo one, the clarity so spectacular she could almost see rainbows.

"You sure?" Dev grinned and held out his hand.

She put the ring in her brother's palm. "I'm positive. This one has my vote."

He sighed, his knees giving way a bit. "Thank God."

Behind the counter, Mr. Larkin, the town's top jeweler since 1970-something, chuckled.

"What?" Anna looked back and forth between them.

"Your brother had that ring special made. I think he would've up and died if you said it was ugly." Mr. Larkin turned to get a ring box and cleaning cloth.

Sophie stared at Dev. "You had the ring made for Anna?" The pleasant burn of tears returned.

"I did." His grin grew, and then fell. "Uh-oh. Don't you start. You'll be all blotchy when we get back and people will start asking questions."

"It's so romantic." One tear welled up. "You're getting married."

Dev handed Mr. Larkin the ring and took her by the elbow, leading her away from the counter. "Not today, I'm not. I'm . . . preparing. No waterworks yet. I need you to keep it together if I'm going to get through this."

"Why? Are you nervous?"

"What do you think?" He held up his right hand, and it trembled.

Who would've ever thought? Devlin Bradley. Nervous.

"You don't have to be nervous." Sophie pushed his hand down.

"What if it's too soon?"

Sophie laughed. "It is quick and maybe it's too soon for some people, but you and Anna aren't some people. The timing is perfect."

Devlin was never going to be the kind of guy to date Anna for a year, be practical about time and wait patiently. Heck no. Her brother was in love and leaping, and she bet Anna wouldn't have it any other way. "She's going to say yes. You know she'll say yes."

"Will she?"

"Come on." Sophie made a show of rolling her eyes. Anna and Dev loved each other so much it was a little bit sickening. "Of course she will. When are you going to ask her?"

"I don't know. I had to get the ring first, and now . . . now I guess I better figure something out. I want it to be special."

Her brother. Getting married. Earlier this year, she would've laughed in the face of anyone who said Dev would be hitched before Christmas. But the truth was, he would be, and they were perfect together.

Anna accepted Dev for exactly who he was. She didn't want to change him, but having her in his life made Dev happier, and that made him a better person.

Sophie was thrilled for her brother, and shamefully envious of what he had.

What she wanted didn't make sense. She longed for that kind of relationship and was simultaneously scared to death. To have that connection with someone might be wonderful, but it made you vulnerable.

Too vulnerable. Even as she coveted what she saw in others, she couldn't imagine herself in Dev's position.

She'd never been in Dev's position.

After a few dates, she ran off every guy she dated. Even the two or three decent ones didn't last. The longer they stuck around, the closer they became, and as they grew closer, she got nervous.

Intimacy, not only the physical but the emotional, was terrifying.

The last guy she liked, she drove crazy, right before she'd driven him away. To this day she hadn't lived down that reputation.

There were still rumors about her messing with poor Paul's head. That's what they called him. *Poor Paul*. She'd gone out with him for almost two months. A record for her.

They'd even had sex, but he kept insisting she was "distant" or "indifferent." When she did finally open up to him, she wanted reassurance from him. She needed to know that he was there for her, that her feelings, and fears, were valid.

Suddenly she was too "needy" and "paranoid," and that's when they'd broken up in dramatic, glorious fashion.

Paul's friends still gave her wary looks if they ran into her.

"I should probably tell Wright I found a ring." Dev leaned over to look at a case of watches. "He might have some suggestions about a way to pop the question. He always has suggestions."

"Yeah. He's good at suggestions." Among other things.

Lord above. And now there was Wright.

"So you two are talking again?"

Sophie stared blindly at the case in front of her. "Uh-huh."

"That's good."

Good, except what was she supposed to do now that they'd gone from talking to making out? Eventually they'd go from making out to sex and from sex to . . . being together? The way they were going, they were moving as fast as Dev and Anna did and—

Oh god, no.

Sophie stared nervously at the sea of diamonds before her. She wasn't ready to be *here.*

No, no, no. She couldn't—They could not.

Not because she didn't care about Wright. She did. But having sex with Wright and having a serious romantic relationship with him were two different things.

Even as friends, he didn't know about her fears, all of her doubts.

She was the master of looking like she had her shit together, even though she had nothing together.

She was held together by the grit of supporting her family and the glue of a demanding family business. Honeywilde made her whole. Without it, she was fractured pieces and ugly scars.

If she and Wright got too close, got serious, he'd find out. Her insecurity would be impossible to hide and she'd cling to him, in fear of losing him. She always did. And that's what would drive him away.

Dev turned and went back to the counter to talk with Mr. Larkin, and she tried talking herself out of a panic attack.

She was freaking out for nothing. Some passionate kisses, even sex, did not a relationship make.

Dev was the one getting hitched, not her and Wright. Wright didn't want to marry her. That was absurd. He'd marry a girl like Kate.

And even though it'd break Sophie's heart, she'd let him. Because Wright deserved someone wonderful and whole. Not a scared little girl who'd need him to constantly reassure her that everything was okay. That he wouldn't walk out the door and never come back. Or drive across town one day and die.

"You ready?" Dev passed her on the way to the door.

Sophie willed away the dark thoughts.

In the middle of a jewelry store, mourning a twenty-two-year-old loss and the loss of something she didn't even have yet.

Yep, she was *totally* great relationship material.

"Soph?" Dev studied her, concern wrinkling his brow.

She forced herself to snap out of it. "Yeah, I'm ready."

"Come on, then. It's been a lot longer than thirty minutes. We better get back."

They climbed into his SUV, which was parked around back, and he handed her the bag to hold. "Thank you for coming with me. I'm still nervous as hell, but not about the ring. I know you wouldn't bullshit me, so if you think it's perfect, I know I got the best of the best."

Because she would never bullshit Devlin.

Out of their whole family, the two of them were always up front with each other. He'd never told her all about Anna because he didn't have to. Sophie had figured out their secret herself.

And it would only be a matter of time before Dev figured out something was going on with her and Wright.

With her luck, it'd be the day Dev and Anna got engaged or some nightmare like that.

There'd be a huge family drama, and for what?

So she could satisfy a craving? She and Wright didn't have any chance of growing into something sustainable, like Dev and Anna.

She didn't have the nerve to make a relationship work with a guy who had nothing to do with her family or career, never mind a guy who was all up in the middle of both and irrefutably a part of her life. She was with Wright because it felt amazing to do so *now*. But what about later?

This wasn't fair to Wright, and she couldn't risk her family's peace and happiness just to satisfy some teenage fantasy.

She'd find Wright and tell him they had to stop what they were doing.

They couldn't touch. Or kiss. He couldn't look at her that way, and she couldn't want him.

But they could be friends.

"I don't want to be your friend." Wright planted his hands at his waist.

His undershirt was still damp from five plus hours in the kitchen, and it clung to his chest as he scowled down at her.

"Excuse me." She wasn't feeling particularly friendly either, with him in his wet T-shirt, but like hell was he going to use that tone with her.

He half-bothered to take a look around. They were in the kitchen alone and it was almost eleven, but Wright knew as well as she did, this was a conversation no one else needed to hear.

He moved closer to her and lowered his voice. "You know what I mean. I am your friend. I'll always be your friend, but . . . I don't want to be *just* friends. After last night. After today? I know you don't want that either."

With a step to the side, she eased away, putting some distance between her and all the gloriously frustrated manliness. "You, I do. We can't keep this up."

"Why?" He followed. "Because your brothers might find out?"

"Yes." That was only half the reason.

"We're back to that? They don't have to know."

"So I lie to my family? That's the solution?"

"Or we tell them. I'll tell them right now." Wright turned to go and she went after him.

She grabbed his arm and dug her heels in. "No! You can't tell them we're screwing around.'

Wright turned and pinned her with a scowl. "Screwing around? Is that what you think this is?"

That wasn't what this was, but to ponder it under any other terms put her brain on overload.

She still clung to his arm and couldn't let go. His thick forearm filled her grip, the ripple of muscle warm in her hands. With concerted effort, she managed to meet his gaze. "I . . . I don't know."

Wright peeled her fingers from his arm and took her hands in his. Another quick look around and he tugged her toward the large pantry. Once inside, he faced her, still holding her hands. "Technically, we haven't even had sex yet, but when we do, it won't be screwing around. I want to have sex, but that's not all I want. I want to be with you."

"But . . ." Sophie barely shook her head. But that would never work.

Being together or dating or, heaven forbid, a relationship? She'd never been able to sustain it in the past, there were always problems, *her* problems, and that was the last thing she needed right now.

Even if she wanted to be Wright's girlfriend, it was impossible, and not because of her family.

And she didn't want to lose Wright.

Sophie shook her head, harder this time. "We can't be together. Not like that."

His shoulders stiffened. "You really think Dev would be that upset? I mean, yeah at first, he might be pissed, but in the long run—"

"Long run?" Her chest tightened. How could he talk about long term? They'd only made out the day before yesterday.

She pulled away. "No. Dev would forbid it." The false words were like acid on her tongue. "This . . ." She freed one of her hands to point back and forth between them. "What happened has to stay between the two of us. And we can't do it again."

He blinked, his expression stricken. "You seriously want to go back to only being friends?"

She swallowed hard, a knot like wad of dry oatmeal in her throat. "Yes. Friends. We can't do this anymore."

One eyebrow crept up as Wright studied her, his lips pursed like he was ready to call her out on her bullshit. She knew because she'd seen that look on his face before. And he wasn't wrong. She was full of it. Full of it and frightened.

Sophie backed away before he could challenge her claim. Paper thin and flimsy, it'd crumple under his scrutiny if she stayed.

She was a coward for running, but self-preservation won out over pride. Her hip hit the pantry's door frame as she turned, and ran.

Chapter 10

L ike hell they were going to be just friends.
Wright tossed his duffel bag across the den of his apartment. He had half a mind to boot it up and down the hall, but he really liked that bag, and kicking it wouldn't help matters.

Sophie was scared of getting close, and too scared to admit it.

"Dammit!" he yelled at his empty apartment.

Well after midnight and here he was, alone in his sparsely furnished apartment, instead of here with Sophie in his arms, his lips on hers and her legs back around his waist.

"This. Sucks." He jerked the refrigerator door open, rattling all the condiments in the door.

After checking to make sure the various sauces and spreads were okay, he grabbed a beer and drank half of it standing in front of the open fridge.

It wasn't that he didn't understand where she was coming from. He did.

He knew how Sophie could be. She backed away from every guy who ever wanted to date her more than twice.

But he'd assumed he was different. That *they* were different.

He wasn't some dude bro she didn't know.

Wright grumbled and cursed, scanning his stock. He might not have much for furniture and décor in his apartment, but by god, he had plenty of food. Cooking would help him process what Sophie said—and what he was going to do about it.

Even after being in the restaurant's kitchen for hours, this was still the best therapy.

He grabbed the chicken breasts, mushrooms, butter, and his meat mallet. Careful not to take too much aggravation out on the food, he pounded the chicken to thin it out.

Sophie wasn't fooling him. She couldn't deflect his interest, and hers, with talk of how upset her brothers would be.

Yes, Dev and Roark and Trevor would take some issue with the two of them dating or sleeping together or doing anything other than being platonic buddies. They would flip out about it for a few days and be protective older brothers, but they wouldn't oppose them to the point they'd try forbidding Sophie and Wright to be together.

They were reasonable men, who loved Sophie and liked and respected Wright.

Accepting Wright and Sophie as a couple might take time and hell of a lot of getting used to, but everyone would get there.

No, Sophie's big issue was her.

His attraction and affection freaked her out because they were already close. He wasn't interested in a couple of dates and some sex on the fly, and she knew it.

Wright had more than a smidge of insight into how she operated. He'd known her for double digit years now. They were in each other's lives. If they took this thing further—no, not if, *when*—she couldn't run and hide from him.

Wright grabbed his flour and spices, mixing them in a wide bowl. He put his skillet on to heat up, added a healthy dose of olive oil, and set about coating and placing his chicken.

Come to think of it, he couldn't name one guy in Sophie's entire adult life that she'd kept around long enough to be considered a boyfriend. Except Paul Pearson.

On the other hand, every time Wright dated someone, it lasted at least a season.

Her breakups weren't always the guy's fault either. Some of them? Absolutely. They were losers who didn't deserve her. But many of them Sophie broke off with no explanation.

She'd say she wasn't into them, which was fair enough, if that were true.

But she couldn't make that same claim about Wright. She'd already admitted, in words and action, she was into him. So she used her brothers as the excuse.

Wright sliced his mushrooms with perfect precision.

She'd been fine at the lake, fine before their meeting with Roark.

It wasn't until later today she'd gotten skittish, and downright deer-in-headlights when he'd said her brothers would get used to them together long—

"Son of a bitch." Wright stopped slicing.

Long term.

His words. Exactly.

"You're a damn idiot."

Sophie was going to pull the plug on them because he wanted more from her than a little down and dirty in the lake shed, and he'd gone and opened his big mouth with words like "long" and "term."

Well, hell no. He was not letting her pull the plug on them.

If all she could handle right now was casual, the down and the dirty, then that's what he'd give her. At first.

Then he could work his way toward long term from there.

Of all people, he should've known better than to throw a bunch of serious relationship talk at her. He'd tossed too much in the mix, but as with any recipe, he could fix the issue of adding too much sugar. All he had to do was even out the sweetness with other ingredients.

Sophie was skittish when it came to relationships outside of her brothers.

Understandable with her childhood and basically losing two sets of parents. He would simply sidestep the whole relationship and feelings ingredient for the time being. Add a little saltiness to their interactions. Not a difficult task since they'd be working on the fund-raiser together.

He added the mushrooms to his skillet, delighting in the rich brown color and mouthwatering scent.

One wrong ingredient did not a disaster make. Not in food and not in love.

All he had to do was stick to the recipe and adjust as needed. Tomorrow, that's exactly what he was going to do.

"What if we use the patio underneath the verandah for staging the event?" Dev drummed his fingers on the arm of one of the great room's chairs.

In lieu of an early Roark meeting, Dev was meeting with Wright, Sophie, and Trevor to discuss the Midsummer Night Gala before any guests were up.

Sophie shook her head, looking at one of the many property layouts she owned. "I think the patio for dancing and music. Save the verandah for the food and beverage."

"Life would be easier if we keep the food up here near the kitchen." Wright agreed.

"True, true." Dev nodded. "I was thinking of creating the mood. Lights all above, that kind of thing."

"We could still do the lights." Trevor got up to refill his coffee. "I went to this party where they used streetlamps in the corners and the twinkle lights went back and forth between them. Oh hey, and if you had a centerpiece light, you could do a whole tent effect with strands of lights. A canopy of illumination."

They all stared at him.

"What?" Trevor sat back down, smirking. "I have ideas. I know things."

Everyone nodded in surprised agreement as they laid out the major logistics of the event. Dev would be in charge of communications and take the lead overall. Wright would head up the menu, obviously, and Sophie would work with the vendors, since that was already her wheel house. Trevor would do whatever they needed.

Once they got the basics down and everyone had enough tasks to keep them busy through the week, they were done. Different from the end of Roark's meetings, Dev didn't so much dismiss the group as announce he was hungry and wander off.

Trevor didn't budge from his spot on a sofa, which left Wright and Sophie staring at each other, neither one of them jumping to be the first to speak.

"I . . ." Sophie glanced at her watch. "I should make a few calls before we get busy."

"Yeah, I have some prep work." Wright headed straight for the restaurant. That's where she'd choose to make her calls.

Sure enough, she followed, settling near the hostess station to use that phone.

Normally, Wright would immediately start on breakfast, but now, with Marco to help, the prep work would already be in process. So Wright lingered.

He went behind the bar, grabbed a few lemons and oranges, taking his sweet time about it.

Sophie was on the phone all right, but her lips weren't moving. A couple of minutes passed before she hung up, leaning on the hostess station to study him. "Shouldn't you be starting on breakfast?"

"Shouldn't you be on the phone?" Wright tossed an orange into the air.

"Don't be snide."

"I'm not." He made a pouch with the hem of his shirt to hold his citrus stash. "I know you have a lot going on. I'm trying to help you remember. You said you needed to make calls."

"Now you're being a smart-ass."

With a genuine smile, he approached her. He'd be whatever he had to be to get her to talk to him. "Sorry. I'm not trying to be."

"Look, I know this is weird, but I ... I'm trying to do the right thing here. I have to consider the consequences."

The consequences being they might be great together, and that terrified her.

"I know." He leaned against the hostess stand too, inches from her. "I respect that. Might not agree, but I respect where you're coming from. You think you're doing the right thing."

She tilted her head. "But you don't."

"I think we should be taking advantage of the opportunity we've been given. I think we should be right back in that lake shed or you should've been at my place last night, finishing what we started."

"Wright—"

"Doesn't have to be complicated. Doesn't have to be anything we don't want it to be. And what we do isn't anybody's business, especially if we keep it casual."

She studied him, probably searching for signs he was bluffing.

She wouldn't find any. He meant it. Right now, they could be whatever she wanted them to be, as long as it meant they were together.

"And, not for nothing, but I made a mean Marsala last night that you would've loved. We could've eaten, had some wine, enjoyed dessert. Enjoyed each other."

The tops of her cheeks went pink.

"But if you want to cool it, we can cool it."

She glanced away, her stern expression wavering. "I ... I think we should."

"Okay then. Done. I'll leave you alone." He made a point of casually accepting her pronouncement, even as she faltered.

As he headed to the kitchen, her gaze burned into the back of his skull.

Once in the kitchen, he slid on a clean chef's jacket and readied his workstation.

His goal wasn't to piss Sophie off, but to make her see she was fighting something they both wanted. If she didn't long for him the same way he did, he really would cool it, but what sparked between them when they kissed wasn't the kind of thing you ignored.

A lack of desire wasn't what held her back.

Fear and guilt. They kept her from doing what she wanted. Some kind of deference to what others expected from her, or whatever expectation she'd created for herself.

Sophie was always sacrificing, and while everyone appreciated her and relied on her, she ought to do *something* for herself.

He'd love it if that something was him.

Halfway through breakfast, the doors of the kitchen swung open. He didn't look up from buttering a pan of biscuits, but he knew Sophie had joined them.

"Hey."

"Hey." She lingered on the other side of the prep table.

He put the pan in the oven and began cracking eggs into a bowl. A table of four wanted four omelets, fully loaded.

Sophie stood back, out of his and Marco's way, not saying a word.

With all of the eggs in a large bowl, he held it against his side and grabbed a whisk. "Can I help you with something?"

Her gaze shifted from where he whisked to his face to the bowl and back again. "Um . . . no. I got hungry. Thought I'd grab a biscuit when they're fresh out of the oven."

"It'll take them a few minutes."

"I can wait."

Wright turned toward the range, hiding his grin. Sophie was more than welcome to hang out in the kitchen. Once upon a time, she'd loiter in the kitchen, off and on, throughout the day.

Before they hired Marco, Sophie was his extra pair of hands, if she happened to be around.

An idea came to him. "Hey, Soph? Would you grab a bag of onions from the pantry? I used the last one I had out here."

"Okay." With a spring in her step, she walked to the pantry.

This time of day was the slowest for her. If he kept her busy, she might stick around for the rest of breakfast service.

She returned with the onions and hung back as he chopped and diced and prepared four omelets. Once those were done, he checked the biscuits.

Perfect.

He pulled the pan from the oven, and Sophie hovered closer.

"You have to let them cool a minute," he warned, using a spatula to separate them from the pan.

"I like mine hot." She grabbed one from the pan, tossing it from hand to hand like a hot potato.

"Here." He picked up the nearest clean dish and held it out for her biscuit.

"Thanks." She put her biscuit in the bowl and clutched it close to her chest.

Wright chuckled. "I'm not going to steal it back from you."

"Can't be too sure. I'd steal one from you."

He transferred the rest of the biscuits from the pan to serving baskets. "I know you would. You do it all the time. Because you're greedy."

Her mouth fell open and her eyes went narrow. "I am *not* greedy."

"The other night at the Tavern, you ate your half of the sandwich, a quarter of mine, and probably two-thirds of the rarebit."

"I was hungry."

He grinned. "If I remember correctly, so was I."

With a pointed look, she jerked her chin toward Marco, who was too wrapped up in his prep work for lunch to take any notice of them.

"I was talking about the food, Soph."

She broke off a bite of biscuit and chewed.

Wright served up the omelets and set them on the pass for the wait staff. Next to them, he put the baskets of biscuits. He had about a three-minute break before the next order came in.

He moved closer to Sophie and lowered his voice. "Don't worry. If you're greedy, so am I. You're hungry for food and I'm hungry for—"

"You said you'd cool it."

"Dessert. I was going to say dessert."

"Sure you were." She glanced down at her bowl.

"For someone trying to do the right thing, you certainly have your mind in the gutter."

"I'm leaving."

"Okay."

But later that night, he saw her again. He checked the time and it was almost midnight, yet she remained up, sitting at one of the few booths at the far end of the restaurant, typing away on her laptop.

She wore shorts again, God help him, and one of Honeywilde's apricot-colored polo shirts. The shade should look awful with her red hair, but she did the damn thing justice. She was a warm, radiant light, with her bare legs pulled beneath her, criss-cross, the glow from her monitor illuminating her face.

He ought to walk right out of the restaurant and head on home, but that'd never happen. For years, he'd gravitated toward her like a moth toward light. Why would tonight be any different?

"What are you still doing up? And why are you working?"

With a heavy sigh, she dragged her hands through her hair. "The company we've been using for our coffee? You know, the coffee everyone loves so much?"

"Yeah."

"They're going out of business."

Wright lowered his duffel bag. "Shit."

"Exactly. The guy called me this afternoon. I felt so sorry for him. He sounded pitiful. It's a family business, and they can't compete with the huge roasters. I asked, but he said there's nothing we can do to help. We were one of their biggest clients."

He slid into the booth next to her. "And he's definitely shutting down?"

"Definitely." She uncrossed her legs, allowing him closer.

"Who are you thinking about using once he's gone?"

"I don't know. I don't want to go with a big corporation if I can support a local business. The markup on some of these places is astronomical, though. I want to help the little guy, but we can't break our budget either. I'm coming up with nothing."

"There's this place I went to last summer, near Greenville. Here." He reached for her laptop, turning it toward him. "You mind?"

"No. Please."

As he typed in the name of the local coffee beanery, he caught a whiff of her perfume.

Almost midnight, at the end of an almost eighteen-hour day, and

Sophie still smelled sweet. His arm brushed hers, her shoulder pressed near. When he shifted, moving minutely closer, she didn't slide away.

He turned the laptop toward her. "This is the one. They specialize in fair trade Kenyan coffee."

Sophie leaned closer, scanning the website. Her lips moved as she read, stirring the still-too-clear memory of what those lips felt like on his; how they tasted as sweet as she smelled, how delicately they parted as she gasped, climaxing, and how softly she spoke when asking him if they should stop this.

She kept reading, shifting in the booth. The longer they sat there, the smaller the gap between them became, until her leg rubbed his, practically connecting them at the hip.

"This looks . . ." She glanced up. "This looks perfect. Thank you."

Her lips were so close. All of her was close, too close to resist. He struggled to respect her wishes. The two of them cooling off was a horrible idea, but being together needed to be her choice.

He didn't intend for his voice to come out rough and barely above a whisper. "You're welcome."

Her gaze flitted to his lips, then back to look him in the eyes.

He angled himself toward her. "You know I'm always going to help you out and have your back, right? No matter what. Even if we're just friends."

Slowly, her chin bobbed. "I know."

A beat of silence passed before she swept a strand of hair from her face. "I'm sorry."

"For what?"

"I know I'm difficult sometimes. If everything wasn't so complicated—"

"Eh. I'm used to you being difficult," he teased, bringing a small smile to her lips. "Seriously though, I get it, Soph. You want everyone to be happy all the time. But the thing is, that's not your responsibility."

With a sigh, she tilted her head. "I know. I'm trying really hard to do better."

"That's part of the problem." He lifted his hand to touch her, not realizing until his fingertips brushed her hair that he was crossing the cooling-off line.

Screw it, though. This was Sophie, and even if they were only friends, he'd still comfort her.

He held her shoulder, rubbing it gently. "You try really hard at everything. You don't have to try so hard. Just being you is enough. If you're a joy to behold one day and an ill-tempered nag the next, that's okay. You're allowed to be who you are."

She bumped her shoulder against him with a smirk. "I'm never an ill-tempered nag."

"Never?" He cocked an eyebrow. "Not even that time you told me if I didn't hurry up and get you the order for the apples from Stewart Farms, I could—and I quote—sit and spin on my apple crumble?"

She nibbled at her bottom lip. "Did I say that? I don't think I said that."

He laughed through his words. "You said those *exact* words, because I remember picturing myself spinning in a giant casserole dish of apple crumble. And then you told me, at the time, that the restaurant, and my talent as a chef, was what kept the lights on at Honeywilde."

She stared into his eyes, her gaze swallowing him whole.

"That compliment meant a lot to me. I don't think I've ever been so flattered, and yet so bullied, in my entire life."

She laughed, covering her mouth.

Every knot of tension that'd built up within him since last night began to unwind.

"You're right. I did say that. Oh my god, I'm such a witch to you sometimes."

"You are not. You're able to be yourself without trying so hard." Wright moved his arm lower, holding her in a half hug. "Plus, I forgave you the second you called me a talented chef."

Sophie startled him, putting her arms around him too, hugging him back. "Thank you," she said again. "For tonight and the coffee reference, and . . . for knowing I don't mean half the stuff I say when I'm stressed."

He held on tight, savoring the feel of her in his arms. "You're welcome. You should know I don't pay any attention to anything you say."

She laughed again, the sound causing a vibration that bounced around his body.

Letting her go wasn't even an option. She'd have to be the one to pull away.

When she did lean away, she kept her gaze lowered, not letting go completely. Her hands drifted down his arms, and there she stopped.

The top of her head was only inches from his chin, her breath warm against his neck. When she finally looked up, meeting his gaze, he saw the crystal-clear edges of his own desire.

"Wright." His name was a quiet plea, and he knew. He knew exactly how she felt, the conflicted yearnings inside. She wanted the same thing, but she was unsure. Scared of all that could happen, worried about how a relationship with him might affect others, thinking a thousand things could go wrong, because of her.

He wasn't the least bit unsure. Sophie was who he wanted, and all the complications in the world weren't going to change that.

Carefully, he reached up, brushing back a lock of her hair. "I am paying attention to what you said, about us cooling off, but I'm not going to lie. I'm not enjoying it. It's damn difficult, trying not to want you."

Again, she nibbled at her lip.

He leaned in, brushing his lips against her temple, letting his hand fall away. "Which is why I better go."

Sophie leaned into the light kiss, her breath coming quick and low as she nodded.

Before he could go back on his word and ruin his recipe by pushing for more, Wright slid out of the booth and grabbed his bag. He didn't look back. He couldn't. It was all he could do to resist her while not even looking at her.

The entire drive home he replayed the moment, minute by minute, dissecting their exchange, every second, questioning if he'd done the right thing.

Need told him to go for what they both wanted, push the issue, and maybe that's what he should've done. But the part of him who cared about Sophie, cherished a friendship decades in the making, wouldn't allow that.

And he *knew* her. He knew the apprehensive little girl inside her, knew what she'd been through.

Backing off was the right thing to do, but damn if he didn't doubt his actions.

He kept on doubting them, right up until the knock on his door after one a.m.

Wright only got the door half-open before Sophie pushed her way in, her hair a tousled mess, eyes wide and slightly panicked.

His stomach dropped. "Is something wrong?"

"You mean besides me?"

He wasn't going to answer that.

"You know what I said before? About how we couldn't be together because of my family? That we had to stop what we were doing. Because I was freaking out." She dug both hands through her hair, pushing it back.

His stomach flip-flopped, nerves thrumming on overload. "Yeah."

"Well, I'm still freaking out, but . . ." She fisted her hands at her waist, then dropped them, looking everywhere but at him. Finally, she took a ragged breath and lifted her chin, her pupils darkening her gaze. "Can we forget what I said and go back to you kissing me again?"

Chapter 11

S he'd never seen Wright move so fast. She'd never seen anyone move so fast.

In a rush of movement, he had her. His fingers in her hair, her back bumping the wall beside the door, his lips hot against hers.

"Yes." His answer was a low-pitched rumble, and she clung to it. To him.

If Wright said they could forget her crisis of conscience, her irrational fear and all of the complications, then it was true.

They could have this, and to hell with everything else for now.

She pulled him close, wrapping her arms around him and digging her fingers in the thick muscle of his back. She didn't want to think or doubt. All she wanted to do was feel; feel Wright and the pleasure he promised to bring.

He swept her up into his arms, her feet leaving the floor.

At first she dangled there, tottering on the edge of bliss and a restless need for more.

Then Wright shifted his grip, scooping her up until her legs were around his waist, her back against the wall, harder than before.

Hot and greedy as he plundered her mouth. The sweetness from before, in the booth, was gone. No tentative brushing of his lips, no cool behaving.

Thank God.

"Soph." He dragged his lips over her cheek, down her neck, rough sucking kisses near her collarbone.

She let her head fall back against the wall with a thump.

He took advantage of the surrender, licking and nibbling his way to the other side. "I didn't want to stop. Not at all." His voice was rough, thick with desperation.

"Me . . ." Her chest was so heavy, she could hardly breathe. Her heart thundered, making her pulse roar in her ears. Cowardice only slowed the gravitational pull. It wasn't enough to stop something they both wanted. "Me either." She sucked in a deep breath. "I thought we should, and I tried, but . . . I want you."

Wright lifted his face, his lips full and wet from kissing her. A dark need filled his gaze, and though he didn't say a word, she knew the level of longing all too well.

Without saying anything, he turned and walked down the short hall of his apartment. She tightened her legs around his waist to keep from falling, drawing an appreciative rumble from his chest.

He bumped open his bedroom door with his shoulder, a small table lamp left on, probably because he always came home in the late, late hours. It struck her; she'd never actually been in Wright's room.

She had visited his apartment many times, but entering his bedroom stepped across some odd line she'd created. Years ago, she'd compartmentalized whatever they were to each other, and that included not going past the threshold of his bedroom.

Wright went straight to his bed, dropping her on it and climbing over her, obliterating her lines and compartments. Above her, he glowed, the soft lamplight warming his rugged features.

"You're beautiful," he whispered, shifting his weight to one arm and using his free hand to brush his fingers along her cheek and down her exposed collarbone.

Her knee-jerk reaction was to argue with anyone who made such a claim, but right now, she felt a little bit beautiful.

He slid his hand under her neck, cradling the back of her head, and dove for another kiss. His mouth was gentle but persistent, his kisses leaving no room for debate.

Shifting beneath him, she parted her legs. Wright fit perfectly between them. He kissed her lower, and lower still, his other hand moving down her body, cupping her breast. A sharp inhale and he hummed at her reaction, a pleased sound that skated across her skin.

He worked the two buttons of her shirt open, tugging the collar wider to kiss her there.

She arched into the sensation, Wright cupping her breasts, kissing his way over her cleavage, gently kneading until her nipples hardened. He pinched one, hard enough to send a bolt of desire to her core. She squeezed her legs against him, her sex tightening.

In the lake shed, he'd touched her, even made her come, but they were going to have sex.

Something she hadn't done in . . . she couldn't concentrate long enough to tally how long it had been.

Too long.

Her nerves danced more toward eager than anxious, and still. What if she'd forgotten how to do it?

Wright moved his mouth lower, pulling at her collar until her shirt was going to be a stretched-out mess tomorrow.

With a puff of air, he leaned up, holding himself over her. "I want to put my mouth on you. All over you."

The carnal edge in his eyes startled her, but in the most delicious way. Even at the lake, Wright hadn't looked like this. Driven, a little bit dangerous. Her nice guy, gone off the rails.

All she could do was nod. She wanted his mouth on her too.

He tugged at the hem of her shirt, pulling until he got it over her head and tossed it aside. He didn't waste a second, stripping the straps of her bra down, working at the clasp, until she was completely topless, lying on Wright's bed.

Before she had a second to be self-conscious about it, he kissed her. Everywhere.

Across her collarbone, between her breasts, the top of her tummy. Hot and wild, he closed his lips over her nipple, making her cry out at the relief. He pressed her back into the bed, his hands huge on her rib cage, smoothing down her sides, before cupping her breasts like a feast, moving his mouth back and forth between them, flicking his tongue and nibbling gently with his teeth.

"Wright." She gasped. "Wright . . . I . . ."

He dragged his mouth up to her ear. "I'd love to make you come again. Just like this."

She squeezed her eyes shut, the rising tide of sensations threatening to drown her. He went back to work until she arched her back, pressing into him.

She knew what her hips were up to. All but dry-humping him, chasing after the kind of climax that only he'd given her before.

Her breath came out in quick pants, the release barely out of reach.

Then Wright let go. His mouth never slowed in his quest, but he held himself up, propped on one hand, the other working the button of her shorts.

Wright was going to touch her, and the thought alone had her clenching.

With deft fingers he popped the button, sliding the zipper down, moving lower, before slipping his hand into her panties. The first brush of his finger against the cleft of her sex yanked a sharp inhale from both of them.

With enormous effort, she resisted clamping her legs shut or doing something completely insane like grabbing his hand and riding it for him.

He moved his hand lower, exploring, sliding his fingers between her lips until she turned her head to the side, biting back a curse.

Wright groaned, made her look up.

As she turned her face, he kissed her. "You're so wet for me," he whispered against her mouth.

She couldn't respond. There were no words.

Wright shifted lower on the bed, his hands between her legs and his lips on her breasts. He rubbed and teased in tempo with his kisses, slipping one finger inside her as he swirled his tongue around her nipple and nipped sharply.

Sophie grabbed his hand, a curse escaping, but holy crap, it felt good.

Wright panted. He moved away and she was about to go clawing after him when he started tugging on her shorts. "I have to see you," he said as an explanation before stripping her bare.

She was completely naked, in Wright's bed, and he still had every single article of his clothes on, except for his shoes.

Any other time, the vulnerable position would've shot her anxiety into overload. But not with him. He covered her mouth with his, and she forgot all about who was dressed and who wasn't. Again, he kissed his way over her breasts, rubbing and pressing his fingers into her until even she could feel how wet she was.

He took a nipple into his mouth, gently closing his teeth around it, humming as he pumped his fingers, playing her until she writhed and bucked against him.

"I'm—Wright. I'm going to—"

"I know, baby. Let me feel you come."

Like an avalanche that struck without warning, her orgasm swallowed her whole. Covering her, dragging her down. Wright's words penetrated some primal part of her brain that wanted him to feel her. Needed him to. In that moment, she could be honest enough with herself to admit, she'd wanted him to feel her for a long time.

Biting down hard on her lip, the pinch of pain washed past as she came. And Wright didn't stop. He kept touching her, a gentle swirl of his fingers against her sensitive clit until she was twitching and flinching against him.

"S-stop for a second." She stayed his hand. "I need to catch my breath."

"You need mouth-to-mouth?"

The question was so desert dry and deadpan, she began to giggle.

"I'm volunteering." He smirked.

When she blinked and gathered her wits enough to look, the sight was enough to send her spiraling again.

Wright loomed above her, one hand on her hip, his gaze devouring her as it swept over her body.

"I think I'm okay now," she said. A total lie. She had passed okay about a million miles back.

"Good." With another smug smile, Wright shifted down the bed, hooking his hands under her legs, making her bend them at the knees.

He situated himself between her legs and tugged her down near the foot of the bed.

"What are you—" She couldn't get the whole question out before he closed his mouth over her clit.

"Oh—" She dug her fingers into the bed.

Wright was half on his stomach, kneeling on the floor, and he worked his tongue against her sensitive flesh, picking up exactly where he left off.

Her body, still sparking for her last orgasm, required very little for the sensation to build again, her responsiveness shocking. She'd never climaxed twice in a row before, definitely not within a minute.

He sucked, his teeth brushing against her, and she went from clawing at the bed to reaching for him. His hair, his shoulders, whatever she could get her hands on.

"Wright." She panted. "Holy shit."

He let out a deep, satisfied noise, the vibration filling her. Her body bowed, her hips thrusting up with the surge of her second climax. She came and came, Wright's mouth never leaving her as she fell apart.

At some point, she found earth again. Even as she trembled, a smile made her face hurt.

Maybe she hadn't forgotten how to have sex after all.

She rubbed her eyes, her gaze falling on the man laid out beside her, still fully dressed, currently threading their fingers together. He dropped featherlight kisses up her arm, his shit-eating grin the most blatant she'd ever witnessed.

"What the hell?" She was too breathless to add any inflection to the question.

"What?" He moved closer to her side, dancing his fingers up her rib cage, making her flinch and turn into him.

"Why are you still dressed?" She tugged at his T-shirt.

He took advantage of lying this way, smoothing his hand across her hip, around and over her bottom. "Are you saying you want me to get undressed?"

"Yes. That is what I'm saying."

His grin was all too familiar, yet lying naked with him so totally different, her body fluttered and sparked as though made of fireflies.

Wright pushed off the bed and stood, reaching back to tug his shirt over his head. She rose to her knees, facing him, and helped by pulling at his belt. In a few seconds, he was finally, gloriously naked.

She'd seen him without his shirt many times, every summer, but this time, everything about him was different.

The dusting of hair across his chest was sexier than it'd ever been before. His shoulders had never been that strong and defined looking, nor had his arms. And his face. His friendly, wonderful face had never held the kind of carnal expression or rough edge that it did now.

Mostly, though, she'd never seen Wright McAdams naked from the waist down.

She'd felt him the other day, yes, and as promising as that sensation was, it was nothing compared to the real thing.

"Wow." She mouthed the word.

"Come here." He took her elbow, smiling as she moved closer.

She brushed her fingers over his chest, up to his shoulders as he smoothed his hands around her waist, squeezing her bottom. He kissed her. Not as desperate as before, he took his time, brushing his lips back and forth, before moving to her neck and taking a deep breath in.

She let her head fall to the side, her gaze settling on the dresser mirror by the bed.

They were there, in the reflection. She and Wright, completely naked, pressed together, their hands and mouths all over one another. Like a modern-day Adam and Eve tasting the forbidden fruit, yet she felt no guilt.

Not right now anyway.

What she saw reflected back at her was amazing. Sensual and wonderful, and okay, maybe a little bit naughty.

A puff of laughter escaped.

"What?" Wright nuzzled into her neck.

"Nothing. I can't believe we're doing this."

He rained warm kisses along her cheek. "I can't believe we didn't do this sooner."

He had a point. Maybe he'd spent the same amount of time hating her dates and bemoaning her life choices as she had his. Maybe this was all bound to happen, eventually, unless one of them vacated the other's life—and that was never going to happen.

Wright wasn't going to leave Honeywilde any more than she would, and perhaps the two of them being together was only a matter of time.

She smoothed her hands down his arms, relishing the solid muscle beneath her fingertips. Arms that she'd ogled for years. Down his forearms until she drew her hands together, sweeping them across his stomach, until the muscles of his abdomen tightened.

There were exactly two guys she'd touched this way before.

Once, when she lost her virginity, and the whole experience was horrible, and Paul.

Poor Paul.

Other than them, she was an amateur. But she sure as hell wasn't going to act like one.

As she placed a delicate kiss at the corner of his mouth, she slid her hand lower, down the length of his cock.

Wright gasped into her mouth, and she took it as a good sign. Down, farther still, she cupped his sac, gentle, curious.

Touching him felt amazing. His reactions caused a thrill of . . . power? A sense of control she hadn't expected.

She wasn't going to look smug at his reaction—at the way he tensed as she stroked up and down his length, as his breathing skipped—but she felt it. She hadn't expected to feel high on the proud satisfaction, but she did.

Wright took her mouth in a plundering kiss, sucking on her lips in between panting for breath as she stroked him.

She'd wondered about this part of him for years, and it was better than she'd imagined.

He twitched in her grip, as if knowing what she was thinking.

Brushing her thumb over the head, she used his slickness to stroke underneath, making Wright grind out a moan.

"Do you . . ." She rested her forehead against his jaw, the realness of asking *him* this hitting her. "Do you have a condom?"

He nodded, his stubble like soft sandpaper, and dipped his mouth lower. "Hang on."

Pulling himself away, he hurried to his bathroom, the view of him from the back almost as good as the front. He was back in an instant, tearing open the foil.

She took the condom from him and, with some awkward effort, rolled it on. Once she'd scooted over on the bed, she realized he wasn't following. With a tilt of her head, she considered him. "Everything okay?"

Chapter 12

Sophie looked good in his bed. *So* good.

He felt like he was going to have a heart attack, but sure. Other than that, everything was great.

Wright crawled onto the bed next to her, his heart pounding like he'd raced five miles. As spectacular as the sex had been so far, as certain he was of what he wanted and how much they both enjoyed it, this was still a big damn deal.

This wasn't any girl he was sleeping with. This was Sophie. And it mattered.

With a delicate hand on his neck, she tugged him down and kissed him. "Your heart is racing."

"Yeah, no kidding."

"But I'm supposed to be the nervous one. Not you." Her sweet smile was his undoing.

He wasn't nervous out of doubt. His worry came from wanting this to be perfect. Even though it was already as close to perfect as anything had been before, he didn't want to muck it all up now.

"Hey." She stroked his hip, tugging him toward her. "I'm kind of glad I'm not the only one with jitters."

Wright never got the jitters, but that was the best way to explain how he felt.

He eased his way over her, concentrating on the pale beauty of her skin, the swollen softness of her lips, thinking of the delicious noises she made when she came and how desperately he wanted to come with her. Focusing on her, thinking about her, made his nerves fade away.

This time, when he kissed her, he put the wealth of everything he felt into it. Even with all that they'd done so far, he'd never had sex with Sophie. He wanted it to be amazing. Special. Perfect.

With the tips of his fingers, he touched her again, slipping his hand between her legs to find her still wet, waiting for him.

Sophie hadn't been with many guys. Not that it'd matter to him if she'd been with dozens, but they were close enough he had a fair idea of her experience. The last thing he wanted was to go too fast.

"If you need anything from me, all you have to do is tell me, okay?"

He waited until her gaze met his and she nodded. Then he took himself in hand and pushed into her, slow. Painfully slow. The urge to take was strong; to be one with her, those delicious legs wrapped around him again. But he held back.

She relaxed more as he nuzzled her ear, kissing her neck, and he kept touching her until finally, he was deep inside her.

Without moving his body, he caught her gaze. "You okay?"

Sophie caught her lips between her teeth, and nodded. "Yeah. Give me a second?"

She could have forever. He wasn't going anywhere.

A moment later, she shifted beneath him. Pleasure licked up his spine. He closed his eyes and moaned.

"Are *you* okay?"

As an answer, he kissed her, plundering her mouth the way he wanted to plunder her. Somewhere between the kissing, her fingers digging into his shoulders, and her legs finally encircling him again, they began to move.

Not just him as he rocked into her, but Sophie too. She pushed up, counterpoint to his thrust, the contact bringing bursts of ecstasy.

He grabbed her hips, encouraging her movement, helping her along. Beneath him, with her fair skin and pattern of freckles, pert breasts bouncing as they moved, Sophie glowed. She was radiance come to life. Her hazel eyes dark, lips kiss-stained and swollen, nipples darker after his attention.

He would never get enough of this. Could never satisfy the need that gnawed at him, not if he was buried deep inside her now and still wanted more.

He couldn't say it to her, couldn't confess what she did to him, for fear of scaring her away, but Sophie meant *everything* to him. She was vital. Like air and water. He'd always had her in his life and couldn't imagine his world without her in it.

And now, to be sharing this. To have this with her too.

Did she have any idea what it meant? How many times he'd fought his desire for exactly this.

"Oh god . . . Soph." He bent over her, digging his hands into the bed on either side of her head.

Her hands were soft, fluttering across his skin until she found his face.

She cupped his jaw and urged him down for a kiss. "I know," she said, as he thrust into her, over and over, his orgasm building at blinding speed, already threatening to push him over the edge.

No, she didn't know. Because if she knew, she'd run scared.

But she could know how wonderful this was, that compatibility and potency like this didn't happen very often, if at all. And he could show her, by carrying her with him as he went over the edge.

Wright held himself up with one hand, using his free hand to reach between them.

As he ground against her, he tweaked one nipple before going lower, to find her clit. He pressed and rubbed against her until her little gasps and moans told him he'd found the right spot.

Never slowing or hesitating, he worked her clit until Sophie thrashed beneath him, her hair wild against his pillow, panting with "yes" and "there."

"Wright . . . *Wright.*"

"I know. Me too. I want to feel you come for me. One more time. Come on, baby."

Sophie cried out, head tossed back and nails biting into his arms as she tightened around him.

Wright came, pulsing and throbbing inside her, feeling like he might leave his body if it weren't for her legs anchored around him.

"Soph." He thrust into her and panted. His body shook as he buried his face into her neck.

He didn't want her to let go, ever.

Chapter 13

At 6:00 a.m., Sophie rolled over, slapping at her phone to make the alarm shut up.

A little sore and a lot tired, she had no interest in getting up. The only bad thing about staying in bed was it was hers, and not Wright's, and she was in it alone.

She'd finally made it home last night, well after three in the morning. He kept urging her to stay. Spend the night. But they both knew she couldn't roll into Honeywilde when her family might be awake, looking like she'd been doing exactly what she'd been doing.

She'd crowbarred herself out of his bed last night and snuck home to collapse in her room.

Two hours was plenty of sleep to be a functional human, right?

The alarm beeped again and she blindly reached toward her bedside table to make it stop.

She bumped the picture of her and her parents—her birth parents—and turned off the alarm before righting the frame.

A picture of her and her parents, taken on the Fourth of July, the day of their accident.

Why she'd kept that picture close, of the hundreds locked away in storage, she couldn't explain.

Heck, she didn't even understand why.

A silly little moment, frozen in time. They looked so happy

She sat up and brought the picture to her lap.

Framed by lush green trees, a fiery-haired child held hands with a pretty, petite redhead. They smiled and stared back at Sophie. Next to her mother, only slightly taller, a boyishly handsome man grinned, looking proud as punch.

Her parents made an adorable couple. Through childhood, Sophie had been told how much everyone loved her folks. They were friendly and kind, the only couple who truly socialized with Robert and Sue Bradley.

The truth was, her parents could've named one of half a dozen couples in Windamere as her guardians, if the worst were to ever happen. Everyone swore they loved her birth parents.

For some reason, they'd chosen the Bradleys to be Sophie's family.

Had they known how rocky the Bradley marriage could be behind closed doors? They couldn't have predicted the tumultuous future, but surely there were signs. Did her birth parents choose her adoptive parents simply because they had the room? Or because they had three boys and no girl?

Sophie shook her head. Their choice was baffling, even though now she couldn't imagine her life any other way.

Her brothers meant the world to her. Without them and Honeywilde, where would she be? No job, no purpose. No foundation.

But she did have them. And right now she had to shake a leg if she was going to make it to Roark's morning meeting.

With a groan, she forced herself out of bed. Today was going to suck.

As she stood, the tenderness of her body sent memories of last night washing over her, and she grinned. Totally worth it.

No matter how exhausted she was or how much coffee she had to mainline in order to stay on her feet, her amazing night with Wright made any of today's struggles acceptable.

And that's what she was still telling herself when the post-lunch narcolepsy struck.

"Soph. Hello?" Dev snapped his fingers together and waved a hand in front of her face.

She shoved him away from her spot on their favorite great room sofa. "What? I'm listening."

He sat back on his end of the sofa. "No, you aren't. You're sleeping with your eyes open. What did I just say?"

"Something about lights," she muttered.

"Something? I listed off about ten different options for the Chamber's gala. You know, the stuff Trevor mentioned with the lights."

"A canopy of illumination." Trev provided the proper term.

"Yes, that. Did you hear any of what I said?"

"I stopped listening after 'twinkle lights.' Is there any coffee yet this afternoon?" She craned her neck in search of the trolley.

Dev made a show of bellyaching at her lack of enthusiasm, but shoved off the couch, hopefully in search of caffeine.

As soon as he left, Trevor leaned forward from his chair. "You okay, Sis? Late night?"

"Couldn't sleep," she muttered.

When he didn't respond, she peeked out from beneath her lids.

Trevor studied her, one eyebrow raised, lips quirked.

"What's the look for?"

"Nothin'." He put his hands up and slid back in the chair. "Nothing at all."

The squeak of little wheels drew their attention as Wright rolled the coffee trolley over from the kitchen.

He handed a cup to each of them and took the chair opposite Trevor. "Figured you might need an afternoon pick-me-up. Both of you." He tossed in the quick save.

Rather than respond, she took that first, delightful sip, letting her eyelids flutter shut. "Thank you." Her words came out breathy.

Trevor shoved up from his chair. "I have to go."

Sophie roused at his carrying on. "Now?"

"Yeah." He checked his watch. "I have to leave now or I'll be late."

Rather than ask the obvious, she imitated his look from moments ago.

"Tell Dev I had an errand, okay? I'll be back before dinner. Later, y'all." And with that, Trevor took off.

"What was that about?" Wright watched him go.

"Hell if I know. Trevor does more coming and going than anyone I've ever known. I'm too tired to move and he's zipping off to parts unknown."

His chuckle was soft and deep. "How are you feeling?"

"Other than sleep deprived?"

"Yeah." Wright wet his lips and smiled, and the expression on his face was a double shot of espresso to her system.

"Other than that, I'm doing exceptionally well. Thank you for asking."

"Good." He sipped his coffee.

"Great." Dev rounded the corner with empty hands. "I'm looking all over for this thing and the two of you already have coffee."

Time was, Dev would've griped more, all day to be exact, but today he poured himself a cup of coffee and got down to business. "Now that you're both here, and Sophie is conscious again—wait, where'd Trevor go?"

"No one knows." Sophie took another sip. "He'll be back before dinner, though."

Dev took about two seconds to look confused and surprised before moving on. "I was talking about the lighting for the fund-raiser. You know how Trevor mentioned the lanterns and long strands of bulbs? The canopy of lights?"

"Yeah."

"I found this place in Newton, a lighting warehouse, and it has all kinds of stuff, at discount. I'm thinking that's our best bet to check out the options. Everything is in stock; it's in person and better than trying to figure out how it'll look by an online picture."

"Sounds good. When are you going?" Sophie asked.

"*We* should go right now."

This time, she almost choked on her coffee. "What? No."

"Why not? This is the quietest time of day, it won't take a couple of hours, and if I go alone and get something and it looks stupid, I know I'll hear about it. Namely from you."

Fair enough. He would definitely get an earful. She wasn't the type to sit silently by if her brothers jacked something up.

"Fine, but how about we go tomorrow?"

"Because tomorrow I have too much going on. After brunch, I have to go on a call with Roark and review some plan he has about the Chamber."

Sophie's eyes went wide. "Look at you. Going on calls. Wheeling and dealing. Roark Junior."

"Do not call me that."

She made a show of rolling her eyes. Dev called her Roark Junior when she took notes on her phone. Turnabout was fair play.

"Come on. Today is the only free time I have. Run over there with me. You can sleep in the car for the twenty minutes it takes to get there."

A twenty minute nap did sound divine.

"If it's all right, I think I'll go with y'all."

Her attention jerked to Wright. "You what?"

With a casual lift of his shoulders, he rested his coffee mug on the arm of the chair. "This is the only free time I have, the cookie dough is already made and Marco wants to try his hand at finishing them, and I'm on this committee too. Unless you don't want my input or help."

"We do," Dev answered for her. "If you can get away from the kitchen for a couple of hours." He and Wright shared a smile, which meant Wright was going with them.

It would be fine. She and Wright and Dev could run an errand together, no big deal. They might've had earth-shaking sex last night, but that didn't mean Dev would know.

They were able to be low key about it. At least, they better be.

As soon as they piled into Dev's 4Runner, Sophie in the passenger seat, Wright behind her, the car-colepsy set in. They weren't halfway down the mountain before she was asleep.

She woke to Wright nudging her arm.

He stood at her open car door, blocking out the sunlight. "Soph. We're here."

She rubbed her eyes. "Did I snore?"

"No." He chuckled, holding her steady by the elbow as she climbed from the car. "Are you fully awake or should I carry you inside?"

She did her best to give him the evil eye but screwed it up by yawning. "I'm fine. I think the nap helped."

He closed the car door behind her and they followed Dev toward what looked like an abandoned warehouse, except for the ornately lit sign on the roof.

Luanne's Lighting Warehouse.

"Where does Dev hear about these crazy places?" Wright muttered the question.

"God only knows."

They reached the steps, and she wasn't as awake as she thought. Her toe caught on the second step, making her stumble. Wright caught her, grabbing her by the arm and waist.

His rescue was appreciated, and nothing unusual, except that as they climbed the stairs, he didn't let go.

"You sure you're okay?" He grinned. "I can pick you up if you'd like."

Sophie dug her elbow into his side.

Wright laughed and rubbed where she struck. "Well, don't say I never offered."

They reached the platform of the warehouse to find Devlin scowling at them.

Beside her, Wright tensed. "Sophie tried to face-plant on the stairs."

A decent enough recovery, but to be sure they covered up the moment, Sophie kept walking past Dev, griping the whole way. "I'm tired and I tripped. That's what happens when you drag an exhausted woman out to the middle of nowhere."

She tromped into Luanne's Lighting Warehouse, and her footfalls echoed in the enormous space.

"Hello?" Dev called out from behind her.

The warehouse was the size of a football field. Indoor lamps, outdoor lampposts, string lights, displays of recessed lighting—it was wall-to-wall lights of every kind imaginable.

"Let me see if I can find the office." Dev gave her one more little scowl before walking down the wall near the entrance.

As soon as he was far enough away, Sophie turned and gave Wright her own bug-eyed glare.

"What'd I do?"

"Besides grope me in front of my brother?"

"I wasn't groping you. I stopped you from wiping out. Am I supposed to let you fall on your face?"

"Yes."

He tossed his hands up.

"This way, guys," Dev called out and waved them down the wall to follow him.

They went all the way down the wall and headed toward the back.

"Luanne was on the phone, but she said all exterior lights were in the back."

Turned out, "the back" was the whole back third of the warehouse.

"Jesus." Wright sighed. "There's no way you're going to find what you want in an hour, Dev."

Dev cursed and did a three-sixty in the middle of the aisle. "Okay . . . here's the plan. We all know the kind of look we're going for? Think soft glow, Midsummer Night, enchanting, unique."

"Got it."

Dev scanned the layout of aisles. "I'll take these two; Soph, you take the next two; Wright, take those two over there. If you see something that looks cool as hell, how about taking a picture on your phone and texting it to us? Divide and conquer. Go."

He sounded so much like Roark, she had to fight the urge to salute him.

They split up, Sophie taking the middle aisle, and shelf after shelf of boxes and displays blurred together into nothingness. A few hours of sleep didn't result in the best decision-making skills.

The minutes passed as she wandered, and then came a "pssst" from the next aisle.

"What do you think of these?" Wright rounded the corner, holding two Japanese lanterns in each hand, all of them different colors.

"I think that's not the look Dev was talking about."

"No, not exactly." He moved closer. "But he did say anything that looked cool as hell. These are cool."

She shook her head to hide her grin. "They are, but they're wrong. We need something more like these." She pointed to a box of twinkle lights and the strand that lit up the shelf as an example.

"Let's get those, then."

"Not these, but *like* these. And we need them in a quantity larger than a strand of a hundred or we'll be stringing up lights for hours."

"Still an option, though." Wright passed her two lanterns and pulled out his phone. He snapped a picture of the twinkle lights and then one of her holding the lanterns.

"You did not just take a picture of me holding these stupid lanterns."

"I did. And come here, there's something else I want to show you."

Shuffling around to his aisle to return the lanterns, she was blinded by spinning balls and two strobe lights.

"Those are disco balls."

"I know, but look." He flicked on another light. This one was red. "We're supposed to be working."

"Since when are you the stick in the mud?"

"I'm not, but . . . you saw how Dev looked at us before. When we were laughing. I know that look. He's suspicious enough already. We should pick out some lights and go."

Ignoring her, Wright flicked on a colored spotlight, and a mirrored disco ball began to spin. "Tell me you don't want one of these for the inn's game room."

She bit at her bottom lip to keep from laughing at his face, awash in red, then blue, and then green. "How are you not tired after last night?"

He stepped closer, his voice low. "I'm exhausted, but I think the delirium has kicked in. We should sneak one of these disco balls and spotlights into the game room."

"Or Roark's office."

Wright choked on his laughter. "Holy shit, yes. At the start of his next meeting, hit the lights and turn on the mirrored ball, cue up some techno. Can you imagine the look on his face?"

She began to giggle. The ridiculousness of the vision, mixed with exhaustion, bubbled up into a fit of laughter she couldn't stop. With her hands over her face, she gave into the humor of it all. They were in some godforsaken warehouse in the middle of nowhere, and lights were flashing on Wright's face like he was a disco queen.

As she wiped a tear of laughter away, patterns of soft white light in her peripheral vision caught her attention.

She turned and moved away from the aisles to the very back corner of the warehouse.

"Fine. Just walk away from the dance party, then," Wright called after her.

Tucked away in the dark, farthest reaches of Luanne's was about a ten-by-ten square of what appeared to be artificial turf. Centered on the fake greenery was a white arbor with an artificial vine along the sides and top, with tiny white lights woven into the vine.

Up close, the fake greenery was tacky, but from a distance, the little round bulbs held the natural magical feel Dev was going for.

The real catcher was the rustic-style lanterns, made of glass and metal with patterned cutouts, hung high above the ground. The cutouts scattered light across the floor, the strands giving everything a soft glow. On either side were tall metal lampposts that matched the lanterns.

Unique and enchanting.

"This is perfect," Wright said, standing right behind her.

"Right?"

"Of course, ours will look better since we'll be in the actual out of doors and not in a warehouse with fake plants."

Sophie moved closer to the lanterns, trying to test the weight and sturdiness in her hands.

"Here." Wright reached over her and unhooked one to hand it over.

The metal was light, making the lanterns easier to place, the light inside operated on a small battery. "These are perfect." She turned to him. "We could put them anywhere without driving a bunch of nails and hooks in all over the place."

He put his hands over hers, lifting the lantern a little higher to observe. Satisfied, he nodded, his gaze settling upon hers. "They have my vote."

They were only talking about lanterns, but with his warm hands enveloping hers, the mellow light somehow making the moment quieter and intimate, her mind went back to last night.

In his bedroom, the very same seductive look in his eyes.

The rest of the warehouse fell away as he stepped closer, her brother a distant thought as Wright brushed his fingers across the back of her hands. "I can't wait to see how good you'll look the night of the gala."

She hadn't thought that far ahead, but the fund-raiser party was a little over a week away now. She and Wright would still be together then—doing whatever it was they were doing. Would they be each other's secret date for the evening? Normally they could dance together without anyone thinking anything of it, but now . . .

How would she ever be able to dance with Wright again like it was nothing? With his mouth near her ear, his breath ruffling her hair, his hand at the small of her back as he pressed her close to his body.

"I want to kiss you right now," he whispered.

She blinked, tilting forward. "Me too."

"You guys did it." Devlin's voice echoed across the warehouse, making her jump.

Wright jerked away with a grimace.

"You found it. This is *exactly* the look we want. These lanterns are perfect." Dev held his hands out.

Sophie handed him the lantern while avoiding eye contact with Wright. She was too scared to look right at him, but she sensed his tension.

"How many do you think we need?" Dev stepped past them to look at the different pattern options hanging all around.

"Um . . ." Wright scrubbed a hand over his face, sharing a look with her. "Depends on if you want them downstairs or up."

"Both. Along with this style string lights. The exposed bulb look suits the inn and the vibe we want. Don't you think?"

Sophie coughed a fake cough. "That's why the display caught my eye. And I'd say fifty of these. At least."

"Done. Nice going." Dev clapped her on the shoulder before heading to the front of the store, leaving her off balance, her mind a whirl.

"He didn't notice anything," Wright tried to reassure her.

She worked to breathe normally. "Maybe not, but I don't know how." Dev wasn't the type to *not* notice. Over the years, he could be accused of a lot of things, but being oblivious wasn't one of them.

"Come on, we better go help him get the lights ordered."

Yes. They better. Then perhaps they could stay out of trouble.

Once the lights were ordered, set to be shipped next day, the three of them piled back into Dev's car without a word.

They were halfway home before anyone spoke.

Dev took a deep breath and opened his mouth. Sophie's insides turned to stone as she waited.

"So, Wright." Dev stared into the rearview mirror. "I think I know the answer, but I need to ask you something."

Oh no, oh no.

He knew. Dev knew and he was about to call them on it.

Worse, there could be serious repercussions. What if Dev really did get furious? Hurtful words would be said, arguing, fighting. Slamming doors.

She couldn't go through that again. Back to the turmoil. The anger.

Sometimes she missed being needed, but she cherished the peace and contentment of her family more. If she ruined their opportunity with her own selfish desires, she'd never forgive herself.

"I was wondering, if things work out, would you be my best man?"

Sophie stopped breathing.

"You . . ." Wright cleared his throat, clearly caught off guard as well. "*Yeah!* Of course I will."

"And . . ." Dev glanced her way, and her insides were still fish-flopping around. "I want you to be my other groomsman. Woman.

Grooms . . . person. I don't know what to call it, but I want you up there with me too."

She blinked, trying to keep up. Her face was hot, and she was starting to sweat. She rolled down the window to get some fresh air.

One second her world was unraveling, the next she was a groomsman.

At a stop sign, Dev turned to face her more fully. "I've got the air on. You can put the window up." He cranked the AC higher. "Please say yes. I know it's odd and against tradition, but so is everything else I do, and I want you up there with me. You don't have to wear a suit. I don't care what you wear. Hell, I don't know if I'll wear a suit, but that doesn't matter."

"Wh-what about Roark?"

"Roark will be there, but I don't want a huge wedding party standing up. Neither will Anna. I want you two with me." He waited, eyebrows raised, his eyes impossibly blue.

Like she'd ever said no to him.

"Of course I'll be your groomsman." Her heart clenched as she agreed.

Her brother was really going to get married, and he wanted her with him.

Wright leaned forward, his hands on the side on Sophie's seat. "Did you already ask Anna to marry you and not tell us?"

Dev grinned, looking proud as a peach. "Not yet, but I'm going to. I have it on good authority she won't reject me, but I want your help on figuring out what to do." He glanced back at Wright, then at her. "I thought you already knew I was planning to ask. Figured Sophie would've told you."

Her mouth fell open in righteous defense. "I would not. That's your job. I'm not going to steal your thunder." Never mind that she and Wright had been too preoccupied to discuss Dev's love life.

"I was thinking I'd ask next week. Maybe you guys can help me come up with the perfect way to pop the question."

"Sure. We can help, but you know, the details have to come from you. Only you know what would mean the most to Anna."

His advice was almost identical to Sophie's, and she smiled.

As the two of them tossed around days and times to ask, she zoned out, staring at the passing trees.

Dev had never been happier than since he met Anna. Wright sounded thrilled at the prospect of being best man, and an upcoming wedding and fancy fund-raiser would have the entire resort in a state of giddy anticipation for weeks. Everything at Honeywilde was wonderful. Calmer and better than it'd been in years.

All she had to do was make sure no one found out about her and Wright, or all of that contentedness could come to a crashing halt.

Chapter 14

They reached Honeywilde with about ten minutes to spare before Wright had to start on dinner prep. Didn't leave him much time to talk with Sophie alone, but he could make it work.

As soon as they parked, Dev homed in on the black Lexus in employee parking. His soon-to-be fiancée worked out of town several days a week, but she made a point to be at Honeywilde on weekends.

"I'll see you two later." Dev leapt from the driver's side and took off inside, leaving Wright and Sophie alone.

"Guess he missed her." Sophie got out of the SUV and stepped right into the cage Wright had made with both passenger side doors and his arms. "What are you doing?" She rolled her eyes, but a smile played at her lips.

"Taking a moment. How come you didn't tell me Dev was going to propose?"

"That's not my story to share. I knew he'd tell you about the ring soon enough."

He leaned forward. "Dev bought a ring?"

With her eyes to heaven, she avoided his gaze. "Yes. He got the ring the other day. I went with him, but I thought he'd tell you. I didn't want to steal his thunder."

He straightened, brushing his hands down Sophie's arms. "Good for Dev. He's happy. Too happy to notice anything today."

"Not for lack of us being obvious. I almost kissed you in the middle of Luanne's Light Warehouse."

"You did?" He smiled so big he felt it in his toes.

"We don't need to go on any more work errands with Dev. He's going to find out, or at the very least be suspicious."

"I wish you would've kissed me."

"You're missing the point. I don't want my brother finding out about us that way."

Wright studied her, something clicking in his mind like rusty gears working their way into place. "So you wouldn't mind him finding out, just not in that way."

Sophie blinked. "What? No. I don't . . . I don't want him finding out in any way."

"You sure about that?"

She stepped up into his space so she could close the car door, her breasts brushing against his chest. "Yes. I'm positive."

He shoved his door closed and moved forward until she was pressed against the SUV. "All right, just checking."

Sophie grabbed the front of his shirt and dragged him down, crashing their lips together before pushing him away. "You're irritating."

Considering they were in Honeywilde's parking lot and Sophie was kissing him where anyone could see them, he wasn't sorry.

"I'm not coming to your apartment tonight," she told him.

"I don't remember inviting you."

She inhaled sharply, as though wounded. Even though she was far from it, he still couldn't drag out the taunt.

"However, I would like to invite you on an errand for the gala tomorrow. No Devlin. No Trevor. Only you and me."

"We don't have time for that. We have work to do."

"This is work. Did you hear me say it was an errand for the gala?"

She side-eyed him. "What kind of errand?"

With one last quick kiss, he backed away, his hands up. "Don't worry about that. I'll coordinate the scheduling, you be ready to go right after brunch."

Sophie popped her hands to her hips, the picture of frustrated and so sexy. "Wright McAdams, what are you up to?"

"Don't you full name me like I'm in trouble. I'll see you tomorrow."

The next day, he left Marco to clean up the last of the brunch service. He'd also be in charge of the cookie and coffee hour. Good experience for a new chef, and Marco showed talent.

Wright threw on clean clothes and hurried toward the great room. Would Sophie be waiting on him or would she let guilt and family obligation trump her personal wishes?

The reality of the situation was he stood a fifty-fifty shot of being stood up or having a wonderful afternoon away with his girl.

Or rather, the girl he wished was his.

His phone chirped in his pocket.

Hoping it was her, he checked the screen.

Nope. A text from his dad.

Heard anything from New York? Charleston? Chicago? You need to follow up with them if not. Don't let the big one get away.

With a shake of his head, he put his phone back in his pocket.

He wasn't letting anything get away. Not a job and not Sophie. He essentially had his pick of restaurants, but he had to decide on the right one. Maybe that was Charleston or Asheville. He had a little more time to decide, and he would.

But he didn't need his father's pressure to do it.

As he rounded the corner, he held his breath as he scanned the room. No redheads, no redheads, no redheads . . .

Then he saw her.

On the steps between the reception area and the great room, she stood, leaned against the hand rail, typing on her phone.

"You ready?" He kept walking right past her. If he stopped, he'd touch her. And if he touched her, he wouldn't be able to stop.

"I don't know." She followed him out the front door. "Are you taking me off into the wilderness? We going to the farm for produce? I have no idea if I'm ready since I have no idea what we're doing."

He opened the Jeep door for her and went around, climbing in the other side. "I told you. We're running an errand. For work." He winked at her as he buckled up.

"That look on your face isn't instilling more confidence."

"Relax. This really is for the fund-raiser, but coincidentally, it's fun as well."

His phone chirped again and, after a ten-second debate with himself, he checked it.

And call me. Let me know what's going on. Updates. We haven't heard from you in over a week.

He flipped the sound over to vibrate and didn't reply.

His parents could wait. Today, he had plans.

Twenty minutes later, they turned down the long driveway leading to the vineyard and Chateau Jolie.

Sophie turned toward him. "The competition. Really?"

Chateau Jolie was an estate built in the 1920s, inspired by the chateaus of France and sold off to the highest bidder in the eighties. It was also Honeywilde's closest competition for an upscale mountain getaway.

"Why are we at the chateau?"

"Would you relax? And trust me. You little control freak."

"I'm not a—" She clamped her mouth shut.

Even she couldn't argue that point. Sophie was generous and kind, but she absolutely preferred to be in control, with no unforeseen circumstances or curveballs. She didn't so much care if she was in charge, as long as she got to be in control.

For someone who didn't actually share any DNA, she was frighteningly similar to Roark.

Wright parked and faced her. "I am capable of multitasking, you know? I do it every day in the kitchen. I've arranged some time away from Honeywilde that includes accomplishing something for the gala *and* something for us."

She glanced at the chateau, a beautiful stone structure, four stories tall.

The family who owned it had added a vineyard a good many years ago. It was an ever growing work in progress, but already they had a reputation for some delightful reds, along with a rosé and a sparkling wine that were hits.

With her bottom lip between her teeth, she knotted her fingers together.

He leaned over, peeling one hand away from the other, brushing his thumb across the back. "We're going to go in here as representatives of Honeywilde, enjoy a wine tasting, and order a few cases for the party that will perfectly accompany my dishes. We're going to have a nice afternoon, together, and that's that. Got it?"

Her gaze shot to his, and he made sure his expression was certain. "Okay." She nodded.

He lifted the hand he held in his and placed a kiss on her knuckles. "Come on. They're expecting us."

Once they let the concierge know of their arrival, they were escorted downstairs to a cellar that must've taken up the entire bottom level.

There, the chateau's manager, Brooke, took over.

Wright had spoken with her on the phone when he called about some special wines for the gala.

A statuesque woman he'd place maybe in her early thirties, she gave them an extended tour, clearly enamored with her job.

And who wouldn't be? She got to work with wine for a living.

"We're still working on expanding our selections, but in another year, our stock should be full." She showed them the reserves of red and the brut he'd heard so much about. "Are you ready to try some?"

He watched Sophie as she turned one of the bottles of Brut Reserve in her hands. "I would say so."

"Then follow me." Brooke led them outside, down a path, to a stand-alone patio of stone pavers and hearty wood tables and chairs, a waiter standing near a fully set table.

At the far end of the patio, an outdoor kitchen took up an entire corner.

Wright grabbed Sophie's hand and pulled her toward the beauty, all wine temporarily forgotten.

"Wow, this is gorgeous," she gushed.

She had no idea.

He ran his fingers across the knobs of the range, opened the oven door, and caressed the stonework of the structure. "I'm a little turned on right now," he whispered.

Next to him, Sophie giggled and clutched his arm. "Easy. We have wine to taste."

"I want one." The words fell out, so true, yet so impossible. At least for now. Honeywilde was doing well, but not that well.

"Maybe someday." She tugged him toward the table where Brooke and a waiter watched them. "If we get one or two more big rock-star weddings."

Wright watched the kitchen as he walked away.

The thought was nice, but highly unlikely. Roark wasn't the type to spend that extravagantly, even if the resort had the means. And chances were Wright wouldn't even be there by the time Honeywilde had another celebrity wedding, or two.

He had to decide by month end, and month end was drawing near.

"We have a small plates menu ready for you," Brook announced. "Eric will be your waiter, but I'll keep check on you in case you have questions."

Once she left, Eric, looking all of a day over twenty-one, stepped up to their table. "For starters, we have our Brut Reserve, served with cheese-filled brioche."

Sophie shared a smile with Wright as she sat. "I'm going to be full and drunk after this, aren't I?"

Wright spread his napkin over his lap. "Depends on how much you like the wine. We're only trying six and they'll pour conservatively, but . . . given your size, yeah. You're probably going to be tipsy."

The waiter popped a bottle of bubbly, poured, and left them to enjoy the brut and brioche.

"You aren't going to try to take advantage of me later, are you?"

"No." He laughed as he cut the brioche in two, placing a half on each of their plates. "But I'd be okay with you taking advantage of me."

She smiled as she bit into the bun, chewing with her eyes closed before picking up the champagne flute.

"Wait." Wright grabbed his glass. "A toast. To the two of us, and finally doing something about it."

Sophie tapped her glass against his.

The flavor hit his tongue, crisp and alive. Not too sweet, not too dry, the wine went down smooth with the bite of bubbles at the end.

The brut lived up to the reputation and then some.

"Wow, this is good." Sophie took another sip.

"We have to get this for the party."

"Definitely."

Next up was a pinot grigio, followed by a small salad and a rosé. Then they ventured into the reds, starting with a noir and filet medallions, then a syrah.

The glasses of wine were conservative, but not as small as he'd predicted. By the fifth tasting, his face was warm, his muscles relaxed.

He glanced at Sophie over a sip of syrah.

Her cheeks were pink, her eyes shining. She was well on her way to tipsy, in the middle of the day.

But dammit, good for her. She never got out and did things for herself.

Anything.

She worked as hard as, if not harder than, anyone else at Honeywilde, and she deserved something special. A break from the everyday routine.

She needed someone who'd do things like this for her. Someone who'd set it up and treat her to something nice, and fun, because she'd never do it for herself.

Not for the first time, Wright was grateful to be that guy.

She really could be with anyone, even if she didn't realize it, but she wanted to be with him.

What happened to that when he left Honeywilde? Assuming he could keep her from running from him until then.

A pit opened up in his stomach.

Whether he moved to New York or down the highway to Asheville, casually dating—secret or not—would be impossible. They would either be a couple, or they wouldn't.

He knew better than to press her about the future or any kind of commitment, but the thought of not being with her, her going out with some other guy, enjoying dates and laughter, being with someone else . . .

Wright set his fork down, the tender filet turning to rubber in his mouth.

Sophie with someone else was no longer an acceptable option. He'd observed that for years, as she had with him, and he wasn't interested in moving backward.

A secret affair that gave her a thrill was fine, for now. But he didn't want to be a secret forever, or short term. He wanted the rest of the summer, and then the fall. Months and months after that. There'd be no going back to buddies for him.

"Why are you so serious over there?" Sophie reached over, walking her fingers along his forearm. "Is your steak no good? I know you're a foodie perfectionist and all, but this is good beef."

"No, the steak is delicious."

She grinned, the action slow and lazy.

"And you're lit."

"I am not." She flapped her hand in the air before patting his arm. Then she went back to touching his forearm, skating her fingers up to the sleeve of his shirt.

"You're feeling me up."

With a toss of her head, she blew him off. "You think this is feeling you up? Please." She squeezed his arm and sighed.

Naturally he felt a little ripple of pride. "If this isn't feeling me up, promise you'll show me later? I need to understand the qualities of a proper feeling up."

She took her bottom lip between her teeth, her gaze sparkling, and nodded. "You know . . ." With the tip of her pointer finger, she traced a pattern down his arm. "I don't think I've ever told you this, but I have a thing for your arms."

"You're definitely tipsy."

Adamant, she pointed to his upper arm. "You have good arms. And I like the little bit of freckles."

Wright studied his arm, confused. "I don't have freckles."

Sophie had freckles. Delightful, sinful little things, delicately decorating the bridge of her nose and upper cheeks, a few on her shoulders—they drove him wild.

He had plain skin.

"Seriously, you don't see these?" She lifted his arm and pushed it closer to his face.

A bark of laughter escaped him. "I see my skin. I've never thought about it as freckled, though."

"Well." She sighed, propping her chin in her hand. "To be fair, I've probably thought about your arms a whole lot more than you have." The heat from her gaze sent ripples of pleasure right down to his crotch.

The wine was making her loose-lipped, and if she could admit how she felt about his arms, then he was going to fess up to his feelings about her freckles.

Wright scooted his chair closer, leaning toward her with both elbows on the table. "Do you want to know what I think about your freckles?"

"Probably not." With a squeak of embarrassment, she buried her face in her hands.

"Good. Because I'm going to tell you. You remember a few summers ago we had the day off and I was over, visiting Dev?"

"Uh-huh." She kept her face covered.

"We all went swimming, out to the floating dock, with a little cooler full of beers. Dev was still drinking then and he somehow managed to swim out there with a cooler and not drown. We sat around, swam a little, and drank a lot. I worked up a decent buzz, but . . . I can still picture it like it was yesterday. You had on this green bikini and I remember thinking no one had any right to look that good in a *green* bathing suit, but you did."

Sophie peeked over the tips of her fingers. "I remember that suit."

He could envision her, sun-kissed and snarky, and his cock twitched at the memory. "Yeah, so do I. Little strings tied it together, and I don't know if it was because of the beer or too much sun, or because I hadn't seen so much of you in a really long time, but . . ." He shook his head at the memory.

The night after that swim, he'd been riddled with guilt as guess who kept popping up while he got off in the shower. Fight though he might, nothing would do but to picture Sophie and that damned bikini, and he'd shot off like a rocket.

His mouth still went dry at the image.

He downed the last of his syrah. "I was obsessed with the freckles on your shoulders," he confessed. "And the few you have right . . . here." He touched the front of her blouse. "I couldn't get them out of my mind. I wanted to touch you so bad."

Sophie's face went bright pink. "You did?"

"Of course I did. Then you dove into the water and I was like thank Christ because I was fighting a hard-on something awful. I jumped in the lake too, praying neither of you noticed."

She shook her head, eyes wide.

"Sometimes now, I get all distracted, thinking about these freckles. Wanting to kiss your shoulders. Wondering what it'd be like to drag my mouth across your skin, into your cleavage."

She placed both of her hands on his arm. "You . . . you like my freckles?"

He leaned in, his nose inches from her. "Oh yeah."

Her breath came out shaky, and she licked her lips. "You know . . . you could do that now. If you wanted to."

"Kiss each and every one of your freckles?"

She nodded.

"And put my hands on you."

The nodding came faster.

He didn't say a word until the waiter moved in his peripheral. "We're going to need the chocolate and cabernet sent to a room," Wright told him. "We're staying the afternoon."

Chapter 15

Sophie walked into the guest room like she was walking on clouds. Chateau Jolie had a completely different feel than Honeywilde. More opulent and formal, the guest room boasted thick drapes and rich bedding in cream and chocolate brown.

Wright closed the door behind them, setting their glasses of cabernet down on the dresser.

Sophie held a small tray of four chocolate-dipped strawberries and two chocolate truffles. Dessert meant to accentuate the flavor of the wine.

Reaching around her, he took the tray from her hands and set it next to the wine before pulling her into a kiss. He swept his tongue against hers and she leaned into him. The wine and Wright's attention had her loose-limbed.

He kissed her until her mind swam with thoughts of what was to come.

No one here to bother them or care about what they might be doing.

She and Wright already had sex once, alleviating the nerves she'd carried with her about their first time together. He'd seen her naked, and she'd seen him. She could relax into the moment and think only of how it felt to be with him. What it might be like to do more.

Wright tucked her hair back, placing soft kisses along the shell of her ear. "We should at least try a sip of the last wine before we're completely distracted."

"Too late."

He plucked one of the chocolate-covered strawberries from the tray. "Open up."

She parted her lips and he slipped the tip of the fruit into her mouth. The chocolate was soft and sweet, the strawberry a burst of juicy tartness on her tongue.

"Mmm." She fluttered her eyes closed.

She opened them to see Wright take the rest of the fruit into his mouth. As he chewed, he reached for one of the wine glasses.

"Here." He put the glass to her lips, tilting until rich cabernet ran over her tongue and down her throat. Then he took a long sip, leaving a dark droplet on his lips.

Sophie rose up on her toes and licked it away. "I'm probably biased, but the cab is my favorite."

He kissed her, long and unhurried, skating his lips across hers. "Mine too." With another sweep of his tongue, he urged her lips open, slanting their mouths together. With the lightest touch, he caressed her sides before tucking her against him. He kissed his way to her throat, nibbling at her neck, small fireworks setting off all over her body.

He cupped her ass, humming appreciatively as he took her lips again.

Wright kissed her like they had all the time in the world, touched her lazy and slow, flicking one button of her blouse open and then the other.

"You know we have to get back before dinner," she reminded him.

"Shhh." He cupped her breast through her bra. "I'll have you back on time. Stop worrying."

A few more buttons and he had her blouse open and began sliding it down her arms.

As much as she'd enjoyed it, she wasn't going to be the only one naked at the start again, at Wright's delicious mercy again.

She eased away and tugged his shirt up, trying to get it over his head.

Wright let out a small laugh and helped her get his shirt off. Then she went to work on his pants.

He stepped out, toeing off his shoes in the process, only his boxers remaining. "We don't have to be in any hurry. We've got hours."

"I'm not in a hurry. I just want you undressed."

A smile split his face.

Heaven help her. She took his hand and led him toward the bed. "Last time you wore clothes for entirely too long."

He reached for the button of her capris. "Then let's not make that same mistake again."

She let him strip her of her pants, stepping out of her sandals and standing before him in her underwear.

Wright smoothed her hair back, touching her face, brushing his fingers down over her shoulders. "You are so beautiful," he murmured, before dropping a kiss on the freckles of her left shoulder.

Then he kissed his way across her right shoulder.

"These are the ones I was talking about before." He pressed his lips to her collarbone, dragging his mouth down into her cleavage. "I love these. I was so caught up the other night, with you showing up at my door, I didn't have time to give them the proper attention."

Maybe not, but he'd paid plenty of attention to other things.

Exactly as he promised, Wright began kissing every one of her freckles, across her cheeks, down her arms. Then he turned her around and kissed the freckles across her back, praising their beauty and hers. Her insides turned to liquid lightning, her sex aching for his touch, leaving her squirming where she stood.

His effect was so unfair.

She'd at least gotten him out of his clothes, but she was still the one trembling with need.

Then she turned around, a renewed intent to follow up on her plan, to find the front of his boxers damp, his erection impossible to ignore.

She ran her hand up the length of him, through the cotton, and he shuddered, arching his neck, eyes squeezed closed as he let out a shaky breath.

"See what you do to me?" His voice was raspy and rough.

Rather than answer, she pushed him onto the bed.

Wright sat and scooted back as she climbed up next to him.

Her plan was to turn have him pleading her name, the same way she'd begged the other night.

She eased the band of his boxers down, his cock springing free.

The other night was the first time she'd had sex in a while, and she'd done fine with that. At least, Wright seemed pretty damn pleased.

She brushed her fingers down his length, touching him the way he'd liked the other night. But after a few strokes, she leaned over, said a quick prayer that perfection wasn't necessary, and wrapped her lips around the head.

Wright made a strangled noise, fisting his hands in the bedsheets.

She opened her mouth wider, taking him in, as he muttered a curse. Gently at first, she slid him in and out of her mouth, and Wright praised her. With her hand around him, she let him pop free from her lips, only to take him in again.

His stomach tightened. Both legs bent and straightened like he wasn't quite sure what to do with them, and his grip on the sheets began pulling them from their neat corners.

He was falling apart.

A swell of pride grew at his reaction. She swirled her tongue around the head, investigating every ripple and ridge with the tip.

"Sophie." His entire body tensed, muscles taut, releasing the sheets only to dig his fingers in again.

She hummed, swallowing him down. Using her hands, she stroked in time with her mouth, using his reactions as her guide.

Apparently, she was doing all right.

He arched his lower back, pushing farther into her mouth. She stroked him faster, pulling a guttural sound from his throat. He thrust into her mouth again, a little deeper.

Wright was . . . endowed, and she wasn't expecting it. She gagged a little but eased back, using more of her hand.

"Sorry," he whispered.

She kept sucking and working her hands but flashed a glance up at him. He had nothing to be sorry about.

Wright shuddered again, harder this time, and bit into his bottom lip. "Shit, don't look at me like that."

She released him with another pop. "Like what?"

"Like . . . *that.* With me in your mouth. I . . . it's going to make me come before I want to."

Her laugh came out lower than normal. Sultry, even to her ears.

Wright suddenly sat up, kissing her hard, his tongue tangling with hers. "I want to be inside you. Right now."

Sophie nodded.

She slid off the bed and grabbed his wallet from his pants pocket. When he pulled out the condom, she took it from him. Pushing his shoulders back, she got him to lie back and rolled the condom on.

"Damn. You have any idea how hot you are? Especially right now."

"Am I?"

"Hell yes."

She tossed her head to the side, her hair swinging as she straddled his lap, her hands on his chest for balance.

"Now you're just torturing me."

"This isn't torture." She eased down his length, his cock filling her, stretching her in delightful ways. With her hands on his shoulders, she lowered herself until he was all the way in.

Wright's pupils were wide, his gaze hungry. "You're right. This is heaven."

He looked at her like he'd devour her. And she would let him. Knowing now that Wright was capable of such a look, that he looked at *her* this way . . . she was empowered. Strong, but desperate for more.

Arching her lower back, she leaned forward, easing up and back down again.

He bit off a curse and moaned, placing his hands on her hips. "You feel so good, baby."

Sophie did it again, easing up and back down his length, until she moved easily and tiny sparks of pleasure began to glow in her core. "So do you."

With his hands on her hips, he helped the movement. Up and down, up and down. She arched and tilted her hips, making him wilder with every second.

He cupped her breast, flicking his thumb over her nipple before pinching it.

The sparks grew brighter, stronger.

"I love the way you bounce when you're riding me." He pinched the other nipple.

She squeezed around him, feeling reckless and dirty in the best possible way.

"You like this, don't you? Being on top of me."

She jerked her chin in a nod. Did she ever.

Wright, all long and strong beneath her, holding her hips but letting her lead, letting her do whatever she wanted and loving it.

"I knew you would. Me too." He lifted his hips in counterpoint to hers, thrusting into her harder, a little deeper. "You can go faster. You know you want to."

Sophie rocked on top of him faster, using the leverage of his movement. With every deep thrust, he hit something inside her that made her brain short-circuit, her nerve endings buzzing like live wires.

She was fire and light and brightness. Unrecognizable and wonderful.

Sophie dug her nails into his chest, her hips pounding against his as he filled her over and over and over again.

She was lost to it. Her need for him, the things Wright made her feel, the person she could be with him.

He groaned again, his grip on her hips tightening. "You're perfect like this. Go on, baby, take it."

The light inside her exploded, a thumping in her ears like a bass drum and a shower of a thousand stars in her eyes as she came.

Wright cried out with his orgasm, pulsing within her. Still gripping him, her legs clamped around his hips, his cock deep inside her, she spun apart, and it was glorious. She let herself spin, letting go, until all she knew was this feeling, and how it felt to share this with him.

Sophie lay sprawled, half across him, her face pressed to his skin.

The image of her above him, her hands on his chest as she rode him to climax, would be forever inked onto his brain.

He'd never forget. Didn't want to. The most provocative thing he'd ever seen, and he played it over and over, in awe that the reality was his.

Time floated by and he drifted deeper and deeper into sleep, sated, with Sophie in his arms.

When she finally stirred, he lifted one eyelid about a millimeter, to find her peeking up at him, her chin on his chest.

"Hey, baby." He grinned.

"I thought you were asleep."

"I was. We've got another hour or so. We can nap if you want."

She laid her head back down. "Ohhh, I love naps."

And she rarely got them. Whether it was because she felt she didn't have time or they were too self-serving, Sophie didn't allow for something as indulgent as napping. Unless she conked out on a car ride.

She rubbed his chest, her eyes sleepy and her gaze warm. Her fingers passed over the red marks on his skin.

"Did I do that?" She sat up and inspected them.

Little half-moon red marks dotted his chest. Exactly the size and shape of her nails, if they were to, say, claw into him.

"Yep."

"I . . . I'm sorry."

"I'm not." He tugged her back down, grinning. He'd dreamt of her marking him like this. "You didn't break the skin, and I think it's hot."

"Not hot if you have to wear a bathing suit."

With a shrug, he tried to get her nestled into the nook of his arm. "I don't think I'll be wearing a bathing suit in the next few days, but I'd be willing to make the sacrifice if so. Knowing I can turn you into a wild woman is worth the price."

She nudged him, giggling as she settled back down.

He meant what he said, though.

The way sex overtook her today was wild and new. Seemed it was wild and new for her too. Neither of them were blushing virgins. They'd even talked about one or two of their experiences before, but he got the feeling Sophie never . . . let go.

She was enthusiastic, but far from reckless. With brothers who ranged from too cautious to foolhardy, she was the balance in between. The middle ground that kept everyone from going to their extremes. And he wasn't sure how much, if at all, her family recognized that.

He'd realized it years ago, and even then, when she was fresh out of college, taking on a lion's share of responsibility at Honeywilde, he wished she'd cut loose from time to time. Act like the kid she was.

But she hardly had the chance.

A few times, he'd argued with Dev about not helping out enough and Sophie picking up his slack. Before Dev got his shit together, she always covered for him. Everyone knew it, and one day, Wright had had enough.

He'd chewed Dev out until his voice was raw, knowing Sophie wouldn't speak up for herself, so he was going to do it.

People weren't off the mark, accusing Wright of being too protective of Sophie. He always had been, but sometimes she needed someone to push back for her, even against her brothers.

Sure, she'd get her feathers ruffled and snap at people, but to *really* push back, hard, stand her ground and flat out say no, without eventually caving in . . . that wasn't Sophie.

Nowadays her brothers had their act together and didn't lean on her quite so hard. Which afforded things like slipping off to a winery with him.

Wright threaded his fingers through the red and gold waves of her hair, smoothing his hand over her back.

Sophie had no problem stepping up to him. She'd done it in the parking lot of the Tavern when she thought he wasn't defending her, in the kitchen when she told him they were *not* going to sneak around, and pretty much any time she disagreed with his opinion on anything.

With him, she pretty much said and did what she wanted.

And he wouldn't lie. Knowing he could push her to places that made her nails bite into his skin, made her temper spark and her spine stiffen, gave him a sense of . . . something.

Not pride. Not importance.

Distinction.

He was the one Sophie would talk to, candid and unabashed. She didn't worry about being perfect or perfectly polite with him. He was the one she'd go toe to toe with and not back down an inch. And he was the one she'd run to in the middle of the night, sneak off and have sex with, risking so much simply because this was what she wanted to do.

Whether or not she could ever admit it, to him or to herself, what they had was special. What they had was different. And it mattered to her as much as it did him.

If they kept going, it would only matter more.

Next to him, she stirred. "If we don't make a move soon, it'll be tomorrow before I get out of this bed."

Wright wrapped his arms around her, holding her close before they sat up. "Guess we have to go, then. You look sleepy, but if I miss dinner, someone will notice."

"You can buy me a coffee on the way back." She slipped from the bed and crossed the room to collect her clothes. The late-afternoon sunlight, diffused as it shined through the sheer curtains, made her fair skin glow. Her form, petite and lithe, took on a mystical quality thrown into sharp contrast with her riot of red bed head.

Wright broke out into a grin, his chest expanding with a pleasant ache.

"What?" She scrunched her nose at him as she stepped into her panties.

"Nothing." Only that he couldn't imagine life without her.

"You're so weird." Her hands behind her back, she hooked her bra on and grabbed her pants.

He felt weird. All knotted up inside, but full of joy. Life didn't feel this way, not normally. His life was one of working hard and striving to be the best he could. He wasn't that different than Sophie. Trying to be a great chef and please everyone with his skill, seeking to please his parents without sacrificing his own happiness, and putting forth every effort to impress this or that girl he was dating at the moment, but consistently falling short because . . .

Because this or that girl wasn't what he really wanted.

He wanted Sophie. In some way, he probably always had.

He'd always worked so hard, he didn't take the chance to stop and soak in the moments with her. He refused to let this moment go.

Wright leaned back against the headboard and watched Sophie get dressed. By the time she slid on her shoes, he was in a trance.

"Wright. What are you doing? We're going to be late. You're the one who needs to get back, and I need coffee."

He held his arm out, waving her over. "Stop talking and come here for a second."

"Excuse me?" She cocked her head but moved closer.

As soon as she was within reaching distance, he grabbed her and pulled her onto the bed next to him.

Sophie squeaked, but didn't put up any resistance.

"I wanted to say I'm glad we did this today. Took the time to get away and come here, together. This was . . . this was special."

Her expression went blank as she blinked. "I . . . I'm glad we did too." Smoothing her hair back, she glanced away.

"Hey." He turned her chin toward him again. "What is it?"

With shining eyes, she put on a smile. "Nothing. Like you said. This was special." She pinched her lips together for a moment before speaking again. "And you're a sap who's going to make us late."

He kissed her, knowing she wanted to say something beyond calling him sappy, but she wasn't ready. He kissed her until her shoulders weren't so stiff, her compact body held tight. When she finally relaxed, he tossed off the covers and grabbed his clothes.

She reached down for his boxers and handed them over. "Look at that. This time you're the one with no clothes on."

Wright laughed and snatched his boxers from her. "Hey. Any time you want me naked, all you have to do is ask."

Chapter 16

They made it back with maybe twenty minutes to spare before dinner service. After rushing through a drive-thru for coffee, Wright swung into the parking lot, barely managing to keep his Jeep on all four wheels.

"Jeez!" Sophie grabbed the "oh shit" bar and held on for dear life. "Told you we needed to get going. You're late."

Wright killed the engine and hopped out. "Worth it," he said, before closing the door. "I'll find you later," he called to her around the car and sprinted toward the front door of the inn.

As he rushed through the entrance, he almost knocked down a baffled-looking Trevor on his way out.

Trevor spun to avoid him, wide-eyeing Sophie as he passed the portico. "What the hell was that about?"

She put on her best casual expression. "I think he's late. Or something."

"Yeah, no shit. Where have y'all been?" Trevor checked his watch.

"Been?" She scratched at her ear, then her hair. Trevor shouldn't be asking about a "y'all" at all.

"Roark said the two of you were going to try some food or wine or something for the fund-raiser. Where'd you go?"

She forgot Wright had given them the perfect cover for being gone all afternoon. "Oh, right. Chateau Jolie."

"The competition. Nice. And fancy." Trev drew out the word. "And?"

"And what?"

He tilted his head to the side, thick brown hair flopping over. "And, details?"

The details that really mattered were none of his business. "How about some details on where you went when the rest of us had to go light hunting at Luanne's Warehouse?"

Trevor quirked his mouth and squinted at her. "I had stuff to do."

"Exactly. And we had stuff to do today."

With a quick glance around, the youngest Bradley moved closer, his voice barely above a whisper. "I'll give you details about the other day if you'll tell me what's going on with you and Wright."

She balked, taking two steps back. "Nothing. Nothing is going on."

He gave her that look again, blue eyes narrow and homed in on her. "If you say so. But you sure do look funny. You're not high, are you?"

"No!" Warning bells went off as she pushed past him. High on great sex, but she sure wasn't going to tell him that. "I'm fine."

Trevor followed her. "Then how was the chateau? Did you guys try wine? Find anything you like?"

She'd found something she liked, all right. Having the time and attention of Wright was proving addictive, the way she felt with him even more so. He made her stronger, willing to take a chance on feeling something. In return, she found pleasure, ecstasy, and a person she didn't have to hide from.

Wright had seen more of her than anyone, and he liked what he saw. So far.

Maybe he'd like all of her, even the scared, little heart she resented. If anyone was capable of accepting her faults, it'd be him.

"Seriously, Sis." Trevor stopped her. "You're all glassy eyed. Maybe it's a fever."

Sophie wasn't suffering from any fever. She was developing feelings for her closest friend.

More feelings. New, different, complicated feelings that went beyond sharing stories and humor, confiding in one another about crap dates. Feelings that went further than great sex or the rush of adrenaline they got from sneaking around.

How long had it been since she had hope?

Hope that someone would like her for her; accept her exactly as she was. Hope that maybe, just maybe, she could be loved and love in return, without it all falling apart.

Hope was terrifying.

"I'm not sick. I'm tired." She walked faster, eager to get away from her brother.

Once inside, she went straight to the elevator. He wouldn't follow her to her room, so that's where she'd go. Surely no one would need her for the next few minutes and she could take a moment.

She needed time to think. Collect herself and her thoughts. Today, something had shifted. Didn't matter that she and Wright had already slept together and that, in a way, this was their third time. No, today was something new, and there would be no going back.

As the elevator door opened, she hopped on and punched the third floor a few times for good measure.

Trevor stuck his hand in the door. His expression softened, but he didn't move his hand. "You should get rest. But did you find some wine? Because you still haven't said."

She almost smacked her forehead.

The whole point of their day and their outing had escaped her. Wine and food wasn't what weighed on her mind at the moment. "We found three options for the fund-raiser that will complement Wright's menu for the perfect pairings of food and drink." As she spilled out the same lines the waiter used on them, the elevator began to ping in protest of the open door.

"Good." Trevor moved his hand, but his inquisitive look was back. Not good. "I'm sure it'll be awesome. And hey, Dev wants to see you in a few minutes," he called through the closing doors. "He asked me to find you since he couldn't."

The elevator doors closed and she slumped against the far wall.

She could not face Devlin right now. She couldn't face anyone. Her glazed-over look was a postcoital, precrisis haze. And it had to be *super* obvious if Trevor noticed.

Once in her room, she sat on the edge of her bed and took a deep breath.

On her bedside table sat the photo of her parents. The parents she barely knew.

"I can't face Dev right now. That's a fact," she told them.

Great, now she was talking to their picture like they could answer. She hadn't spoken to them, aka talked to herself, in years.

It was the stress.

Lying to her family and hiding what she and Wright were up to, was driving her mad. The last time she'd talked to her parents, she was in college. Scared to death she was going to fail Statistics, flunk out of school, and let her brothers down when they were counting on her, she'd cried and vented to her dead parents almost every night for the last weeks of her junior year.

Sophie smiled, her bottom lip wobbling.

She'd felt crazy talking to them, but it'd helped. If only for the comfort of telling someone she was scared and alone, sharing with them, saying it out loud had helped.

"Ah, screw it, why not?" She scooted into the center of her bed and crossed her legs. "I'm sleeping with Wright—my friend, Dev's best friend—and now I don't know what to do. I can't just tell my brothers, but today was so . . . so . . ." She blinked away the burning in her eyes. "It was wonderful. Perfect. I didn't know . . . no one ever told me I'd feel this way." Sophie gestured toward their picture. "I mean, you couldn't have told me, I'm not blaming you, but . . . now what do I do?"

She wasn't ready to tell her family about her and Wright, but she knew they were no longer just messing around.

"If you were here, I promise I wouldn't have kept it from you," she told her parents.

Would they have judged her if she had, though? Would she even know Wright if they were still alive? Chances were, if they'd survived, she would've never been close to Wright. Never gotten to know him enough to kiss him. To trust him. To care.

She shook off the thought, refusing to obsess over what-ifs.

"Anyway, I have kept it from my brothers, and now Wright and I are . . . well, I don't know what we're doing or what we are, but I'm in a pickle, that's for sure. I'm about to pop for someone to talk to about all this, but there's no one, and now I have to go talk to Dev about *whatever*, and I'm not sure how I'll pull that off when even Trevor is giving me the side-eye. Ugh." Sophie flopped over onto her side.

She lay there for a few minutes, a little calmer after blurting out the truth at her parents.

"I know. I have to go downstairs," she told them. "I have to shower and pull myself together and act like I've got some sense. I can do that."

She got out of bed before she could dawdle long enough to second-guess. She put out clean clothes and took off the ones she'd worn to the chateau. A shower and a few minutes to gather her senses, that's all she needed.

All she got was the shower.

As soon as she stepped out and wrapped a towel around her, her phone pinged with its fifth text message. Four from Devlin asking her to find him as soon as possible, and one from Wright.

Dev is freaking out and wants to talk to us. He said it couldn't wait until later tonight. Be warned.

Her stomach plummeted and she had to sit down again. She was growing weary of the worry about being found out, but this couldn't be what she thought it was. How would Dev possibly know she and Wright had spent the day doing more than tasting wine? Everything was fine. It had to be.

Visions of Wright beneath her, his bottom lip trapped between his teeth, head thrown back to reveal the strong stretch of his throat, the first hints of a shadow beard along his jaw.

Go on baby, take it.

A delicious shiver ran through her at the memory.

Everything was not fine. Her life was flipping over, upside down and right side up, again and again. Cartwheeling out of control. If Devlin confronted her now about Wright, she'd never be able to lie. She might actually break down and start talking gibberish.

There was a big possibility she couldn't be around Wright tonight without her skin flushing and her hands automatically seeking him.

This reaction wasn't going to improve with time either.

She could only hope her brother's urgency had nothing to do with her afternoon at the winery. But if Dev suspicioned they were up to something, dealing with it tomorrow night wouldn't be any better than tonight. And putting off the moment of doom would only make her more anxious.

She sent a quick text off to Dev.

Got your texts. I'll be down in fifteen.

So much for having a moment to herself.

When she reached the lobby, Dev was waiting on her. "Come on in the kitchen. I have to talk to the both of you." He turned and all but marched toward the restaurant as though leading her to the gallows.

Dev shoved open the kitchen's swinging doors. "Marco. Could you give us a few minutes? This won't take long."

Her stomach lurched again. She couldn't meet Wright's gaze, her hands growing clammy, her neck hot. Without looking at Wright, she knew he was tense. His unease radiated across the prep table between them, washing over her.

Once Marco was out of the room, Dev let out a rough sigh. "I'm sure you're wondering why I had to talk to you immediately."

She dug up the courage to glance Wright's way. His face was white with a hint of green.

"I know what I'm doing, but—*Shit.* I'm not scared. I think you call this freaking out? If so, that's what I'm doing. I'm freaking out."

She wrinkled her nose and met Wright's gaze full on as they echoed one another. "Huh?"

"About popping the question. Asking Anna to marry me." Dev dug his hands into his dark hair and began to pace. "I'm rattled about it now and I don't know why."

"Oh." Wright shot her a look.

"I love her," Dev insisted as he picked up a serving spoon and set it back down. "I can't imagine not being with her. It won't always be easy, but we can handle whatever life throws at us. Why am I scared all of a sudden? I'm never scared."

Wright's pop of laughter was not the tactic Sophie would've gone with.

Dev spun on his best friend. "What the hell?"

"Of course you get scared. We all do. You didn't want to deal with the people in town about the Blueberry Festival because you were scared. And you know why?"

His jaw held tight, Dev shook his head.

"Because you gave a damn. It mattered to you. If you don't care, it's easy not to be afraid. Afraid of failure or rejection. You wanted that festival to happen. You want Anna to be your wife. You care about her answer, and that's why you're scared."

"But she's not going to say no. You know that, right?" Sophie touched her brother's arm.

Dev turned to her, his pale blue eyes wide. "Do I?"

Sophie's heart clenched. As obvious as it was to everyone else that Anna was in love with him, Dev would always have frayed threads of doubt. Just like Sophie.

They'd both had turmoil and loss in their lives, everything from insecurity to abandonment. And though Sophie's parents couldn't help that they were ripped away from her, that didn't make their absence any easier to bear.

Finding someone didn't remove the damaged thread from Devlin and replace it with something perfect and new. It merely tied off the weak edges and wove around with something stronger. The kind of love that held a person together.

Anna wouldn't say no to Dev, and she would never let him go.

Sophie hugged her brother, and Wright's gaze locked with hers as he spoke. "She's going to say yes, Dev. I guarantee. Anyone can see how she feels about you."

As she stepped back, she swiped at her eyes. "Anna is going to say yes. All you have to do is ask."

"But the longer you wait, the more it's going to mess with your head."

"You're probably right." Dev dragged a hand through his hair again.

"Of course we're right. Now, why don't you tell us how you've decided to ask?" Wright deftly maneuvered him to talk about his proposal plans, and Sophie took the moment to start breathing again.

There for a second she knew the ax was going to drop. Instead, Dev was worried about his future and his future wife.

She inhaled slowly, urging her nerves into check.

Dev reviewed his choice of proposal options, he and Wright delving into the details of each while her mind was a whirl of worst-case scenarios.

She wasn't normally the negative one in the bunch, but right now she was worrying more than Roark did.

Wright was spot-on about being scared because something mattered. She and Wright, what they had, it mattered. Her family mattered. As much as she tried not to let people get close, get their hooks into her deep enough to tear her apart, these were *her* people. They'd been hers her entire life.

There would be no getting out of this situation unscathed. Whether she fessed up about Wright or broke things off with him, the hurt was unavoidable.

In the distance, she heard Wright and Dev decide that Tuesday night was ideal for a proposal. They'd have a family dinner, throw Anna off the trail, and then he'd pop the question.

Dev clapped his best friend on the shoulder before giving Sophie a squeeze. "I don't know what I'd do without y'all."

As he left, Wright stepped closer, but she couldn't bring herself to meet his gaze.

"Hey," he finally said, touching her arm.

"Hey." With effort, she looked up.

"I thought he'd figured out what we were doing."

Did they even know what they were doing? One second, she had a grasp, but the next, doubt made her hold slippery.

"You look like you've seen a ghost. It's okay, he doesn't know. Breathe." Wright turned her to face him, rubbing her arms like she'd come in from the cold.

"I'm..." She didn't have the words to finish the sentence. She didn't know what she was right now, and there wasn't any time to figure it out.

"I know." Wright pulled her closer, tucking her against him, his chin touching the top of her head. "It's a lot for me to process too."

Whether he was talking about Dev proposing or the connection growing between the two of them, she didn't know. All she knew was that in his arms, she was incapable of reason.

She was fire and light and passion. Her heart wanted, without a thought or care for anyone else. And every time her heart wanted something so much it hurt, that was when the world came crashing down.

Inevitable as death, the prospect of happiness meant disaster, and it terrified her.

Wright stepped away, still holding on, studying her intently. "Are you okay?"

Something tightened in her chest, like a band around her heart. No, she was not okay. Never had been. But she could fake it like a master.

The look in Wright's eyes, the sympathetic tone in his voice, they were more than she could handle right now.

With him, her future held possibilities she'd written off years ago. With him, she could imagine a life of security. Happiness

But with him, there was no way to fake being okay

If she lingered in the kitchen, the band around her heart might snap. Later, she might be able to handle this.

Maybe later, she could act like she was okay.

Chapter 17

Sophie was not okay.

Wright studied her from across the large round table that he'd helped her set up. The entire Bradley family was gathered on the verandah for a late dinner. All around, those closest to her chattered and laughed, but Sophie was quiet. Reserved.

He chewed on dinner and his worry.

The night breeze ruffled Sophie's hair, revealing the tension at her temples and eyes. Her gaze never settled on anything, including him, for more than a few seconds. During dinner, she'd pushed her food around more than eaten it, and that simply wasn't like her.

A little anxious anticipation was normal, given the circumstances, but the hard lines set in her brow were over something more than waiting for Devlin's big moment.

All night, he kept one eye on Sophie, the other on Dev's amateur lighting attempts with their newly purchased strands of gala lights.

Currently, both questionably stable.

They'd closed the restaurant early, using the excuse of setting up lighting and testing it for the big gala. Wright had cooked a special meal for the family. All of the effort was to set the stage for Dev's proposal. Everyone knew but Anna, and everyone knew this was a big damn deal.

This was *Dev*. Planning to get married.

When he paused long enough to think about it, Wright still couldn't believe it. His best friend, the guy who had struggled for so many years to find direction and the confidence to follow it, and here he was. Dev was taking a huge step that, months ago, Wright would've never believed possible.

Dev coughed, drawing Wright's attention. With one last look of mild panic, Dev clinked his knife against his water glass and cleared his throat. "If I could have everyone's attention for a minute."

The table went quiet, everyone sharing knowing looks except Devlin and Anna.

She looked at Dev all right, as he scooted his chair back a bit and gathered himself. Anna's emotions were crystal clear. Even though her expression only changed slightly—a soft smile, a knowing twinkle in her eyes—how she felt about Dev rolled off her.

Her love and acceptance, even admiration, was so obvious, it took Wright's breath.

For years, he'd wondered if Dev would ever find himself, much less find someone who loved him. But he'd found Anna, and she suited him perfectly.

"I, uh . . ." Dev cleared his throat and picked up his water glass. "First, I want to propose a toast."

As everyone raised their glasses, Wright caught Sophie's gaze. A smile spread across his lips. He was happy for his friend, but even happier to have Sophie.

She returned a smile that didn't quite meet her eyes.

"To us," Dev said. "To each of you. We've gone through a lot over the past few years, but we made it. We'll continue to make it. And I want to take this opportunity to tell you all how much the support and love of this family means to me. How important it is."

Uh-oh.

If Wright was getting a little tight in the throat, he bet that . . .

Yep. Sophie's eyes were shiny, as were Roark's. Madison, who normally did a good job of schooling her reactions, blinked a lot more than necessary.

"So . . . here's to us."

Everyone leaned up to clink glasses and say cheers.

Then Devlin put his glass down and turned to Anna. "And here's to you. My sweet, strong Anna." He cleared his throat again, glancing down and fidgeting with the edge of the table. "Even with the love and, let's be honest, long suffering support of my family, I never completely believed in who I could be until I met you."

Anna twisted the cloth napkin in her hands.

"I don't know how I got so lucky, to have you pick this place for your R and R, but I'm glad you did. I'm glad you found what you were looking for, and something you weren't." He grinned. "I'm so grateful I found you. I knew when I met you, you're something special. And one thing you told me, months ago, was that if I wanted something, I had to go after it. I did, and I . . . I'm not about to let go."

Dev scooted his chair all the way back and knelt down beside her.

Anna's hands went to her mouth, tears filling her eyes.

"I know this might be a little old-fashioned," Dev said with a shrug, "but you're a classic kind of girl, and I love that about you."

She laughed through the tears.

"Anna, will you let me love you for the rest of our lives? Let me be there for you, and be the man you see in me. Make me even happier than I already am. Will you marry me?"

Anna laughed and cried as she nodded, a watery "Yes!" when she finally spoke.

Wright clapped, everyone cheered. Sophie's eyes were wet too as she hugged Dev, then Anna.

Everyone began making the rounds, congratulating one another. A real hug-fest for the newly engaged couple. Immediately the tales began about how they'd planned it, the lights, the dinner.

Dev pointed to the glow all around them. "Wright and I strung all of the lights out here."

Wright eyed the extension cords. "I'm pretty sure they're still a hazard. They need more work and I'm going to unplug them as soon as we're done."

Anna gushed over the setting they'd provided, blotting her face with a napkin.

After Wright congratulated her and Dev, he reached Sophie.

They had to hug. It'd be odd not to when everyone else was doing the same. People might think they weren't speaking again.

"Great news, huh?" He dipped his chin and winked at her.

"Very great." She reached up to put her arms around him, and he opened his, welcoming her in.

His embrace was entirely too long, way too close, and he didn't care. He placed his hand in the small of her back, holding her close, bent low so his mouth was by her ear.

"You smell nice," he whispered.

She poked the back of his shoulder as she eased away.

"Are you okay?" He got the question out before she went far.

Her plastered-on smile made his protective streak rear up. "I'm great. Why?"

Refusing to look away, he waited, their gazes locked.

Sophie was the first to glance down and, with a flip of her hand, insisted she was okay. "I'm tired. That's all."

A load of crap. No doubt she was tired, but that wasn't all.

Wright took another step closer, keeping his voice low. "We can talk later."

"I don't—" Sophie's words got stuck in her throat as she shook her head. "I don't need to talk. I'm fine."

Her stubbornness was endearing at times, and often, people let her get by, insisting nothing was wrong.

Not him. Not before and definitely not now.

With a hand at his mouth, feigning an itch, he leaned closer. "Then maybe I need to talk to you. Ever thought about that?"

Her eyes widened. "Yeah, I . . . of course we can talk."

As the words left her mouth, the lights around them began to twinkle.

At first, he thought it was some cool effect. Then he remembered the hundreds of tiny bulbs they'd finally decided upon didn't come with a twinkling option.

"Uh-oh," Trevor said as the lights blinked twice and went out completely.

The verandah was plunged into darkness, except for the moon and stars and three candles on the table.

"Damn." Dev bumped into the table.

Sophie spoke up, moving past Wright in the dark. "Don't worry, I've got it. I'll get the regular lights on."

"Won't work if we popped the breaker," Roark called out.

"I'll go with her and check the panel." Wright followed her to the French doors.

As soon as they got inside and closed the door behind them, she flipped the useless switches. "Must be the breaker."

Sophie marched toward the kitchen to find the panel.

"Slow down for a second."

"I have to get the lights back on outside."

"And I want to talk to you." He pushed open the door for her and waited as she flipped the switch for outdoor lighting back over.

"That ought to do it." She turned to go, but there was no way in hell he was letting her go that easy.

"Wait." Wright reached for her, taking her wrist and turning her around.

"What? We have to get back." Her expression was nothing short of terrified.

"What is going on with you? Talk to me. You look scared to death right now, same as last night. This is supposed to be a happy occasion."

"I know that," she snapped. "It is a happy occasion."

"But you look so upset."

"I am!"

He took a step back at her vehemence. "Why?"

Dev was engaged; she and Wright were essentially a couple, if in secret; Honeywilde was doing well, he hadn't told her about his opportunities to work elsewhere—what was there to be upset about?

"Because everything is going well. Everything is so great, it's almost perfect. Too perfect."

With a slow, steady breath, he tried to comprehend. This was Sophie. She might be given to emotion and sensitivity, but she wasn't irrational. Somehow, this made sense to her. Though he couldn't figure out how.

"I'm . . . I don't follow."

She ran her fingers through her hair, tugging all of it back. "I know. Because it doesn't make sense." With a sigh, she turned away, pacing the length of the prep table.

She kept walking, back and forth.

"Hey. Stop for a sec." When she paced by him the second time, he caught her, holding her arms, waiting for her to look at him. "Talk to me. Tell me what's going on up there."

Slowly, she met his gaze. "You don't want to know."

He smoothed his hands down her arms, taking her hands in his. "Yes, I do. Normally, I can take a decent guess, but I'd rather you tell me. Come on, Soph. It's me. You can tell me."

She stared into his honey-brown eyes.

This was Wright. If there was anyone she could tell, it was him. He might think she was crazy, but he wouldn't judge her for it.

"I'm scared because things are going *too* well."

He nodded, encouraging her to continue.

"And—this is going to sound nuts, Wright."

"That's okay, say it anyway."

"Things are going really well and . . . as much as I want them to, as much as I've wanted this family to be happy and content, no longer fighting and all of us together again, being with you, having that as reality—having happiness and good things in my life—it scares me to death."

Wright wrinkled his brow, his lips pinched together.

She didn't blame him for looking confused. "I told you this was going to sound crazy."

"No," he quickly replied. "I'm trying to follow."

"I don't know what to do when things go well."

He gave her hands a squeeze. "You don't have to *do* anything. Your family isn't falling apart at the seams anymore. You can enjoy this."

"No, I can't. That's the problem. You don't understand."

"Then help me understand."

Her gaze drifted away as she shifted on her feet. "I'm afraid to be happy. I can't let myself get used to it because as soon as I let my guard down, that's when I lose people. There's never really been a time when this family wasn't in crisis or recovery mode. And the few times, the one, maybe two times things went well, the next thing I knew, it all came crashing down."

Sophie pulled her hands away, flinging her arms out wide. "I don't know how to enjoy this. Any of this—not for more than a few days—because I'm too busy waiting for it to fall apart. And that's nuts, I know, but all I've ever known is trying to keep this family together. My whole life. From the day I moved into Honeywilde, my parents were dead and my new family was always moments away from crumbling. Then it did. Sue Bradley walked out and then Robert finally did."

She would never forget the look on Roark's face when Suzanne Bradley said she was leaving.

They weren't exactly kids anymore, but it didn't matter. Their parents were divorcing, and their family was finally breaking up.

The only parents she really remembered, and Sophie was losing them too.

Days before, Sophie had thought they had turned a corner. As a family, they were a bit happier, a little calmer. Dev hadn't been in trouble for weeks. There'd been no huge argument. Nothing was broken in anger for almost a month. They finally had peace.

And then, *I can't do this anymore. Your father and I are separating. You'll stay here with him.*

"All I've ever known is struggling to keep this family together." Sophie swiped at her eyes. "And I know, if things calm down, when things are going great, if I get used to it, if I take happiness for granted, if I take my eye off the ball, everything will go to hell again."

The corner of Wright's lips pulled down, something too close to pity in his gaze. "And you think it's your fault."

She couldn't stand for him to see her, so she looked away. "Whenever things go well, while everyone else is busy celebrating, I'm waiting for the bottom to fall out. It happens every time. Not once has any happiness ever lasted, Wright. Not once."

"Soph—"

"No. I know this for a fact. Did you know, the night my parents died, we'd spent the whole day together? It had to be one of the best days ever. Did you know that?"

"No." His voice was quiet.

"I was so little and I don't remember much. But I know we'd gone up on the parkway to go hiking. Me and this ridiculous teddy bear backpack, because I probably insisted on having my own. There's a picture I keep by my bed, of me and my parents, on the trail. Sun on our faces, not a cloud in the sky. We looked *so* happy. That night, we went out for pizza. Fourth of July, right? Gotta celebrate."

When she finally looked at him, Wright's lips were pinched into a thin line. He knew how this story ended. Everyone in Windamere knew how this story ended.

"That was probably one of the happiest days of their lives, even though it rained out the fireworks that night. I remember music in the car. I remember my parents in the front seat and I remember music." Sophie's voice cracked, the pain in her chest making it hard to breathe. "I can't remember much about either one of them, but I remember the music and the rain, and being happy."

She even remembered the song that was on the radio. Now she couldn't bear to hear it. That song made her a child again, alone and scared.

The aching inside spread, tears stinging her eyes. Not tears of sadness. She was angry. Angry at them for dying, and angry at herself because it still hurt so much. Over twenty years later, why did it hurt so much?

Wright reached for her, his face blurring in her tears.

Sophie stepped away. "I was happy and then there were screeching brakes. That's all I remember about that night."

His face crumpled with hers.

"Why? *Why*, Wright? We were so happy."

He reached for her again, and she was too tired to reject his comfort.

Her tears piled up and spilled over, trickling down her cheeks. "Why couldn't they just be happy and be okay?" Her question melted into a plea. "Why did they have to die?"

Wright's arms surrounded her, one hand on the back of her head, tucking her against his chest, the other on her back, never letting go.

"I can't lose anybody else." She cried.

"You won't. You're not going to lose anyone."

"I hate summer time! I always lose someone."

He murmured words of reassurance, but she didn't absorb a single one, too caught up in her bottled-up fear to hear. "Everyone is finally happy and . . . and I know something bad will happen. It always does."

Wright held her until the tears dried on her cheeks. Until she stopped railing against the injustice of what she'd lost. And then he held her some more.

When she finally settled down, he leaned away without letting go. "You're not crazy for the way you feel. What you've been through—I don't care how long ago it was, you lost your parents—you carry that with you. Forever. Survivor's guilt or something. I don't know, but then you lost the Bradleys too, and for years this family has barely held together." He rubbed her arms. "I remember being little, after you moved here, and I was scared my folks would die in a car wreck because yours did. I guess I didn't know parents could die until it happened to you. It scared the shit out of me. Of course you're scared. Nervous that it will all fall apart again, to fear that someone you love will be taken from you."

She blinked and rubbed at her face. "Is this where you promise they won't? That I won't lose anyone and I'm . . ." She lifted her shoulders. "Overreacting?"

"I don't think you're overreacting at all. And no one can promise us that we'll have the people we love forever."

With a shake of her head, she laughed. "Nice pep talk."

Wright squeezed her arms. "I'm not going to bullshit you. You know that. Yeah, if we love people, we might get hurt. But the people we love, they're here now. Right now. Your family is happy and safe. You have them, and you have me. And I have you."

She *did* have him. She'd always had Wright.

He leaned back a little more, tilting her chin up to meet his gaze. "And you don't have to be scared about enjoying what we have. Our happiness isn't going to hurt anyone. Your happiness won't cause everything around you to fall apart. That much I know."

She wished she were as certain. Her logic was crazy; she knew that. But after years of feeling like disaster might strike at any moment, how did she turn it off?

For so long everyone around her was a hairbreadth from falling apart. Her job was keeping them together. Now they were, and she was the one who was lost and afraid.

Fear had held her back. Her family needed her to be the glue, and if she wasn't there, somehow any failure was her fault. Fear kept her from loving, from letting anyone too close, because they'd see how dysfunctional she was, and then it'd be so easy for them to hurt her.

She didn't want to hold back from Wright.

Finally, she'd found something and someone who understood her. And what he didn't understand, he still accepted.

Maybe she could be happy without the worst happening. Maybe she could live and love without fear.

There was only one way she'd ever know for sure.

With her chin still in his hands, Sophie closed the distance between them and kissed him.

Up on her toes, with every tumultuous thought in her mind and all of the emotion inside, she kissed him. In the kitchen, where they'd first started down this path, she reached out and took what she wanted.

Her mind was too busy for sweet and slow tonight. She needed to forget and feel only him.

She grabbed the front of Wright's dress shirt, twisting her fingers into the cotton, licking her way inside his mouth. Soft pulls on his lips, nibbling until he rumbled with the desire for more.

Normally, Wright instigated sex. Spurring her on, pulling her in, making her world spin out of control. Tonight, she would kindle the fire between them. She needed him, needed what they shared.

With a firm push, she got him to back into the pantry, the room full of mingling scents like cinnamon and rosemary. His back bumped the shelves, making jars rattle. Then his lips were hot on her neck, down into the front of her dress.

With a desperation that swept over her, she was the one to plunder his mouth.

She wanted to be pulled under by the power of what she felt when she made love to Wright. She needed to get carried away.

"I want you so much," he murmured against her skin, echoing the same. "I always want you. But sitting across from you all night, worrying about you, wondering what was wrong, needing you to be okay—"

"I want to be okay. Touch me," she pleaded. "Touch—"

He slanted his lips over hers, stealing her words and all reason.

Good. She wanted them both gone.

In a hot stripe of lips and tongue, he moved from her mouth, down her neck, slipping the straps of her dress down, tugging at the fabric until he revealed her breasts, sucking and kissing until she writhed against him.

Sophie slid her hands around him, clinging, holding him close as she arched closer.

He went back to nibbling at her neck, then turned her and reached under her skirt, caressing her leg, farther up and farther, until he hooked her knee.

Her back was pressed hard into the shelves and he held her with one arm. Using his free hand, he squeezed her ass through the cotton and satin, sucking kisses against her neck as he moved his hand. Under the cotton, barely brushing her flesh. Heat rushed to her core and she sought his touch.

He breathed against her neck. "You're always so wet for me."

His words seeped into her brain, making her body tighter, needier.

"I want to rip these off and take you right here."

She needed his hands on her, wanted him inside her. Wanted to forget but remember. To feel and believe this was something real, something she wouldn't lose. "Yes." The word rushed forth.

His low rumble of a chuckle coasted down her skin. "You'd do it too, wouldn't you?"

"Wright, please." She needed this. After a night of love and laughter and everyone having something for themselves, except for her. This she could have.

She had it already.

Wright didn't hesitate.

Her leg lowered, he reached under her skirt and slid her panties off in one swift tug. Before she could catch her breath, he had his hand between her legs, fingers gliding over her, making her bite back a moan as her body sang.

"This, baby?" he whispered in her ear. "Is this what you want?"

She jerked her chin in a nod.

He slipped a finger inside her, stroking her until she rocked in motion with him. Then two, opening her, his thumb coasting over her clit each time he went deeper. "I can't wait to taste you again. Feel you on my tongue."

"Yes." The word came out sounding more like a moan, and suddenly, Wright was on his knees before her. Under her skirt, he pushed the material up, held her against the shelves with one hand, and used the other to caress her flesh before his mouth descended, covering her, one gentle flick of his tongue before sucking hard against the cleft of her sex.

Sophie cried out and pressed the back of her head against the shelf, making some bottles clink together.

With his mouth and his hand, Wright worked her, until her legs trembled and threatened to buckle.

"I—" Her mouth was desert dry. "I'm going to . . . fall over if you . . . keep—"

"No, you won't." His words blew hot against her swollen flesh. "I'll catch you. Come on, baby. Come on my tongue."

He licked and stroked her, merciless in his ministrations. Until the first wave of her orgasm hit her, her hips pushing against him, seeking more.

Wright moaned against her, giving exactly that, and Sophie came. Forgetting where she was, forgetting to worry, she called out his name and came, all of reality and its burdens falling away.

When she opened her eyes, Wright held her upright, his lips warm on her temple.

"Come upstairs with me," she said.

He straightened, studying her face, but she knew he would never decline.

Wright wanted her, wanted to be with her, and he said he didn't care who knew about them. She was the hold up, and now, her reservations were spent.

"Stay with me. Spend the night."

"You're sure?"

"Never surer."

He stepped back, adjusting himself, and then he was gone, leaving her alone in the pantry, only to reappear seconds later with his duffel bag in hand. "Let's go."

She smiled at his certainty, his total lack of hesitation.

While she second-guessed her every choice, each whim and desire, Wright always knew.

He held out his hand, hers for the taking. As soon as she slipped her fingers into his palm, he headed to the elevators.

Before, she'd fret over everyone wondering what she was doing, why Wright's car was still here. A litany of things to worry about would chase away the pleasure of being impulsive.

Tonight, she didn't care.

Tonight she was only going to think about the two of them.

Wright bent low and covered her lips with his.

As soon as the elevator doors dinged open, Wright had her hand again and they were halfway down the hall before she could blink.

He took her key and opened the door, closed it behind them, and tossed the key aside.

With his hands on her waist, he backed them to the door. He was on her, hands in her hair, reaching for her legs around his waist.

And she let him.

She was delirious with the feel of it. His hot, wet lips on her neck, his strong broad hands under her skirt again.

"I . . . I think . . ." She could barely catch her breath. "You like that you can move me wherever you want me."

"I'm picking up where we left off."

Her feet barely touched the ground, so she grabbed his shoulders and lifted them, wrapping her legs around his waist.

"Yes," he growled.

With her fingers in his hair, she held him against her neck, letting him kiss and suck, certain he'd leave a mark, but she'd worry about that later.

He shifted his hold, his hands back on her ass, right where he'd left off. Wright pushed against her, rocking into her sex, the hard line of his erection rubbing and pressing, driving her insane.

She couldn't see his face, couldn't see anything, but she wasn't worried. Wright had her and he'd never let her fall.

She wanted him inside her. The urgency scared her, but not enough to stop or even slow down.

"I want you inside me. Right now. Like this."

Wright lifted his head, hair tossed, color in his cheeks.

He lowered her down to one foot as he worked his pants open.

His cock stood up straight, flushed and shiny. She had to touch it. Gently, she caressed the tip and slid her hand down his length. Again she stroked him, until he grabbed her hand, wrapping her fingers around him fully. "You won't break me."

She didn't get to touch him long before he had her leg around his waist again.

"Like this?" he asked.

Her back against the wall, the nearby bookshelf the only thing to grab onto beside him.

"You want it like this?"

"Yes." God yes. "Wait! Condom."

"Oh shit." Eyes wide, in a flurry of movement, he let her down and rummaged through his bag, grabbing protection.

She hurried to help him, so eager her hands shook. Once it was on, he hoisted her up again. They banged off the wall, knocking a trinket off her bookshelf, and laughed.

"It's okay, I've got it together now." He grinned, and when he touched her, her entire body clenched.

As she moaned with the need of it, Wright took his cock in hand and pushed inside her. Slow at first, but not for long. He filled her, the stretch perfect.

She clung to his shoulders as he thrust into her, over and over, deeper, filling her until she was only this sensation, this need, and the sparks brought to life in her body.

With her fingers dug into his skin, she panted his name.

Wright's breathing hitched, already heavy.

Neither of them was going to last long like this. "A little harder," she encouraged. "You're not going to break me either."

He groaned against her neck, his teeth and lips closing on her skin.

When he came, he kept pushing into her, until she came too. Everything else forgotten, she floated on the ecstasy of now.

Chapter 18

The sun wasn't even up as he rolled toward Sophie. Her night light shined just enough so he could see. After brushing back wild strands of red hair, he found her face.

Eyes still closed, she smiled. "Morning."

"You always wake up this happy before day break?"

With a laugh, she tugged her covers up past her chin. "I never wake up happy."

So he wasn't the only one thrilled with life at the moment? Good. But man, the thrill made him a little stupid. "We almost didn't use protection last night."

Sophie finally opened her eyes to roll them. "I remembered."

"At the last second."

"Yeah, but I remembered. Besides, I'm clean. And you better be."

"Of course I am, but . . ." He lifted his eyebrows and waited.

She lifted her eyebrows right back at him. "But what?"

"Are you on the pill?"

With a groan, she glanced away. "Oh my god. I have been since I was nineteen. Don't worry. I'm not going to trap you by getting knocked up or something."

"Hey." He reached over and turned her toward him. "That's not why I'm asking, and you know it. We're sleeping together. We should be able to talk about this stuff."

Last night he'd almost forgotten his hard and fast rule about using protection because he'd been consumed by the moment, and her.

Being with Sophie could never be a trap for him, no matter the circumstances, because he wanted to *always* be with her. But his feelings for her—feelings about always and forever and wanting things like a life and kids with her—would send Sophie into a tailspin.

Last night, she'd told him about her worries, her fears of loss. Opening up to him was a huge step, and he was going to honor her honesty by not throwing all of his feelings on her at once.

One ingredient at a time, until they reached forever.

She sighed. "Yeah, it's—of course we can talk about this. Just, I'm not used to anyone . . ."

"Asking?"

"Caring."

The flatness of her tone tied a knot in his gut. "Oh."

"You know I haven't exactly had a ton of . . . lovers. And you know I usually run guys off before we can get to this point or have this conversation. I don't know that I've ever had the 'responsibly sleeping together' talk."

"Thank God."

She smacked his bare chest and he laughed, defending himself.

"What? I'm not going to lie anymore. I *hated* the guys you went out with. I'm glad you didn't keep them around or sleep with them. Assholes."

"Except Poor Paul."

"Poor Paul." He scoffed. "Screw Poor Paul. He was an idiot."

Her eyes went round.

"Well, he was. You really liked that guy. I could tell. But he screwed up and then tried to make everyone think you were the crazy one for breaking up with him. He's the crazy one. You needed him to be there for you and he was a flake."

Sophie giggled and curled closer. "Yeah. Screw him."

"Anyway—the sleeping together responsibly thing. I won't forget about the condom next time. But if I do, you be sure to remember."

"Or . . . we could go without. Since we, y'know . . ." With a searching look, she tucked the sheets around her. "Since we aren't sleeping with other people, and I'm on the pill. I mean, if that's okay with you."

It was her roundabout way of confirming they'd be exclusive. Stating they were a real couple without saying it outright, but serious enough about each other to take that step.

And this was more than a little step. They were leaping forward.

Wright bit his lip to keep from smiling. He'd been exclusively Sophie's since the first night he'd kissed her.

"There's no one but you," he promised. "I'm okay with only using the pill if you are."

The corner of her mouth quirked up. "That's assuming there's a next time."

"Oh, there's going to be a next time." He tugged her closer, until she was flush against him under the covers.

Sophie giggled, tangling her legs with his. "Says who?"

"Says me. And I'm not above begging."

She rested her chin on his chest. "Thank you for listening last night. And not judging me. I didn't want you to see that side of me, but—"

He kissed the frown lines away. "I'm glad you showed me."

He'd seen what he suspected was always there, even if he couldn't define the reason for her fears. She didn't realize how much attention he'd paid to everything about her, for years. The ebb and flow of her life, her mood, her relationships. Any scars she tried to hide, he'd figured they were there, whether she'd showed them or not.

And so what if he saw more?

Sophie made him want things, with no uncertainty. For weeks now, he'd been unsure about his future.

Did he want a high-stress, high-paying head chef in New York gig? Or did he want to keep some of this lifestyle and make half of what he could in a big city by going to Charleston or Asheville? Did he want to talk it out with the Bradleys and give them a chance to influence his choice or decide alone, to keep things simple?

With Sophie, he had no questions. He wanted to be with her, whether he was at Honeywilde or not. That meant New York was impossible, Charleston would be a big challenge, but Asheville could feasibly work.

About an hour away. He could keep his place or get an apartment halfway in between locations. They could make a life that way. What he and Sophie had, what they shared, it wasn't common and it sure as hell hadn't come easy. Nothing worth having ever did.

He wanted forever with Sophie, but couldn't tell her all of that now. Not yet.

First, he had a decision to make and a job to firm up. More than that, Sophie needed to be ready. He couldn't pressure her for more if he didn't know what he was doing. The last thing he wanted to do was ruin what they'd so carefully created with a bunch of questions about the future and commitment.

One ingredient at a time, he reminded himself. Patience. A dash of this, and pinch of that, until they got there.

And he had to find a way to tell his parents he wouldn't be leaving for New York or Chicago, or across the country, and all because of Sophie. A Bradley.

He cringed inwardly at the proposition.

His folks would be livid, but they'd have to get over it.

"C'mere." Wright slid his hands under the sheets and over Sophie. Her body was warm, small curves perfectly filling his touch. Their lips met and he kissed her until she was even warmer and loose-limbed against him.

"We have a little while before I have to cook breakfast." He hooked his hand under her knee, tugging her leg over until she straddled him. "Let me make things up to you."

She laughed into their kiss. "There's nothing to make up for."

He brushed his lips down her neck, lower and lower, until he captured one of her nipples, kissing and sucking until it puckered in his mouth. "I know. But I want to anyway."

Wright changed into clean clothes from his bag and ran downstairs, sneaking into the kitchen earlier than anyone else, except for Marco.

Marco winked and went back to his prep work, whistling and dicing.

Once breakfast and lunch were served, Wright had a long stretch of afternoon free.

He wanted to find Sophie and spend the afternoon together, but he still hadn't called his dad back or checked in with his folks at all. Calling them meant facing them, and facing them meant dealing with his looming future.

His parents weren't going to like what he had to say, but waiting day after day to tell them wouldn't change things.

He couldn't say yes to New York now that he and Sophie stood a real chance of being together, but he couldn't ask her for some kind of commitment yet either. He'd have to take it on faith that if he stayed somewhere close, the two of them would eventually be together.

With a quick text to Sophie, letting her know he'd be gone to see his parents for a while, he dialed his father's number.

His dad answered. "You're alive. That's nice to know."

"Yeah, yeah. I know it's been a few days."

"A few days? We've been leaving messages with you for almost two weeks now."

Wright ran over the dates in his head. Had two weeks gone by since they spoke?

"But listen, I'm glad you called. Your mother wanted me to call you about having lunch or a drink."

"I'm working. You know I can't do lunch."

"I realize that, but we're having a late lunch. You need to make this happen." His father insisted he agree on meeting today.

His mother must've reached her breaking point. Late lunch was not optional.

Wright put on his cheeriest voice. "Where would you like to go? I'll meet you there."

"The club. We're on our way there now. You come on as soon as you can get out of that place."

That place.

Like Honeywilde was a sweatshop and not a luxury inn. "Okay, Dad. I'll see you at the club."

His parents had been members of Mountain Creek Country Club for at least thirty years. It was way outside of town, snotty and inconvenient as hell, but it was the only exclusive club in the county and damn if his parents didn't *have* to be members.

Wright hated the place. The food was dry, pretentious, and overpriced.

A lot like the members.

By the time he got there, his parents already had their martinis.

"Would you like a drink, son?" His father stood to shake his hand, and that would be the extent of his affection.

"No, I'm fine." Wright sat and didn't bother looking at the menu. Call him a food snob, but there was no point in getting anything but the soup here.

"It's good to finally see you." His mom leaned over and gave him a half hug.

He loved his mom. She meant well and only wanted the best for him. Only, her ideas of what was best didn't always line up with his. She tried, though. Made sure he always knew how proud they were and how much they expected of him.

And he wanted them to be proud. They'd worked hard to be where they were and to give him opportunities. He was grateful.

He wasn't as concerned with impressing everyone and everything as they were.

"I was beginning to think we'd have to make reservations at that Honeywilde restaurant to remember what you look like," his father joked.

He put on a smile and sipped his water. "The restaurant is called Bradley's." His father knew that. Wright had worked there since he finished culinary school. "And a chef's hours are long. I don't have a ton of free time."

"We know, honey." His mother patted his hand. "We know. That's why we want more for you with as hard as you work and all."

And by more, she meant more money.

He had to work not to roll his eyes, in perfect mimicry of Sophie. "I do fine at Bradley's. I told you, these new opportunities are great, but if they don't work out, it's not the end of the world. Not like I'm living hand to mouth. I'll survive."

"And is that enough? To simply survive?" His father sipped his martini and nodded to their waiter.

Poor wording on Wright's part. He knew better than to slip with any word that could be twisted into a criticism of Honeywilde or the family who owned it. Especially not in front of his father.

When Wright had left for culinary school, a shift took place between them.

His dad wanted him to be something sensible, like an accountant or salesman. Since Wright had insisted on the unstable enterprise of being a chef, his father behaved more like a business partner than a parent.

"I'm doing a lot better than surviving, okay? I enjoy being head chef at the resort. I'd love the challenge of something new, sure, but I told you, I'm not going to accept any old offer. It has to be right."

His mother's mouth turned down at the corners. "What exactly constitutes any old offer?"

He should've known she'd read into that. But there was no point in staving off the truth, only to make lunch tenser.

"I'm not going to move off to Chicago or New York for a new opportunity."

"What?" Her volume went up a notch.

Wright shook his head at her look of shock. "Mom, come on. You really think I'd be happy in some big-city, Yankee kitchen?"

His father sat forward, both arms folded onto the table. "I thought you wanted to expand your horizons. Strive for something better."

"Those were your words, not mine. I want to do something different, get broader experience since I've only ever worked at Honeywilde. But I don't need to move halfway across the country to do that. I don't *want* to move that far away. The southeast has some of the best restaurants in the country. Why should I leave if I can find something in Charleston or Charlotte, or even Greenville and Asheville?"

The waiter approached and his mother stiffened. She didn't approve of private talk around strangers. Particularly not strangers she viewed as "the help."

Wright wondered if she ever stopped staring down her nose enough to realize that for the guests at Honeywilde, *he* was the help.

They placed their orders, and as soon as their waiter was out of earshot, Wright's mom leaned forward. "For what we paid to put you through Johnson and Wales and your level of talent and hard work, it's embarrassing that you aren't getting more recognition. You're too good for that place. Too talented. You should be in New York, with your own restaurant. Or TV show. Now, I know you don't like me saying so, but that's how I feel." She sat back, her eyes glistening, the corners of her mouth wobbly.

He was not going to get a TV show. His mother's dream was absurd, but he wasn't going to say as much and hurt her feelings.

As predicted, his decision upset her. He hated it, but he couldn't live his life for her.

His father sat, stoic except for the thin line of his mouth. "If New York and Chicago are out of the equation, then what about the offers in Charleston and Asheville?"

"I'm still interested in those. We're in talks."

"And you'll accept?"

"Guys." Wright took a deep breath. "I don't have an answer yet, but as soon as I do, you'll know."

Right after he told Sophie.

He wanted her to be the first to know because she mattered.

Before they got together, nothing factored into his decision about the future except his desire to spread his wings. To prove he could do more than work for the family of his best friend and rely on their goodwill to get by.

Now things were different.

If he had the opportunity to go and be one of the top chefs in the region, he wanted Sophie to be a part of it. He wasn't going to move so far away that she couldn't be.

Their food arrived, and the three of them ate half of their lunches in an awkward silence.

"So . . ." His mother was the first to break the tension, as always. "How are things at the inn?"

"Great, actually." He welcomed the chance to talk about something besides his career path. "We're the host location for this year's Chamber Gala. I guess Devlin won so many people over with the Blueberry Festival that the Chamber wanted to work with him. Honeywilde is the perfect location."

At the mention of Dev's name, his parents shared a quick glance and made a point of not looking him in the eyes as they ate and drank.

Regardless of how far Devlin had come in life, the changes he'd made and the man he was today, to his parents, Dev would always be the boy who got Wright into trouble; the one who almost got him wait-listed for college because of a B&E charge. All of that was more than ten years ago, but to his parents, it might as well have been two days ago.

"I was able to completely create the menu too." Wright kept talking about the gala, filling the dead air. His folks hated Dev, and therefore all of the other Bradleys, and he'd learned to live with it.

But if he was going to be with Sophie, living with their animosity was no longer an option.

"There will be dinner and dancing and raising money. We've only had a couple of weeks to pull the details together, but it's going to be phenomenal. Sophie designed a layout to make the patio and verandah look like an enchanted garden. She did an amazing job too."

He went on, in great detail, about the event, and all of Soph's hard work. Anything to fill up the rest of lunch.

But his parents shared looks at every mention of Sophie's name. The heavy glances were different than when he mentioned Dev, and this time he couldn't let it slide.

"Okay, enough with the looks."

His mother blinked rapidly and reached for her martini. "What looks?"

"The looks you keep giving each other like I'm talking about Delilah. The Bradleys are good people. You need to ease up on them."

"Sophie's not technically a Bradley," his father pointed out.

"Dad." Wright's tone had an edge on it like a knife. No one was going take jabs at Sophie. Not even his father.

"Now, now." His mother set her glass down. "Your father didn't mean it like that. But we know how you get about that poor adopted girl, and maybe it's clouding your judgment."

Wright's fist landed on the table, making the silverware jump. His mother's eyes went wider than her salad bowl as she scanned the room to see if anyone was staring.

He kept his voice even and low. "First of all, she isn't a poor anything. She doesn't warrant or want your pity. Secondly, she isn't *that adopted girl*. She's as much a Bradley as the rest of them. And—" A siren suddenly filled his mind as the rest of his mother's words sank in. "What do you mean, you know how I get?"

Her eyes narrowed. "I mean, you do things like bang your fist on the table at me if I say the least little thing about her."

Wright unclenched his fist and put his hand in his lap. "I'm sorry. But I won't let you criticize her for no reason other than being part of the Bradley family."

His father leaned forward, both elbows on the table. "She's why you don't want to move away, isn't she?"

He couldn't argue. To do so would be a lie, and he didn't lie to his parents. Not anymore.

His father huffed with disapproval. "Dammit, son, don't you miss out on the chance of a lifetime for that girl. We know you've always had a thing for her, but you'll regret it if you let her hold you back."

"She isn't holding me back." Wright glared at both of them, then at his half-eaten soup.

Dammit to hell. He was a grown man and they had no bearing on his relationship with Sophie, but of course his parents would see how he felt about her. Why wouldn't they? They'd always been involved in his life, and most of his life involved Sophie. Thinking back, he'd probably mentioned her name at least once in every conversation.

Sophie did this, Sophie said that. Hey, listen to this funny story about Sophie.

He was an idiot for not realizing they'd see the truth. A truth he'd tried to deny or ignore for years. And all the avoidance and disregard, all of the dating around and reining in his feelings had still led him right back to Sophie in the end. What good came from hiding it now? Why lie about an undeniable truth?

"I think I'm in love with her." He blurted the words at his parents.

Neither of them moved. Didn't even look like they were breathing.

Wright flattened his hands on his thighs. "No, I *know* I'm in love with her. But . . . I haven't told her. I hadn't planned on telling you guys, but there you go. That's why I can't let you sit there and talk down about her. And no, I can't move across the country for some job when I might get the same opportunity an hour or two down the interstate."

His parents still didn't move a millimeter.

"One of you, say something."

"How . . ." His mother coughed into her napkin and took a sip of her drink before trying again. "I mean, when did this—"

"Why haven't you told her?" his father asked.

"Because I'm waiting until the right time."

"Not a good sign if you have to wait."

His mom laid a hand on his father's forearm, but directed her questions at Wright. "Does she know about the opportunities in Charleston and Asheville? Or even New York?"

"She's a manager at Honeywilde, where I work. No, I haven't told her about leaving. I told you, the time has to be right." And because bringing up his future would mean talking about theirs.

Asking Sophie to make any kind of plans or commit—no, now was too soon for that kind of talk.

"What if she has no interest in leaving Honeywilde, and you end up in Charleston? Are you going to let her derail your career completely?"

Wright tossed his hands up. "No. I don't know. Jesus, I don't have all the answers right now. I'm waiting to see what happens first. I'm not saying anything until I know. What if none of these jobs become official? What if none of it works out? Then it's a nonissue."

"Wait a minute." His father pressed his pointer finger into the tablecloth. "If you don't get any of these offers, aren't you going to try again later? Are you giving up your goal of working somewhere besides Honeywilde, all because of Sophie?"

"No."

"Then you need to take a moment to think about it." His mother intervened, one hand on Wright's arm, the other still on his father's. "Not to answer us, but to answer Sophie. When you tell her how you feel, when you tell her about these opportunities, you can be certain she'll have the same questions we do. And the offers for other jobs won't stop coming, Wright. You'll continue to be courted away from that place, and she needs to know it."

She already knew it. Sophie was smart. She'd have to know he had offers, but she probably assumed he'd never accept.

Wright took a slow, steadying breath, trying to calm down.

His mother gave his arm a pat before letting go. "And you can't answer with what she wants or what we want. You have to know what *you* want."

Chapter 19

With Wright gone for the afternoon to visit his folks, and most of her work done for the day, she was finally able to take an afternoon off.

Sophie could do anything she wanted, and what she wanted most of all was to do nothing.

A protein bar in her pocket and a bottle of water in her hand, she left the main inn to wander. No intentions or direction. A chance to roam wherever the day took her.

She headed toward Lake Anikawa and hung a left on the path that wound all the way around the body of water. Whether she had it in her to do the full distance, she wasn't sure, and she didn't care.

For half an hour she strolled, the oaks and pines towering above, rhododendrons knotted by the lake side, creating muffled silence and privacy.

Wright had texted her after brunch, saying he was having lunch with his folks at the club.

The club.

She sucked her teeth, loudly, since no one could hear.

His parents had always been members of the country club. Back when her adoptive parents could barely afford to keep the lights on at Honeywilde. Wright got a new car when he was sixteen, while she didn't have one until college.

It'd been selfish and petty to envy Wright those material things, but she had. Living in Windamere wasn't like living in a city. There was no bus or rail system. With no car, she was stuck at Honeywilde unless a friend would come get her.

So often, that friend was Wright.

He'd pick her and Dev up and go into town. They'd drop her off at a friend's and get into whatever they were going to get into that day, all at the very vocal objection of Wright's parents.

Now he was having lunch with them, and she bet if he so much as mentioned her name, he'd get the same, patented disapproval.

Sophie was a Bradley, and to the McAdamses, the Bradleys were bad news. All of them.

Hopefully he was wise enough not to bring her up, even though now they were sort of, almost, dating.

No, he wouldn't talk to his folks about her or what they were doing.

Last night, she'd let herself get closer to Wright than anyone before. Taking a long walk around the lake today, and *not* freaking out, actually made her quite proud. Right now, she should be filled with worry.

Breaking down and blurting all of her insecurities at him, confessing her fears and doubts, was something she swore she'd never do to anyone. But she'd spilled it all into the quiet understanding of his eyes and the warm comfort of his arms.

Her walking ceased.

"Holy shit." She'd spilled everything she'd always kept hidden to Wright.

But she was not going to freak out.

Nope, not going to happen. With a deep breath in and a slow exhale, she put one foot in front of the other.

He was Wright, after all. She could tell him these things. He wasn't going to leave and hurt her. Honeywilde was as much a part of him as it was her and her brothers.

Her steps stuttered once more.

Last night was extraordinary, his acceptance a balm for her raw soul, but letting him in meant she was vulnerable. Exposed.

Like a nerve.

Except, the thing was, he was already in. They were already close. Opening up to him was one more step. All she could do was trust him not to hurt her.

She kept walking, the air heavy and humid, not a breeze to stir the air. The lake lay flat like glass, the sky cloudless.

The cicadas trilled, high pitched and loud. She swore that somehow that sound alone made days feel hotter.

Up ahead, she could make out a dark figure, sitting cross-legged on a shaded rock. He faced the lake, unmoving, eyes closed, back straight, but a sense of serenity flowed from him.

Next to the rock, a hairy brown mass rose from the ground and woofed at her.

"Hey, Beau," she whispered. "Trevor?"

Trev turned his head and opened his eyes. "Hey, sis."

Hey. Like sitting way out here on a rock, meditating, was some everyday thing.

"What are you . . ." A quick glance around told her he was alone. "Am I interrupting?"

"Nah." He unfolded his legs and patted the space next to him. "Come on up."

She passed him her water bottle and got a foothold on the side of the boulder. One foot in, she was still too short to mount the top. "I'll need a—"

Trevor stood and offered his hand, hoisting her up the rest of the way.

"Thanks."

"No problem."

He sat back down and she settled beside him, unsure of what to say. So she said the first thing that popped into her mind. "Are you out here, like, doing yoga or something?"

His relaxed laugh made her smile. "Not *like* yoga. It is yoga."

"Since when do you do yoga?"

"Since Peru." He stretched his long legs out in front of him. "There was a yogi in our group. After a week or so, she could tell I was pretty lost in my head. She talked to me about stuff and started teaching me yoga."

Sophie studied the man beside her.

Her brother, but nothing like the other two. In fact, inside, Trevor couldn't be more different than Dev and Roark, yet on the outside he was so similar. Same tall build, same dark hair and shocking blue eyes, but that's where the common thread ended.

Trevor had always walked to his own beat. Independent and free-spirited, which meant, after childhood, the two of them grew apart.

Trevor didn't need her. He didn't need anybody. And Sophie didn't know what to do if she wasn't needed.

"Does it help?"

"Oh hell yeah." Trev grinned and took a sip from his thermos of water. "Why do you think I come out here?"

She shifted to face him. So much of Trevor was a mystery. His attitude toward life, his absence at odd times, the way he seemed scatterbrained, but whenever she talked to him, he actually wasn't scattered at all. "Trev, until now, I didn't know you came out here at all. I don't know where you are or what you're doing half the time. Is this where you go when you disappear?"

He studied the lake, giving her his profile. His expression went carefully blank as he shook his head. "Not always."

"Then where?"

A slow lift of his shoulders. "Different places."

"Places like . . ."

Trevor turned, mirroring her position exactly, their knees touching. "I'll tell you one place I go, but you have to promise not to get mad and you can't say anything to Roark or Dev."

"Ohhhh . . ." She already had enough secrets. "I don't know—"

"Promise."

Fine. "Okay, I promise."

With eyes as blue as the sky at midday, he studied her. Then he nodded, satisfied. "Sometimes I call or go see Mom in Asheville."

Her mouth fell open.

He went to see—*"What?"*

"I go visit Mom. She's in Asheville now and . . . we've been talking."

She opened and closed her mouth, no words coming out at first, only sounds. Eventually she got out a few syllables. "But. I—When? How? *Why?"*

Trevor gawked. "She's our mother. That's why. I know things were bad and she left Dad, but she still loves us. She did the best she could."

Heat shot up Sophie's spine and she stiffened. "Did she? Did she really? So her best means almost letting the inn fail and then running away and having as little to do with us as possible?"

"Soph. You have to know they tried." Trevor's tone remained calm and even. It was infuriating. "Yes, their best *sucked.* They couldn't handle four kids and a resort, but then they never really had much choice, did they?"

She didn't care about their choices; she cared about their actions. Their absence and anger, and the effect it'd had on her brothers.

"The business was theirs, whether they wanted it or not, and they had us kids. Pretty sure I was an accident, and they weren't about to let you be an orphan. We went through hell, but we're all still here, aren't we? And we're together."

She blinked at her brother, baffled by his new outlook on their family. Baffled by him. "I don't . . . Trevor, I don't get you at all. You can't forgive what they did because they tried."

"And you can't resent them forever and harbor that hurt. It's not good for you."

"I'm not harboring hurt."

Trev stared at her, unblinking, expressionless.

Sophie jerked her gaze away. "You always were closer to Mom. It's easy for you to forgive her."

"Like hell."

His vehemence startled her.

"I'm not saying I have the same anger as Dev or you or Roark, but I was plenty mad. Then guess what. I started talking to her. I told her how I felt. I even yelled at her, and she listened. Crazy, I know, but it helped. Bottling all that shit up? Did not."

"I hope you're not suggesting I call her up for a chit chat."

With a huff of annoyance, Trevor put his hands up, as though they were balanced scales. "No, I'm not saying call her up. But look at it this way. When we started down this road, we fought and bickered, Dev drank and got in trouble. I took off for a year." He lowered his right hand, weighted. "Life is hard and none of us are perfect. But we had each other. The four of us, and some damn good employees too." He lowered his left hand, the right hand rising. "We do all right now, but we survived because we each have three other people—at least—holding us up. Our folks had no one. Not even each other. But they managed to leave this place afloat, just enough, for us to have Honeywilde."

True, she and her brothers had each other, but still. She shook her head. "I . . . I guess. And I know you want peace in your life. If this makes you happy, then . . . okay. But I had no idea you were talking to Mom."

"I told her Dev got engaged."

"Trev." She groaned, burying her face in her hands. The thought of her mom and Dev twisted her stomach. He wouldn't want her to know. After years off the rails, he'd gotten his life together, but he blamed their parents for a lot. Fair or not, Dev was far from being ready to forgive and forget.

"She's happy for him. You should've heard her."

"Does Dev know you talk to her?"

"No. Of course not. And you can't tell him. I want to tell him and Roark, but they'll be pissed."

"Yeah, no kidding. But you can't keep this from them forever. They'll find out, and it'll be twice as bad if you've kept this from them."

Trevor scrubbed a hand over his mouth before leaning back, his hands on the rock to support him. "There's a lot of stuff they'd be pissed off about at first, but in time, they'll have to adjust."

He didn't smirk or wink, but there was something in his eyes; knowledge and a silent understanding. One simple truth settled into her soul.

Trevor knew about her and Wright.

She swallowed hard. "I suppose."

"Sometimes, we have to do what we do in order to make our own way. It's *our* way, whether other people like it or not. And it's nobody else's business until we're ready to make it their business."

Her mouth stayed shut. If she said anything, the truth might come tumbling out.

A gentle smile curled his lips. "I wanted you to know I'm talking to Mom because I hate keeping it to myself all the time. Having her in my life has helped me. She's doing better and so am I. This is a good thing. I trust you to see that."

"I . . ." She did see that. As much hurt as they all shared, if Trev was talking—to anyone at all, but especially his mother—that was a good thing. "I do see that, Trev. But be careful."

"I will." He bumped his knee against hers. "I knew I could trust you. Same way you trusted me when you and Wright rolled in late the other day. Or every time I see him looking at you like you hung the moon."

Her eyes went wide as she reached for him, unsure of why. Maybe to grab him or pinch him, make him swear not to tell.

"Relax." He patted her grasping hand. "I trust y'all know what you're doing. I'm only asking the same from you."

There was nothing aggressive in his tone or posture. He wasn't mad or even a little bit put out.

Of anyone in her family, he'd be the last one to take issue with her and Wright seeing one another. He might even support the idea of them as a couple wholeheartedly. Trevor was all about people doing their own thing. Not living out of obligation, but by choice. And she needed more of that in her life.

She admired that about him, and wanted him to know. But when she opened her mouth, "Why haven't we ever been close?" was what came out.

Another shrug before he leaned back, planting his hands on the rock. "We used to be. When we were kids."

"That was ages ago, though. When do you and I ever hang out and talk nowadays?"

"We're talking now."

"Yeah, but why not before now?"

He stretched one leg out to the side, looking like he didn't have a care in the world. For as relaxed as he appeared, he could be one of the resort guests. "All kinds of reasons, I guess. For a long time, I didn't talk much to anyone. We're closest in age, but . . . I don't know. Growing up, I think you liked having older brothers. Roark and Dev are these big personalities that clashed nine times out of ten. You kept the peace and they were protective of you."

They'd needed her as much as she needed them.

"I wasn't like that. I didn't butt heads with them, but I didn't stick around when the arguing kicked off either."

"No, you got the hell out of dodge."

"Damn right." There wasn't a hint of self-deprecation now, and Trevor made no apologies for his exits. "I didn't do well with confrontation. I couldn't calm those two down or act as mediator, but you could. I left you to it because the things I wanted to say would've only made matters worse. Instead, I shut down. But I admire how you keep the peace and manage everyone."

She sat up a little straighter. "Since when do I manage anyone?"

"Since always. Come on. Everyone knows who the real manager is around here, and it isn't Roark. You're the glue, Soph. You keep this place ticking by keeping all of us from spinning out of control. You're the one really calling the shots around here, which is why I don't understand you hiding how much you and Wright want to be a couple. But whatever."

"Who says we want to be a couple?"

Trevor tossed his head back and laughed. "Please. I keep telling you, I know things. When you're the quietest one in the family, you hear things. And if you want to be with him, no one is going to stop you. Everyone else may have to adapt, but that's not a new experience for the Bradley clan, now is it? Learning to deal and adapt? That's kind of our thing."

She couldn't help but smile. Trevor did know things, even if he didn't say a lot. But his advice was easier given than followed.

To him, any relationship she had with Wright was no skin off his teeth. He wasn't best friends with Wright and he wasn't Wright's employer. He wasn't super protective of her and felt no betrayal at her sneaking around with their chef.

The same couldn't be said for Roark and especially not Dev.

"We've come so far, though." She planted her elbows on her legs and propped her chin in her hand. "Everything is finally on the mend. Our family, the resort. Things are going well. I don't want to be the one who ruins all that."

"You're not going to ruin anything. Give us more credit. All of us. We're older now. Sure, we were a mess for years, and living at the inn was like living in a powder keg. Might've been the end of the world back then, if you were sleeping with Wright, but not now."

She planted her face in her hands. Perhaps he was right, but she struggled to wrap her head around a Honeywilde where she could sleep with Wright, date him, and everyone was cool with it.

He nudged her arm, making her look up. "It's your life, and his. Not Dev's or Roark's or anyone else's."

"That's easy for you to say."

"No, it isn't. You think it was easy for me to live my life, leave and go to Peru last year?"

"Yeah."

"Like hell it was."

Sophie straightened up again.

"It was like ripping off a limb when I left, but I knew I had to go. I wasn't ready to take on the responsibility here, but Roark kept loading me with more. I resented him as much as I ever resented Mom and Dad, and I was starting to hate this place. I saw Dev self-destructing and then trying to recover, but struggling, and there you were, trying to be the rock for everyone. It hurt the worst to leave you because I knew what you were taking on, but I also knew I'd make matters, and myself, worse."

"How? I could've used your help. You're levelheaded. And calm."

Trevor laughed. "*Now* I am. Now I can help you, but back then? Hell no. I would've been more work for you. I had so much bitterness. I wanted Honeywilde to fail."

Her mouth fell open again, but he didn't bother trying to look ashamed.

"I hated this place and what it did to our family. I remember thinking, maybe if our folks had simple, nine-to-five jobs, maybe they wouldn't have been so messed up. I still feel like we could've worked as a family if they had the therapy and help they needed and were out from underneath this responsibility they couldn't handle."

She wasn't so sure about that, but she understood what he meant about their parents being happier if they hadn't had the pressure. Running an inn and resort wasn't for everyone.

"Honeywilde was never their dream. It was Grandpa's and it's Roark's and Dev's and yours. And now mine. But for them, it was all work, work, argue, yell, work some more. I saw Roark and Dev going down that same path and wanted no part of it."

Everything Trev said made sense, though she hadn't thought about that over a year ago and had never understood why he left.

"But when Dev contacted me in Peru, told me how things were going here with the big rock-star wedding, and that Roark was slightly less maniacal in his management skills—"

"Wait. *Dev* contacted you?"

"Yeah."

"I never knew that."

"There are a lot of things we all do that the rest of us don't know about. Point is, leaving all of you wasn't easy for me, but it was the right thing for my life, even with the inconvenience and disapproval of my family. It didn't destroy any of you, obviously. And when all is said and done, it's *my* life. I'm the one who has to live with it." Trevor leveled a look at her, unflinching as their gazes locked.

He was preaching to her, and she needed to listen.

This was her life, and she had to live it her way. She wanted to be with Wright, and everyone else would simply have to adjust. No matter how much it hurt or disrupted Honeywilde while they did.

"I have to tell them."

"That you want to be with Wright? Hell yeah, you do." Trev gave her a crooked smile. "You'll be happier if you do."

But she was so damn scared. Saying it out loud made it real. People would know. *Wright* would know. She'd fallen for him. No schoolgirl crush or simple daydream. She was falling in love with him. He'd have her heart, and he'd be in the perfect position to hurt her. To shatter her world, all over again.

But then, keeping her heart to herself wouldn't work anymore. She'd already given him most of it.

"The gala is Friday. Once we get through that, once it's over, I'll stop hiding."

With quiet consideration, Trevor studied her. She could almost see him rolling the thought around in his mind. "I think we better head back." He gave her leg a pat and slid off the rock, holding out his hand to help her down. "And if I were you, I wouldn't wait too long to say how you feel. Trust me. If you put the best things in life on hold, you'll live to regret it."

Chapter 20

Wright didn't get a moment alone with Sophie until late Thursday afternoon. They'd seen each other in passing the day before, texted in the wee hours of the night, but a few words and stolen glances weren't enough. Not anymore.

There was a time that a text string with her made his day and sent everything within him into high gear.

Now the short bursts of communication barely tided him over.

He finally found her downstairs, arranging planters to spruce up the patio. Her back was to him as he approached.

She was alone, so he slid his hands around her waist, tugging her back against him, and pressed his lips to her temple.

"Steve?" she teased, without looking back.

He held her tighter as he laughed, their bodies flush together. "Steve better not."

"I think he's got a thing for Vivian anyway. So you're safe." She turned in his arms, wrapping hers around his neck.

"Good. Then you're all mine." The words were loaded and out of his mouth before he considered the repercussions.

But she peered up at him, still smiling, her hazel eyes perhaps even a little warmer as she danced her fingers along the back of his neck. "Yep. All yours."

The small proclamation tightened his chest, made breathing hurt in the best possible way.

What might seem like a casual side comment for some couples was a big damn deal for them.

"But if you're going to do something about it, you better do it quick. Trevor and Devlin are supposed to meet me down here and lend a hand."

"Trevor? Really?"

"I know. Kind of surprising, but he keeps being really helpful, and turns out, he knows a lot about a lot. Now hurry. Kiss me before anyone else gets here."

Wright bent and pressed his lips to hers, listening for any approaching footsteps.

The smell of flowers and freshly turned earth wafted up from all around them, a sweet and earthy scent that was perfect for Sophie.

He moved his lips to her ear, a slow inhale as his nose brushed her soft hair. "Did you decide what to wear to the gala?"

"I did."

"Tell me."

"If I tell you, it won't be a surprise."

He leaned away, his gaze caught on the plump pinkness of her lips. "You want to surprise me, huh?"

"Maybe."

"Good. Maybe I like surprises."

"Let me see if I can guess what you're going to wear." She closed her eyes and put her fingers to her temples as though a mind reader. "One of your fancy chef's jackets."

While her eyes were still closed, he kissed her again.

She opened her mouth to say something else, but someone was tromping down the stairs form the verandah.

Wright released her as she stepped away.

Trevor cleared the last step and rounded toward them. "Sorry, guys, but Dev is on his way too. Thought it might be a good idea to make a noisy entrance."

Wright's gaze shot to Sophie's. Trev's tone was a little too in-the-know.

She lifted her shoulders and mouthed, *I'll tell you later.*

Then Devlin reached the patio. "This looks great, guys." He walked around the perimeter lined with topiaries and trees, a few planter boxes with flowers.

The entire center of the patio was left empty for the dance floor and band to set up. "I think people will be lured this way after dinner, no problem," he said.

"Steve is going to set up the portable bar out here," Wright offered. "That will solve any issues of people lingering upstairs instead of dancing."

"Perfect. The chairman of the Chamber said she's saving the fund-raising pitch for later, down here, when everyone's had drinks and is dancing. Loosens up the wallets." Dev peered around the patio. "They're going to love it, guys. Nice work."

Sophie put her finger in the air, calling the small group to attention. "I do have one special request for the night, though."

"Whatever you want. Name it."

"I think, since the menu is mostly small plates and we have Marco for back-up, Wright should have part of the evening to enjoy the gala with us. He's worked as hard as anyone on this event and—"

"I agree." Dev was quick to answer. "We all deserve a little fun at the gala. Why not?"

He shook Trevor and Wright's hands and dragged Sophie in for a side hug. "Look. I know you all did more than originally planned for this event, what with my engagement stuff happening as well. Thanks for that too by the way. The other night was—" He caught himself, coughed, and began again. "The other night was perfect."

"You're welcome, man. We're happy for you. Don't go getting mushy on us." Wright pulled Dev in for a hug, even as guilt gnawed at his insides.

But this time, his guilt wasn't over sleeping with his best friend's sister. This guilt came from keeping the best thing that'd ever happened to him from Dev. Not only was he shutting Dev out of the truth about his new career opportunities, but he was lying about his feelings for Sophie.

Maybe Dev had kept his relationship with Anna quiet for a while, but that was then and this was now. That was Anna, and this was Sophie.

How much longer could he go on hiding? Now that Sophie had let him in, now that he'd told his parents the truth, how much longer could they keep the truth from all of them?

He had to come clean. Not only about him and Sophie, but about the very likely chance he could be leaving Honeywilde.

His announcements—on both counts—would cause an uproar, but he was tired of carrying these secrets.

If he could convince Sophie that it was time to talk to her brothers, then he could tell her about Asheville and Charleston.

"I'm going to go call the chairman and let her know we're all set for tomorrow night." Dev gave him one last clap on the back and headed up the stairs, leaving him and Sophie to stare at Trevor.

Wright shoved his hands in his pockets to keep from reaching for her as he waited for Trevor to make his exit. Exiting didn't happen, and the awkward tension grew with every second.

Sophie frowned at him before glancing at Trev, a light dawning in her eyes. "Oh! You can relax, Wright. Trevor knows about us."

He jerked his hands from his pockets. "Since when?"

"I don't know. Sometime before I told him the truth? He called me out yesterday."

Of the whole family, leave it to the quiet one to have them figured out.

Trev nodded, not a trace of smugness or judgment. "I thought something was up a while ago; back when you two weren't talking to each other, when normally you talk all the time. There was a lot of sexual tension too, so . . ." He shrugged. "I know I was gone for almost a year, but you two have always been thick as thieves, then suddenly there's all this intensity and silent treatment? Not rocket science. Figured one of you screwed up, but hey, looks like y'all got things figured out now, so congrats."

Wright's mouth fell open.

"Don't worry, though." Trev gave him a good-natured punch in the arm. "I'm not going to say a word to anyone. Not my job. That's on you two."

He turned to go and climbed the stairs, two at a time.

Wright trailed the movement, trying to comprehend what happened. "He told you he knew?"

"Yeah." Sophie moved closer, taking his hand.

His heart gave a little kick every time she initiated contact, each time she was the one to reach for him.

"Why didn't you tell me?"

"I wanted to wait until I had time with you, in person." She turned so they faced each other. "He was surprisingly supportive. And insightful."

"Yeah, you said he knew more than you thought, about a lot of things. I didn't guess *we* were one of those things."

"He told me I shouldn't hide the truth about us, and . . . and I think maybe he has a point."

"You do?" His heart rate surged as he tried to remain completely composed on the outside.

"I don't like lying. About us. I don't want to hide forever."

Forever. Wright went from fighting for composure, to losing the battle in a split second. His mouth suddenly dry, he blinked and tried to get a grip. "I . . . okay, I'm with you. I don't want to hide either."

"I know. But I still don't know how to tell Dev and Roark, and the time has to be right. You know the news won't roll over them as lightly as Trevor."

He knew all about timing announcements right, and no, Dev and Roark wouldn't be as easy as Trevor. But he was still ready to take that step.

Sophie needed to be ready as well, and he wanted her to get there on her on. Pressuring her would backfire, and besides, he didn't want to push. Faith and experience told him she'd arrive at that step on her own.

Who would've ever guessed Trev, of all people, could help her get there.

"And I don't want to do anything until after the gala is over." She tangled her fingers in his. "Let's get through this, make sure everything goes off without a hitch, and then you and I can talk about how to tell my brothers."

Wright nodded, a fluttering in his chest. They could talk about his job opportunities too, discuss what they wanted to do with their lives, because they'd be living them together. They'd decide how to tell her family.

Sophie was the one. He knew it, all the way down to his bones. She'd always been the one.

Chapter 21

For the Midsummer Gala, Sophie bought a sleeveless silk chiffon dress in deep purple, cinched in at the waist, with a V-neckline a little deeper than she'd ever worn before.

She smiled at her reflection, feeling like a Greek goddess.

If the dress revealed a lot of those freckles Wright was so wild about, all the better.

On the rare occasion she wore a dress, it was never for such a high-end event. Tonight there would be a band and dancing. Dinner jackets and semiformal dresses.

The crowd that came to these parties always did so in style. And while the Chamber's gala was not about her, she still felt like the belle of the ball.

A pretty dress *and* a date.

How long had it been? Had it ever been? Dates in Windamere normally meant a meal in town and a movie. Not this.

With monumental effort, she managed not to twirl off the elevator as soon as the doors opened.

Then she saw Wright.

"Wow." His mouth fell open.

He'd been waiting on her in the lobby, and the sight of him, all dressed up in a formal black chef's jacket and looking at her like she was a sky full of stars on a clear summer night, sent her heart skipping from her chest.

Unable to resist the urge, she twirled toward him.

"Wow," he said again, catching her in his arms.

"Right back at you." She took a quick glance around before smoothing her hands down the buttons of his jacket. The cut accentuated his broad shoulders and lean waist. This close, the material was clearly a midnight navy, not black. The subtle difference suited his golden coloring, making him glow.

"You like?"

She stopped feeling him up and met his gaze. "I sure do."

Wright cleared his throat and turned, offering her his arm. "Come on. We're going to end up groping one another if I don't escort you to the verandah immediately."

A smile spread across her face. Later they could grope one another. Right now he could escort her to the verandah, and no one would bat an eye.

They'd look like Sophie and Wright, relying on each other as stand-ins because they didn't have dates. No one would know they were each other's dates.

Her hand in Wright's, they were about to go to fancy dinner together, dance, and have drinks, exactly like a real couple.

In her heart, that's what they'd become.

Even if no one knew, even if finding out hurt the people she loved, she was Wright's and he was hers. And this was real.

The truth settled into her soul.

As they crossed the great room, she caught their reflection in the mirror above the fireplace, in the floor-to-ceiling windows and doors across the back of the inn.

They made a beautiful pair. Even she could see that. The smile on her face was the happiest she'd ever seen.

"You took my breath away stepping off the elevator," Wright whispered. "And I don't think I've caught it yet."

Sophie squeezed his arm. "You're going to dance with me tonight, right?"

"Of course. We always have before. It'd look strange if I didn't."

"Promise?"

He put his hand over hers, giving it a squeeze. "I promise."

They reached the French doors and found Devlin and Anna waiting on the other side.

Wright took her to them.

"My goodness, look at you two." Anna gushed over Sophie's dress. "Who knew everyone cleaned up so well? Please look at this. Dev is wearing a tie." She pointed to Dev's black tie, teasing him as she straightened the knot.

"Only for you would I wear this much starch." He winked.

Anna's neck blushed and she touched the waist of her red dress. "I told him, if I have to wear Spanx all night because he thinks this dress is hot, then he has to wear a full suit. Fair is fair, right?"

They both looked gorgeous.

With their dark hair and striking features, Anna and Devlin might be the most elegant couple at the gala, but tonight, they had some competition when it came to being the happiest.

Wright gave her a subtle wink that only she could see. "Duty calls. I'll be back once dinner is served and Marco can manage without me."

He returned, along with dessert, bringing Sophie an extra crème brulee.

They sat with Dev and Anna, laughing and discussing wedding ideas. A casual wedding by the lake was what they had decided on, and it fit them.

After dessert was served, people began to wander downstairs, to the bar and the band. Exactly as planned.

Once they were alone, Sophie turned to Wright, her hand over his. She needed to hold on to say this. "Tomorrow."

"What about it?" Wright set his wine glass aside.

"I want to sit my brothers down tomorrow and tell them that we . . . that you and I are . . ."

"Together?" he offered.

"Yes." She laughed, rolling her eyes at her timidity. "Are you sure you want to be with me? I can't even say that we're dating or that you're my boyfriend without getting vertigo."

"Ooh, I like the sound of that. Say it again?"

"You're my boyfriend?"

He grinned, a hum of satisfaction in his throat, making her laugh.

"Why on earth do you want to be with me?"

Wright leaned on the table, his arm casually draped across the edge so he could brush his fingers against her elbow. "Why *wouldn't* I? I'm crazy about you. I think I always have been."

"But I can be a lot of work sometimes. And being with me and dealing with my family won't be easy."

"Soph. I want to be with you. Trust me, I know. I've had my whole life to figure it out. Nothing worth having is ever easy. We'll manage."

She moved the tiniest bit closer to him. "I was so mad at you after you kissed me in the kitchen that night. But being mad and not talking to you for weeks, *hurt*. Now I'm glad you kissed me and caused us to fight, and everything else. Otherwise, we wouldn't be here."

"Wasn't easy, but worth it." He tapped his glass against hers.

With a quick glance around, she counted five Chamber members still loitering upstairs and her entire family gone downstairs, where the music had already started.

She faced Wright, and the knowing look in his eyes unfurled a ribbon of heat that tickled her core.

"Come here and let me kiss you," he whispered.

Sophie went to him, eager for the day they could do this whenever and wherever. There would soon be a day when she was able to say, out loud, that she and Wright were together and know, in her heart, that he'd never leave her.

Wright kissed her, soft and seeking, gentle pulls at her lips as he slid his arm around her waist.

They kissed until there was no space between them, heating up until she shivered.

With a groan, Wright pulled himself away. "We better go downstairs."

"I think so." She stood and fluffed her dress, trying to get an updraft to cool down. "Besides, you owe me a dance. You promised."

"That I did." He pointed at her before offering her his arm for the second time that night. "Shall we?"

Sophie took his arm and floated toward the stairs. The evening was perfect. Tomorrow they'd tell her family the truth, and happiness would truly be hers. She could have love and everything life had to offer, without the fear of losing it.

"Oh my—" Sophie clung tighter to Wright's arm to keep from falling over.

In a heartbeat, those grand notions and intentions fell away.

Standing right outside the verandah's French doors was Sue Bradley, her adoptive mother.

"Holy sh—" Wright clamped his mouth shut before finishing the statement.

"Hello." Sue lifted her hand.

Sophie faltered, but Wright kept her standing.

"What . . ." She shook her head, certain this was a hallucination. "What are you doing here?"

Her mother blanched and studied the stone flooring at her feet. "I came to see you, all of you, and the place, and congratulate Devlin. I didn't know you had an event tonight. You look lovely."

Sophie shook her head, a million panicked thoughts racing through her mind, vying for first place.

How? *Why?*

Congratulate Devlin? Dev hadn't spoken to her in years.

And that's the thought that came spewing out.

"None of us have heard a word from you in forever." As soon as she said it, the caveat came to her.

Trevor.

Sue nodded, looking as wrecked. "You made it clear you'd prefer not to hear from me for a while, so I stayed away."

"Prefer not to hear from—*what the hell?*"

Wright moved forward, still holding on to her, his touch a solid support. "Maybe right now isn't the best time to do this."

Sue looked from Wright to Sophie and back again.

A quick understanding lit in her eyes as she looked at both of them. Wright with his hand on Sophie's, his presence close and sure. For all she knew, Sue had watched them kiss.

It didn't matter that Sue had been out of her life for a while now. She'd still known Sophie since she was a baby, and Wright almost as long.

Without saying a word, Sue's gaze met Sophie's, a question hovering between them.

And Sophie refused to answer.

She didn't need to know what was going on with her and Wright, but she better have an explanation for showing up out of nowhere.

"You can't show up here," Sophie blurted out.

"I did call. Or rather, Trevor called and invited me."

"He *what*?" Sophie's question boomed across the verandah, and everyone drew up short.

"I wanted to come see all of you, but I didn't know how or think it was a great idea until Trev told me about Dev and how well things are going now."

Sophie turned to Wright, clutching his arm tighter. "You have to find Trevor. We need to fix this before the bomb gets dropped on Dev and Roark too."

"I will." Wright peeled her hand from his arm and held them in his. "I'll find Trevor. Everything is going to be fine."

As much as she appreciated the sentiment, she knew it wasn't true.

Nothing was going to be fine now.

She didn't know why her mom was here or why Trevor had summoned her, but her sudden appearance was not something the Bradley family was ready for. The last years of hard-fought peace and respect could easily fracture in the face of the woman who'd walked out on them.

Old hurts, bitter feelings. There might be a time and a place to come together, someday, but this wasn't it.

Yet here she was.

"It'll be okay." Wright squeezed her hand, probably attempting to bring her back down to earth. Remind her of what was real, of their plans.

But there was no way she could go through with telling her brothers about the two of them now. Not with this shit about to hit the fan. When they all dodged this bullet, then she would talk to her brothers.

The truth about her and Wright would have to wait.

"Thanks for saying so." She squeezed his hand in return. "But I doubt it."

Chapter 22

One look and he knew. The window of opportunity they were going to take to come clean about their relationship, to talk about the future, had closed.

His perfect time to tell her about Asheville and Charleston was gone.

Now everything would be about the sudden reappearance of Suzanne Bradley. Once again, Honeywilde and the family would be in an uproar.

Call him selfish, but he wasn't having it.

He left Sophie's side to go find Trevor and made a vow that he wasn't going to lose her in the chaos. There would be chaos, no doubt. And hurt feelings, but he wasn't going to let what they'd built, the fact that now Sophie had let him in, get shoved aside in the fray.

Her words came back to him.

I don't know how to exist unless I'm in crisis recovery mode. I don't know how to enjoy this. Any of this. Life.

At the first sign of her family fracturing, Sophie would rush to her family's rescue. And he loved her for it, he did. But in her efforts to save everyone else, she'd pull away. He knew it.

She'd put everything she wanted, all of her need and dreams and desires, on the back burner in order to serve others.

That was not going to happen to them. Not with him.

He wouldn't let Sophie weather this storm alone while taking care of everyone else. And once the winds settled, he'd still be with her. They would still be together.

Trevor was downstairs, standing on the outskirts of the party, but well within earshot of Dev and Roark.

"Trev." He tried to wave him over without the other two noticing.

No such luck.

"Yeah, man." Trevor approached him, beer in hand, casual as could be, like he hadn't invited their estranged mother to show up at Honeywilde after years of little to no communication.

Devlin watched them first, Roark's gaze trailing right behind.

Wright kept his voice as low as possible given the music from the band. "We need to talk upstairs."

"What's up?"

"I think you know. The guest you invited?" He glared at Trevor, willing him to follow his meaning without making him say it. "She's here."

"The guest I invi—*Oh.*" His brow scrunched, he looked past Wright. "She's here? Now?"

"She said you told her to come."

"Not tonight."

"Yeah, well, I'm not sure why you thought it wise to invite her at all without telling everyone else, but she's here. And Sophie isn't happy. You need to go fix this."

"Right. Got it. Hold my beer." Trevor shoved the pint glass into his hand and took off for the stairs.

Roark and Devlin confronted him as soon as Trev was gone.

"What's going on?" Roark asked.

Dev's intense stare bored into his skin.

"Nothing. Something Sophie needed help with."

"And Trevor took off like *that*?" Dev's doubtful tone made Wright nervous.

Devlin could smell bullshit a mile away. He'd been distracted enough by Anna and the pending engagement not to clue in on what he and Sophie were doing, but Wright got the feeling all obliviousness had worn off.

"What's really going on? I've never seen Trev move that fast or be urgent about anything. And you look sick."

Roark set his glass down and moved in to complete their circle. "The kitchen isn't on fire again, is it?"

Wright glared at Dev. "You told him about the fire?"

"I had to."

Roark stiffened enough to seem two inches taller, his voice taking on a sharp tone. "Is something on fire right now or not?"

Only everything. "Nothing is on fire. The inn is fine, just . . ."

Shit. As soon as he told them, the storms would blow in. His plans, Sophie finally finding the courage to open up about their relationship, it'd all be swept away by the hurt and betrayal.

But Dev and Roark had a right to know. That was their mother upstairs, and their issues, the same as they were Sophie's.

"Your mother is here. Upstairs, with Sophie and Trevor." He got it all out as quickly as possible.

Roark blinked, his expression blank.

"You're kidding." Dev's voice was flat, but his eyes held an edge.

Wright met his gaze. "Would I ever joke about that?"

A wall fell over his best friend's face. A mask he hadn't seen in months. "No."

As if sensing the shift in mood from ten feet away, Anna quickly joined them. "What's wrong?"

"Nothing." Roark straightened his arms by his side. "Nothing is wrong. You guys stay here. We're not doing this right now. I'll handle it."

He stalked toward the stairs, leaving Anna and Madison to stare at each other. "Doing what?"

"Our mother is here." Dev's words were still without inflection as he turned to Anna. "I need to go with Roark. I'd rather you stay here until I know what the hell is going on."

"I can do that. I think," she said.

They all looked at Wright.

"I'm going with you, man," he told Devlin.

His best friend jerked his chin down in something resembling a nod, and Wright followed him up the stairs.

This was just fantastic.

Of all the times Suzanne could've chosen to return, she had to pick now.

It was some phenomenally shitty timing.

They got upstairs. As soon as they were close enough to see that no one else from the party lingered on the verandah, Roark's question came with a tone that could strip wood. "What made you think tonight was a good time for this?"

Trev's hands went up. "I did not say come tonight."

Right behind Devlin, Wright took in the scene before him and cringed.

Sophie appeared ready to melt into the verandah's floor; her mother stood, stone-faced, while Trevor looked panicked. And Roark was pissed.

Beyond pissed.

Wright had seen the eldest Bradley on a protective tangent, but this was a whole new level. Either because of the family's newly won closeness or because now he had Madison, Roark was on the warpath.

"You said to come as soon as I could," Sue Bradley argued.

"And to let me know." Trevor's volume went up a click. "Not just show up. This isn't helping to accomplish anything."

Dev moved to stand by Roark's side. "What is there to accomplish? She shouldn't be here."

"Trevor told me you got engaged and how well you were doing." The hopeful pleading in Sue's voice made Wright want to hide.

She probably meant well. She was their mother, so she must love them, but as a parent, she'd screwed up. And then left them; her ex-husband not too far behind.

"I'm doing fine." Devlin stared at something past Sue, looking right through her. "Still doesn't explain why you're here."

"I wanted to congratulate you. All of you."

Dev leveled a look at her. "You could've called or sent a letter."

Wright wanted to intervene. He hated seeing Dev like this. Didn't realize how much he hated it until he'd gone months without seeing the icy veneer in place.

And through all of it, Sophie remained stock still and silent.

He wanted to go to her. Shield her from what was happening, soothe the pain that put the lines of hurt on her face.

He could imagine what she was thinking. Her worst fear, now playing out in front of them.

She'd been happy tonight. For the first time in a long time, she had something for herself, with him, and they were both happy.

Now this.

Sue shook her head. "There's too much to talk about, so much I want to say, and it can't be said over the phone."

"So you show up, unannounced. Uninvited." Roark's voice went lower. "Not thinking how it might affect the rest of us. We're not doing this now. You can come back tomorrow or the next day, but tonight, this conversation is over."

"I was invited," Sue rushed to say. "Trevor said it was okay."

Trevor threw his hands up and let them land against his sides with a slap. "Later. *If* you let me know. I told you to let me know when you could visit. I didn't say drop by anytime."

"And you didn't think to let us in on your invitation?" Roark turned on him.

Sophie snapped out of whatever trance she was in and moved closer to Trevor. "Everybody calm down. We have guests downstairs. I'm sure Trevor meant well. Obviously there's a misunderstanding. I think we can all agree, now is not the best time to do this."

"I can't think of a worse time," Roark sneered.

Then Madison and Anna appeared at the top of the stairs and moved closer. Anna shot Dev a look of apology and shrugged, but Madison had her sights set on Roark. "Are you okay? I thought I heard you all the way downstairs."

"You know what?" Roark tossed his hands up. "That's it. We're done talking for now, and that's final. Whatever this is, it can wait until the gala is over."

"It can wait forever," Dev mumbled.

"It's late for her to be driving," Trevor murmured.

"And we live in an inn with plenty of rooms." Roark was already turning away.

"Exactly." Sophie grabbed at the opening for nonconfrontation and ran through it. "You can check in, and we'll handle all of this later. I'll get you some keys."

"No, I'll get it." Trevor stopped her with a hand on her arm. "I did this, I'll handle it."

Dev glared at his youngest brother's admission.

As soon as Trevor convinced Sue to go with him, Wright went to Sophie's side.

With the wisdom not to say anything right away, he stood close enough to brush against her.

"What the hell?" Dev finally spoke at a normal volume.

Anna touched his arm. "Was that your—"

"Yes. That was our mother."

She slowly covered her mouth. "Why would Trevor ask her to come here?"

Sophie glanced at Wright, on the precipice of panic.

She and Trevor had talked the other day. He knew about her and

Wright, and understood. They were closer now, and her knee-jerk re-action would be to come to his defense. To assuage everyone's anger at him and try to smooth everything out.

True to form, she took a heavy breath and put her hands out. "Let's all keep our voices down. I'm sure Trevor had a valid reason, and we can ask him as soon as he gets her settled."

"There is no valid reason for this."

"Dev."

Dev shook his head, his mouth a thin line. "I don't need her to congratulate me. We're doing fine without her. Why now?"

"I don't know, but everyone getting riled up won't help."

He let out a gruff sigh and took a few steps away.

Dev was as shaken as Wright had ever seen him, and with good reason. He'd been more estranged from their mom and dad than any of them, and he'd probably hoped to go a long while, if not forever, without having their involvement in his life.

"I'm sure he meant well." Sophie looked to Wright and then past him.

He'd be damned if he wasn't going to her aid, even though he thought Trevor was batshit for doing this.

"Sophie's right. Trevor is a lot of things, but malicious isn't one of them. If he asked your mom to come here, then it must be for a good reason. Make amends, settle some things. I don't know. But I do know we have a patio full of guests who need to donate a lot of money."

Sophie's eyes widened. "Yes. Exactly. We have a gala to finish, and we can't be up here hashing things out while Roark is down there alone."

"Fine." Dev paced back toward them, his jaw clenched tight enough to crack. "This is bullshit, but I'm not ruining a good thing because she showed up. We can deal with her later."

Anna put her arm under Dev's, her voice low as she spoke to him.

Wright realized Sophie still stood alone, her entire body rigid.

As the others made their way to the stairs, she cast him an unfo-cused look and began to follow.

She was walking away.

Did she intend on facing the rest of the evening alone, all because she didn't want anyone to know about them yet? Deal with the fact that their mother was back and no one really understood why, alone, while everyone else had someone to lean on?

No way.

As they brought up the rear, Wright grabbed her hand. He laced their fingers together and brought her hand up to place a kiss over her fingers. "It'll be okay," he whispered.

Her posture remained stiff, her voice shaky. "How?"

"I have no clue, but it will."

She shook her head, but let him hold on.

The entire night, he stayed by her side. He was there in case she needed him again, but she never did. Eventually, the party drew to a close, and the music ended, but not once did they ever dance.

Chapter 23

The first thing she saw when she woke was the photo of her biological parents.

Sophie rolled away and pulled the covers up higher, praying the day would magically go away.

She couldn't deal with Suzanne right now, she didn't want to see and hear her brothers argue, and most of all, she didn't want to face Wright.

Last night, she'd smiled so hard, pretending everything was okay, that her entire body ached.

Wright had tried to talk as the gala ended, but she'd kept herself too busy, intentionally around others the whole time, so that he couldn't get her aside. He wanted to be there for her, because that's how Wright was, and she appreciated that. But with her family, with this going on, he couldn't possibly help.

He'd texted her several times last night to check on her. Her only reply was to say *I'm okay.*

He'd know it was a lie. Of course she wasn't okay. She'd been okay for a day or two before her mother showed up, and wasn't that the problem? A little bit of happiness led to a whole lot of heartache.

And last night, if Wright had pushed to tell her brothers they were together, it would've been too much. All the pressure and frustration. The wounded part of her that never went away had resurfaced in the face of her mother, and it all would've come pouring out onto him. She didn't want her hurt and anger making a target of him.

With a curse, she pushed herself to sit upright. As much as she wanted to, she couldn't hide in her room all day.

Once in the shower, she closed her eyes and tried to take deep breaths.

She thought about Trevor on that rock, doing yoga.

Poor Trev. What the hell was he thinking?

After a few minutes, her heart stopped jumping, her pulse not galloping fast enough to make her light-headed.

She was a big girl; she could do this. They were all adults. Somehow they'd get through their mother coming back, figure out the real reason why, and deal with whatever came after.

But she was not about to pile the truth of her and Wright on top of everything else. Then the two of them would be a source of problems. They would be the issue, and she had worked too hard for her family's happiness to become one of their problems.

Wright had to understand that.

She got out, dried off, and took in her tired reflection.

Everyone was already keyed up and on edge. Now was not the time to lower another boom.

She pasted on another fake smile. "Hey, guys . . . now seems like a great time to tell you that Wright and I have been sneaking around and having sex for the last week or so. We're seeing each other behind everyone's backs and never said a word to any of you because I was afraid of more family drama. So . . . Surprise!"

She planted her face in her hands.

Putting the truth off for another week or two was the wise choice. Already she'd be walking into turmoil and mistrust. That's not how she wanted her public relationship with Wright to begin.

Wright would totally understand. He knew how her family could be; he'd been around them his whole life.

He practically *was* family.

"Oh god," she muttered into her palms. Her brothers were going to be hurt and confused. More so that she'd lied to them, but also because this was Wright. And he'd lied to them too.

Secrecy seemed a great idea at the start, but they'd probably hurt their case more than helped.

She scrubbed her hands through her hair. They couldn't come out with the truth now, though, regardless. That much she knew.

And Trevor.

Poor Trev. He was going to catch the brunt of everyone's frustration, but surely he had some kind of plan or good intention in inviting Sue here. If Sophie could just keep everyone calm enough to let him explain, maybe things would be okay.

Peace would resume. Ensuring her family didn't fall apart after how hard they'd worked and how far they'd come, *that* was her priority.

She went downstairs, but no one was in the great room. No one on the verandah or having breakfast in the restaurant. She wasn't about to check the kitchen and have to see Wright.

She tried Roark's office.

Inside, Roark sat at his desk. Across from him sat Dev and Trevor, tension stealing oxygen from the room.

"Good, you're here." Roark rose from his chair and ushered her in, closing the door behind her. "Mom isn't down yet."

Trevor turned to her as he got up.

"No, keep the chair."

"It's your chair." He kept his voice low. "Besides, I'd rather not be too close to the action, if you know what I mean."

Trevor took up his spot by the window, and she sat next to Devlin, feeling like a traitor. Maybe it was ridiculous, but she couldn't shake the sensation.

A big, lying traitor.

Dev planted his elbow on the arm of his chair and leaned over. "Trevor was explaining how he's been in touch with Mom since early spring."

"Apparently, she's been excited to hear how well things are going," Roark added.

"And when Trev told her the news about my engagement, she wanted to see us all in person."

Sophie met Trevor's gaze and held it.

Roark scooted up to his desk, propping his arms on the ink blotter. "What I don't get is why you didn't tell us. Why would you keep that to yourself and keep us in the dark, especially about her coming here?"

"Okay, first of all, I didn't invite her to show up last night. I just said I'd like her to come by sometime and we should make plans. My plan was to talk to all of you first and then invite her. Second . . . I don't know. I haven't mentioned talking to her yet because I knew y'all would be weird about it."

Sophie finally spoke. "She's your mother. You're allowed to talk to her, no matter what anyone else thinks."

Devlin threw one hand in the air and let it land on his thigh with a slap. "But never say a damn word about it? You'd keep something like that from us?"

Trev studied her, an expectant light in his eyes.

He wanted her to come clean about their talk. Admit she knew he'd reached out to Sue and that she was, if not supportive, then at least not completely opposed.

She refused to admit anything about her and Wright, but in this, she should speak up.

"I . . . He told me," she confessed.

The total focus of all three of them turned to her.

"A few days ago, Trev told me he'd kept in touch with mom. He asked me what he should do and I told him I understood the need for secrecy. But I didn't know about her wanting to come here or contact us or any of that." She rushed to add the rest. "I only knew they talked."

With a grumble, Roark scrubbed a hand over his face and through his hair. Dev stared at her like she'd kicked Beau.

"I couldn't say anything." She pleaded with him. "He asked me not to, and it wasn't my truth to tell."

He kept looking at her, and her guilty conscience grabbed hold, right before she shoved it back in favor of defensiveness. "Same way I never told anyone about you and Anna, even though I knew. And the same way I never ran my mouth about Roark and Madison. Don't act like y'all have never kept secrets from the rest of us. We've all fibbed when it comes to our privacy."

Her words penetrated the guilty fog hanging around her.

Shocking though it was, she was dead right. Every single one of her brothers had withheld the truth or downright lied about their personal lives. Why should she feel so guilty?

Roark shook his head as he leaned forward. "Dev not telling us about Anna isn't the same as not clueing us in about our own mother showing up after years."

And now the guilt was back.

"Who knows what she might want? What if she wants part of Honeywilde back?"

Trevor's laugh reeked of sarcasm. "Come on. She does *not* want Honeywilde. This place damn near killed her and destroyed our parents' marriage. Why would she want any of that back? Mom wants to make amends. That's it."

Dev turned in his chair to stare down Trevor. "Did she tell you that's what she wanted? What she *really* wanted?"

"Yes."

"Because she always tells the truth, right?"

"This isn't helping." Sophie cringed.

Trevor shoved away from the wall. "I wouldn't have been in touch with her if I ever thought for one second that she'd try to take Honeywilde away from us. You should know that."

"I know you've always hated this place and did everything you could to stay away."

"Stop!" Sophie yelled, the last of her control splintering. Five minutes talking about the past and they were all back to the paranoid, scared little kids they were then.

Her brothers would start snapping at each other and it'd end in her family, her one little piece of foundation that she'd fought for, falling apart. She tried so hard. It couldn't fall apart now. "Stop digging at each other. Stop being hurtful because you're hurting. Just stop."

The room went quiet as a tomb, the three of them staring at her again.

"If we're all on the same side and stick together, it doesn't matter what she wants. Amends or a piece of the inn. It doesn't matter why she's here. We can hear her out, listen if we want or ignore her. Please. If we have each other's backs, we'll be fine."

Her brothers all stared.

She could barely feel her limbs, and she was holding her breath.

Her family had to keep it together through this. She'd fall apart otherwise.

Someone knocked on the door and they all jumped, but when the door cracked open, Wright's sandy blond head popped in. "Just me. Checking to make sure you're all okay."

"We're here. I don't know about okay." Dev waved him in, and Sophie avoided making eye contact.

Along with everything else in her life getting tossed upside down, she had her hidden relationship with Wright.

He might resent her for wanting to push back talking to her family, but she couldn't toss that match onto the tinder pile of her family right now.

Wright took his usual spot near Trevor. At every meeting, she would share looks with Wright. It's what they did, but not today.

She couldn't bring herself to look at him.

He meant too much to her now. What if he got more than a little upset about waiting to tell everyone the truth? What if he hated her for asking him to wait?

What if he left her?

Roark sighed, and planted his hands on his desk. "We can't stay holed up in here forever. We have jobs to do."

They filed out of the office, and Sophie did her best to stay close to Dev. The closer she was, the less likely Wright was to intercept her.

"Soph," Wright called to her once they hit the lobby.

Ignoring him would make her too much of a coward. If she talked to him, surely he'd understand.

Slowing her steps, she created some space between them and the others, but she still couldn't look him in the eyes.

Once everyone was far enough away, Wright brushed his hand down her arm. "You okay?"

No, she wasn't okay. Their mother was back, along with all of the emotions that came with her; her brothers were fighting again; and eventually, Sue would leave and she'd be left with the jagged pieces.

"I know. Stupid question. Why won't you look at me?"

With a shaky breath, she forced her gaze to Wright's. Her eyes burned, the knot in her throat threatening to give way to sobs.

"You'll get through this." He tried to reassure her, but he didn't know the half of it.

The words came tumbling out as soon as she opened her mouth. "We can't tell them about us yet."

Wright blinked, the corners of his mouth turning down. "I kind of figured that was coming."

"You know we can't. Not now."

A gruff sigh as he leaned away, crossing his arms. "I know. We can wait until Sue leaves."

When Sue left, she'd leave the rubble of raw feelings in her wake. They couldn't confess their affair in the middle of that. They'd be asking for a huge family blowout. "We need to give it a few weeks. Let the dust settle and then maybe we can talk to my brothers."

"A few weeks?" Wright's volume rose as he scowled.

"Shhh." She stepped toward him, moving them back toward the office and away from the great room. "Yes, a few weeks."

"I can't—That's too long."

"It's not too long. What does it matter if we tell them now or next month?"

His eyes wide, he searched her face, then the room around them. "It matters to me. I can't wait that long. We shouldn't have to wait that long."

"Before, you were willing to wait however long it took. You said we'd be casual. Whatever I wanted."

"I know, but . . . but things are different now. What if waiting one month turns into two or three? Soph, your family could always have some kind of upheaval."

"No, they won't." Defensiveness stiffened her spine.

"Now it's this, then it's Dev's wedding. There's never going to be a good time. Not anytime soon."

"My family needs me right now. Who do you think holds the pieces of this family together?"

"You do. That's exactly my point. I know better than anyone how strong you are. How hard you work to keep this family and this business together. You bend over backward when it comes to saving other people, but I'm not talking about other people. I'm not talking about your brother or your mother or work. I'm talking about you. About us. And you running and hiding from what we could have."

"When have I ever run from us?"

He gave her a stare hard enough to cut glass.

"We both decided not to tell anyone what we were doing."

"No, *you* decided, because you're scared to so much as bump the apple cart, and I agreed. Because I want to be with you."

"That's not . . ." But it was true. Twice he'd been ready to walk right up to her brothers and tell them. He'd only stopped at her request.

"I've watched you run every time you had a chance at a personal life. A shot at some happiness of your own. I don't want to be that guy."

"You're not that guy. But we can't tell them now. You have to see it's impossible."

"Waiting weeks and weeks is impossible. Because you're not just waiting. You're pulling away. You wouldn't talk to me or even make eye contact last night, and you'll barely look at me now. And you don't want to tell anyone about us for weeks? Months? What am I supposed to think?"

Tears swelled, threatening to spill. "Why does it have to be right now, though? Why can't we wait until next month?"

His gaze shot from hers, his posture stiffer as everything about him tensed. "Because we're ready. You told me how you feel. You know how I feel."

"That's not it, though." Alarms went off in her head. A lifetime of waiting for disaster to strike meant seeing the signs.

Signs she should've seen before now, but she'd been blind. Blinded by her feelings for Wright. "Wright. What are you not telling me? Why can't we wait a few weeks to tell my brothers about us?"

"Because I don't have weeks to wait." He spat out the words before stepping away.

She stared, frozen, as he scrubbed a hand over his face, his feet moving as he went nowhere. "I . . . shit. I wanted to talk to you about this last night. Or today. Before we told your brothers about us. I . . . I have these really great opportunities. For me, for us. And I'm taking them. Well, one of them. And I wanted to talk to you about them before I decided."

"What are you talking about?"

"A job offer, from one of the top restaurant groups in the country. They want me to be head chef at their new flagship location, in Asheville. I have an offer for assistant chef in Charleston too, but that's farther away and—"

"Charleston?" Her heart twisted as it raced, her vision narrowing until the only thing she saw was Wright. And he was talking about leaving her.

"I was going to tell you last night. I didn't officially accept either one yet, but I need to give them an answer sooner than a few weeks from now."

"You're leaving Honeywilde?"

"I'm not *leaving* leaving. If I take the one in Asheville, I'm maybe an hour outside of Windamere."

She shook her head, all of his extra words floating past her. "You're leaving."

"No. Soph. I'm not—"

"Don't Soph me. How long have you known you're leaving?"

"I haven't accepted yet."

"*No.* How long have you known?" It took a while to find any new job, but a chef's job took several months.

"I . . . I'm not sure. I think I started looking early spring. Maybe March."

"*March?*" She raised her voice as well, and didn't care. "And you said nothing?"

"We weren't dating then, and there for a while you weren't talking to me at all. Remember?"

"Don't give me that crap. I've talked to you plenty since then. Done a hell of a lot more than talk too. And not once in that entire time did you even think about telling me you wanted to leave Honeywilde?"

He opened and closed his mouth. Like he had any right to be indignant. "I couldn't even get you to admit you wanted to be with me until two days ago. What was I going to do? Say, 'Hey Soph, check it out. I know you might drop me like a hot rock at any second, but I have these great job opportunities in Charleston or Asheville or New York. And I was wondering, if I left Honeywilde, how you would like to commit to being my girlfriend.'"

She curled her hands into fists. "You got an offer from New York?"

"Yes. I did. And I turned it down because I don't want to lose you. Okay? I know if I go to New York, that's the end of us. And I don't want that."

"So I'm holding you back."

"God dammit, Sophie. That's what you hear when I say all of that? That's what you think?"

With blurry vision, she looked around, shrugging. She didn't know what to think anymore.

"I don't want to go to New York. This is home to me. You are where I want to be."

"Then why didn't you tell me anything about any of this?"

"Because it was too soon. You were scared of upsetting your family, skittish about being with someone. I didn't want to mess things up with you. I knew you'd freak out. Until you told me you wanted to be with me, that you were ready to be together, really together, I was scared I'd lose you."

Her voice dripped with sarcasm. "And leaving Honeywilde is the solution to not losing me?"

"No, but it sure as shit isn't the problem here either. No matter what I do, I'm not going far. This"—he jabbed his finger back and forth between them—"our problem isn't me and some new job. This is about you putting your happiness on hold, again, because your family is a wreck and you're scared. This is about you serving time as . . . as some kind of punishment or penance because you're still alive and your parents aren't."

"Screw you!" Sophie spat out the words, with tears in her eyes and her hands in fists. "Don't you dare throw that up in my face. I trusted you."

"Whoa. What's going on?"

Sophie spun, her gaze landing on Dev. "Wright is leaving Honeywilde."

Dev's face fell. "What?"

Next to her, Wright stumbled over his words. "That's not—I have some job offers. But that's not the issue here."

"Like hell it isn't." She turned on him again.

"What is going on?" Dev stepped right in the middle of their argument, his eyes tired.

"Sophie thinks I'm abandoning her. But I'm not."

He was leaving, had planned to leave for months, and hadn't said a word about it. Not when they were friends, and certainly not when they were lovers. "Then what do you call it?"

"A great opportunity. For me, for us."

A pained noise escaped her throat, clawing its way up from her heart. "How can it be an opportunity for us when you were interviewing with groups from New York and God knows where else, and you never said a word about it to me?"

"I was going to tell you. Last night. But then all this shit happened and you stopped talking to me. Again."

The pain spread, from her heart to her limbs. Everything went numb, her hearing fuzzy. She was too young for a heart attack, but not too young for a broken heart.

"Are you seriously leaving Honeywilde?" Dev asked, glancing back and forth between her and Wright, his expression growing harder by the second.

"I have a job offer in Asheville and one in Charleston. I have to let them know soon, but yes, I want to take one of them."

Dev opened his mouth and closed it. With both hands, he scrubbed his fingers through his hair. "Why didn't you tell us you're unhappy here?"

"I'm not unhappy." Wright's mouth turned down in the corners, his glow from last night completely gone. "But I've never done anything besides work here. I need to know that I can survive outside of Honeywilde, but I'm not unhappy."

"Then . . . why?" Sophie swiped a traitorous tear away. "Why would you . . . I thought you would never leave me."

"Soph." Her name was a plea. "I won't ever leave you, baby. And I would've told you all about the different offers if I didn't think talking about a future together would scare you. But you and I both know you weren't ready for all that."

"Baby?" Dev bit off the question, but they ignored him.

"I knew you might freak out, so why would I bring it up?"

"Because we were together, and I trusted you."

Dev took a step back. "Hold up, *what*?"

"Please don't use the past tense. I knew, even if I was offered a great opportunity with someone else, you weren't ready to have that kind of conversation about us. About me and you, forever."

Dev sucked in a sharp breath. "Son of a bitch." His grimace turned to a scowl as he scrubbed a rough hand over his mouth. "How long have you been messing around with my sister?"

"I'm not *messing around* with Sophie. We're dating. Or we were trying to."

A gasp dragged their attention to Roark as he skidded to a stop. He didn't say a word, but studied her face before glaring at Wright.

The difference between messing around with her and dating her seemed to be lost on Dev. "You start something up with Soph, you're both doing . . . whatever, behind my back, and now you're leaving?"

"I wanted to tell you. *I* didn't want this to be a secret."

Sophie ground her teeth together. He was not going to throw her under the bus for this. "You're all about telling the truth unless it's got to do with leaving. You want me to be open and brave, while you're being sneaky as hell about finding another job."

She was always the first to try and calm things down, have peace. Now she could see how she put her own life aside to ensure her family's happiness. But what difference did it make in the end? In the end, she still got hurt, her heart was still breaking.

Wright growled with frustration. "If I'd said I wanted to talk about us, long term, what would you have done?"

She shifted her gaze away, threading her fingers together.

"Exactly."

She worked her jaw until it hurt. He might not be wrong, but his understanding reeked of condescension. He was too reasonable, too certain and sure, thinking he knew what was best for her, all while leaving her out of this decision. Leaving her out of his life and then planning to straight up leave her, all after she'd opened up to him about her fears, about her parents, about the bizarre way her brain worked.

Sophie pointed her finger, jabbing it at him. "The other night, in the kitchen, you should've told me. Even if you were thinking about leaving, you should've opened up to me the way I opened up to you. You know how hard that was for me when . . . when we . . ."

"When what?" Dev spoke up.

"Stop it," she snapped at her brother. "This isn't about you. This is about me and Wright."

"I didn't even know there *was* a you and Wright until a few minutes ago. So excuse the hell out of me for caring."

Sophie bit off her words, more than enough anger to go around. She glared at Dev, daring him to take issue with the facts. "Well, now you know."

"No. I'm not sure I do." Dev's tone was as waspish as hers.

"Your best friend and I. Me and Wright. For weeks now, running around like you and Anna did. Maybe even more so. Happy?"

Roark muttered a curse and buried his face in his hands.

To his credit, Dev didn't even blink. "No, I'm not happy. And I'm not happy with the tone either."

"Guys, stop." Wright tried.

Dev turned on him. "And *you*. You make plans to leave Honeywilde and you not only keep it from me, but you've been seeing my sister, and you kept it from her too?"

"Wright is leaving Honeywilde?" Roark echoed.

Wright threw his hands out wide before balling them into fists. "Jesus. What is with you people? I wasn't sure I was going anywhere until recently."

After fighting as hard as she did for family peace, and seeing peace still proving to be elusive, Sophie lit a match and threw it. "And why bother telling me the truth when all we were doing was sleeping together?"

Wright grimaced and closed his eyes.

With a growl, Dev backed away from them and paced toward the windows.

She no longer cared about the kind of hellfire her comments would draw. Maybe she wasn't being fair, maybe she was being the bratty little sister, but she felt torn open. Raw.

She'd trusted Wright. She'd given him her heart. And he'd lied. He was leaving, same as everyone else, and he'd lied about it.

Betrayal twisted an ugly knot inside her. Everything that'd started to heal lay frayed and exposed. Hurt.

Everyone else could hurt right along with her. She was done trying to take their pain away while quietly drowning in her own.

"I was going to tell you." Wright kept his voice low.

"When? Whenever it suited you? We've been inseparable for over a week now. And in none of that time you thought it might be something to bring up?"

"I didn't know how you'd take it. How you'd react. It'd be the perfect excuse to throw me away. Why would I tell you?"

"Because it's you," she yelled. "And you keep insisting I mean so much to you. But when someone means something to you, you include them. Even before you make a decision, you respect them enough to let them in. I told you about how all of this, with my family and the inn, how it scared me. I told you how much I worry about my family. Their happiness. I trusted you and cared about you, and that's why I wanted you to know. And look what happened. Everything I was afraid of has happened."

"Nothing has fallen apart."

"Everything has fallen apart. It's over." She took another step away, though she had nowhere to go.

"So that's it, then? I mess up and you push me away. This is the perfect excuse for you to cut me out of your life?"

She stopped, pinning him with a look she could only hope hurt half as much as his words.

Dev stepped in between them to face Wright. "Stop talking. You are not helping this situation. And you're my friend, but I swear to God, not another word. Not now."

This was when Sophie would normally jump in. Tell everyone to calm down and not say or do anything in anger and haste.

But she couldn't see reason. Not with her world falling down around her.

Wright was leaving and he'd lied. Resentment and bitterness were back in Dev's eyes. And Roark was cold and stoic as he'd ever been.

They were all right back where they were before.

She had to get away from them, from Wright, but her feet were nailed to the floor. She couldn't move, even though the sight of him stabbed at her heart.

She'd thought they had a future. For the first time, she'd reached a place where she was ready.

Whatever she thought they had, it was a figment. Something she'd constructed out of her desperation not to be alone. But beyond the sex and flirting and the laughs, they didn't exist. They didn't have what Dev and Anna had, or Roark and Madison.

There was no Sophie and Wright, and maybe there never had been.

Staying in that lobby wasn't an option. If she didn't get out of there, she was going to break down, and she refused.

Dev moved directly in front of Wright, blocking her view.

It was her only chance.

As the two of them stared each other down, she ran.

Out of the lobby, and out the front door. Out of Honeywilde and straight to her car. The tires of her car screamed as she sped from the parking lot with no destination in mind.

It didn't matter where she went, as long as she was the one leaving.

Chapter 24

Wright didn't wait for anyone else to say another word. He'd heard all he could, and the last thing he wanted right now was another opinion about how badly he'd messed up.

"Dev." He turned to his best friend, knowing if they said anything, they'd regret everything. "Don't follow me." He tromped toward the kitchen, daring anyone to stop him.

Cooking always helped, whether he was angry or upset, frustrated or fighting mad. He needed to calm the hell down and figure out how to make this right.

Regardless of how many daggers were being stared into the back of his head.

Marco stared in silence as Wright shoved on his white jacket with a muttered curse. The jacket wasn't necessary, but to hell with it. The jacket was comfortable. A part of him. So much of this place was a part of him, including Sophie.

How could she accuse him of cutting her out his decision? She was the entire decision. She was all he'd considered for the last few weeks.

He knew what was right for his career, he knew what he wanted—what he needed—for himself, but she was the caveat to his plan.

If it weren't for her, he'd leave Honeywilde and go . . . wherever. Anywhere. And probably with the Bradleys' blessings.

Dev might be pissed for a little while, but he'd get over it. Guys like them didn't hold grudges forever. They were best friends, and a career move wouldn't change that.

Sophie, though . . .

He wasn't going to up and leave her and move hundreds of miles away.

And Dev would get over him taking a new job, but sleeping with his sister?

Wright slammed a pan down on the eye of the stove. They were doing so much more than sleeping together. For them, it was never just about the sex.

The physical chemistry, the way they both caught fire when they touched, that was all incredible, but it was a bonus. Cream and a cherry on top of the amazing bond they'd built for years.

Wright knew what they had; Sophie knew too. She had to know. Even her brothers must realize. He would never hook up with her without the best intentions.

He cracked an egg with a heavy hand, bits of shell falling into the bowl. "Dammit."

"Let me." Marco took the bowl from him and cracked the eggs.

He loved Sophie. He'd realized he loved her all along.

As far back as he could remember, she was the one. Why was it so hard for her to understand?

She was the one who made him laugh, no matter his mood. She hadn't put up with his boyish arrogance years ago, and she certainly didn't tolerate it now. Sophie was the first one to call bullshit if he dished any out and, normally, the last one to judge him if he was having a bad day.

He loved when she was the last person he spoke to at night, but he loved waking up beside her even more.

Now it'd all gone to shit.

The chance he'd been given, to convince her forever wasn't a long time with the right person, blown apart.

Marco handed him the bowl of eggs to whisk.

She kept insisting it was because he was leaving. Leaving her like so many people who claimed to love her had done before, and because he hadn't trusted her to handle the truth.

Early on, when he'd tried to move their relationship into a more committed category, she'd balked. Shut him down cold, saying they should stop seeing one another.

So it wasn't like he didn't have proof that's how she operated.

He'd played his cards close because he knew her. All the guys she'd burned through over the years, they all met the same demise for basically the same reason. Sophie couldn't hate him for knowing her MO.

But he did trust her.

He had faith in her when it came to everything. He'd put his life in Sophie's hands if it were to ever come to that.

With a thud, he dropped the mixing bowl onto the prep table.

But believing she could handle commitment? The weight of how much he wanted her forever and always?

He hadn't trusted her with that. When it came to trusting she was strong enough to handle the truth, he'd turned coward.

Her track record of leaving guys shouldn't matter. Because what they had wasn't anything like what she had with those other guys.

They wouldn't be together if it was, and both of them knew that.

What they had was special, and he'd told himself that repeatedly, for the last two weeks.

So why hadn't he trusted what they had to survive the truth?

As a friend, maybe he should've told Dev he was restless, but Dev wasn't just his best friend. He was Wright's employer.

To some degree, maybe that made it more vital he speak up. Even if he had, though, they couldn't help. No matter how much Dev and Roark and even Sophie believed in him, they couldn't advance his career, and he didn't expect them to.

It was not their job to fulfill his dream. It was his.

But he hadn't prepared for that dream to include Sophie.

Being with her had always been some far-off, unrealistic thing. Beyond a dream. Make-believe.

Having her, and that dream, in his hands had made him stupid.

He'd gotten caught up in having something he never thought possible. So worried about losing her and so busy protecting her that he didn't realize the damage he'd do by not trusting her.

He'd tried to be so careful, but he was careless with the one heart he *knew* needed the most care.

"Dammit." He grabbed the skillet off the burner of the stove.

Next to him, Marco cleared his throat. "Maybe I should handle breakfast this morning."

Wright had burned his dish. Again.

Worse this time. He couldn't focus any better after losing Sophie than he could when she was within reach.

He muttered another curse and let his head fall back, staring blankly at the ceiling. Maybe he needed some fresh air.

If he stayed in the kitchen, he might burn the whole place down.

"I think you're right, Marco. You take over for now." He saw nothing as he hit the swinging door and left the restaurant.

Sophie had driven off, clearly upset.

She was out there, somewhere, her world torn apart, like she'd feared—and all he'd done was make it worse.

He'd done a lot of talking about being there for her, but that wasn't how he'd acted. He'd made a bad situation worse and he didn't have the first clue how to fix any of it.

If she wouldn't listen to him, wouldn't even look at him, how could he make things right?

The world didn't come into focus until he was halfway across the great room.

"Wright. Wright!"

From one of the reading nooks, Trevor waved, flagging him down.

Behind Trev, he caught a glimpse of Sue Bradley.

"Hell no." Wright kept walking. He was in no mood or position to deal with them right now.

"Wait." Trevor followed, his footsteps heavy and quick. "Would you stop for a second?"

He jerked to a halt and turned on the youngest of the Bradley clan. "I'm not getting involved in whatever is going on over there. I've done enough. Believe me. Matter of fact, knowing this place, I'm sure you've already heard."

"I already knew about you and Sophie, remember? Dev and Roark are in his office right now, arguing about you and everything else, but . . . you haven't done anything that can't be fixed."

Wright's face twisted. Since when had Trev become the source of family positivity? "You're wrong. I screwed things up with Sophie and her other brothers, and she definitely has." He jabbed a finger toward Sue.

"You're wrong. I've seen how you and Sophie are together. I've heard her talk about you. You can make things right if you try."

"Did your brothers tell you I'm leaving Honeywilde?"

"Yep."

"And that I didn't tell Sophie."

Trev nodded.

"Then how the hell do I make that right?"

"I don't know. But I'm sure there's a way."

A rough exhale was dragged from his lungs. "Really? Because I'm not. I don't think I can do anything but make matters worse, and I certainly can't help Sue Bradley's cause."

Trevor gently pushed his hand down. "I'm not asking you to help her cause. She wanted to say hello to you while I . . . I don't even know yet. I have to go talk to Roark and Dev. Try to get them to stop being angry long enough to hear me."

"They have every right to be angry."

"They do. But they don't have to be."

Wright had seen the effects of Sue and Robert Bradley's marriage, the instability that bred insecurity in every single one of their children. When it came to their mother, how were they supposed to feel anything but hurt and anger?

He couldn't read Sue's mind—see if she really was simply here to make amends—but if that was the point of the visit, everyone stalking around in sullen silences wouldn't help matters. Perhaps, if nothing else, talking to her would give him something to tell Sophie. Some reason for her to listen to him for at least a moment. It was a last resort, but when it came to getting her back, he wasn't above anything.

"Five minutes," he told Trevor. "I'll listen for five minutes, but I am not getting involved."

He followed Trev to the nook and remained standing. This wouldn't take long.

Sue stood as well. "So. You and Sophie?" she smiled.

He scowled at the youngest Bradley. "Trevor has a big mouth."

"Trevor talking too much is better than when he wasn't talking at all."

Wright remembered that phase. A time when Trevor had grown so distant and quiet, he'd all but disappeared into the woodwork.

"But he wasn't the one who told me. No one had to tell me. I saw it in the way you two looked at each other last night. The way you were together. And I'm glad of it. You always did get on well, and Sophie would thrive with someone like you. Stable and strong."

Wrong. "I'm leaving Honeywilde. Kinda like you did."

Her mouth turned down.

"Sorry. That was rude. But I'm pretty sure Sophie hates me right now, so I'm running low on politeness. I screwed up. Didn't tell her about leaving, and you show up and stir up a bunch of crap—sorry, but it's true—and now she's gone."

"Gone? Gone where?"

"Hell if I know. Away from me. Away from you." He needed to find her, but he couldn't go after her with more excuses. He needed something better than *I'm sorry.*

Sue studied her hands, clasped in front her. "Her skittishness is my fault, and Robert's. Don't blame her. She wants stability, someone to be close who she can count on. Always has. But it frightens her more than anything, and that . . ." She shared a look with Trevor. "That has a lot to do with us."

Yes, it did. Wright planted his hands at his waist. "Why did you come here?"

Self-deprecation laced her small smile. "To talk to the kids. That's all. Tell them I'm proud of them. Let Devlin know how thrilled I am to hear he's getting married. Proud of Roark, and all of you, for doing what I never could. And that I … I'm sorry."

Wright studied the woman before him. Divorced and worn down, but still standing. "Yeah, well, you should be sorry." Not the most gracious response of life, but when it came to Sophie, and people who hurt her, he had little grace to offer.

Well . . . Shit.

He'd hurt her. As much as Sue, he'd betrayed her vulnerability, her trust.

With a frustrated groan he scrubbed at his face. "That's not . . . I . . . You're not the only one who should be sorry."

She didn't say anything; neither did Trevor, but she nodded, solemn.

"Sophie struggles with you leaving," Wright told her. "Every day. Though I don't think people realize the same way they do with Dev, because she does such a great job of covering. Coping with it. Hiding."

"And because she's strong." Sue smiled. "She doesn't always know it, but she is."

Sophie was strong. Stronger than anyone gave her credit for, including him.

Wright locked his jaw. Of all the people in her life, he recognized her strength beneath the insecurities. Beneath the fears. But when it came down to it, he hadn't trusted her to be strong enough. Hadn't trusted her to hear about his opportunities, to talk about the future.

She'd run from every guy in the past, but that hadn't meant she would run from him. Not once they'd finally gotten close. Not if he talked to her and believed in her. Stood by her through her fears.

Then, when he'd gotten caught lying, all he'd done was make excuses.

Here he was, thinking he needed to go to her with something more than an apology, when he hadn't ever apologized in the first place.

Sue sighed, garnering his attention. "A couple of years ago, I started talking to someone. A doctor. She helped me...see things I never could. Got me started on medicine that'd help me. I hated Robert when I started treatment, but my doctor kept telling me it wasn't him I really hated. And she told me I needed to get right with my kids. And to do that, I need Sophie here."

Sophie.

Her absence was a sharp pain that wouldn't go away.

Sue Bradley wasn't the only one who needed to make things right with Sophie.

"I have to go." The words spilled out. "I have to go find her."

Sue nodded, her gaze finding Trevor. "I'll wait. I'm not going anywhere until I apologize."

Apologize.

Exactly what he needed to do. Rather than coming up with excuses and defending himself out of pride and purpose, he needed to tell Sophie he was sorry. He'd been so convinced he needed to go to her with something more than *I'm sorry*, but really, that was precisely what he needed to do. Apologize for not trusting that she was strong enough. For not remembering that the two of them were different than her other relationships.

He shook his head. How was he supposed to convince Sophie that he meant well, but he was sorry, and he'd never make the same mistake again? That he'd never lie to her under the guise of protecting her, and he'd trust her and her strength from here on out. For as long as she'd let him. This went beyond a failed recipe. This was the woman he loved.

"That's it." An idea began to bloom, and he refused to go to her empty handed.

He hurried back to the kitchen, intent on one item before he left. And this time, he wasn't going to burn anything.

As he mixed, he tried texting Sophie. As he waited, he texted again. Ten minutes later, the swinging doors opened, and he turned, hoping to find Sophie.

"Can we, um . . . I need to talk to you for a minute." Dev scrubbed a hand over his mouth.

Dread made his stomach turn, but he forced himself to agree.

Dev held himself very still and stiff. Slowly, he inhaled before looking him in the eyes. "This thing, with our mother, it's going to drag on for days. You know that, right?"

Wright managed to nod while Marco acted like he was preoccupied by French toast.

"I'm not happy about any of this, but Roark said I should at least talk to *you*. I . . . I'm not mad about you and Sophie being . . . you know, doing what you're doing."

"Yes, you are."

"Yes, I am." His body sagged as he dragged a hand through his hair. He took a few steps closer toward Wright, but his posture was less defensive. "Maybe I shouldn't be. I don't know. I don't know what the hell is going on anymore, but I am mad. You're my best friend! That's my sister, and that's not even what bothers me most. I mean . . . I know you two have always been close or whatever. And it's not beyond the stretch of reason that you'd be attracted to one another and—" He threw his hands up and shook his head. "Okay, you know what? I can't talk about this because it's weirding me out. But I guess . . . I guess I get it? It's not insane that the two of you would, you know, want to be together. That's what I'm trying to say."

The breath Wright had been holding left on a whoosh.

"*But* what is insane is you lied. Not only to me, but everyone. Lied that you guys were seeing each other and then lied about the fact you're leaving."

Marco turned from the stove top and Wright opened his mouth to argue, to defend his actions again. Except he'd run out of reasons and excuses. He needed to take a note from the Bradleys and own up to his mistakes.

All of them.

"I know, Dev. You're right. I don't have anything else to say except you're absolutely correct. And I'm sorry. I . . . I was so sure I was handling everything the right way. So focused on . . ." *Making your sister mine.*

Yeah, maybe he'd leave that part out for now.

"On doing what I thought was right that I didn't stop to think I could be wrong. I'm sorry we didn't tell you. I'm sorry I didn't talk to you about leaving. For all of it."

He should've told Sophie all of it too. Wanting more for his career, needing to spread his wings beyond Honeywilde. He should've shown her that he believed she was strong enough instead of saying it.

"That's my little sister. You know how much I love her. And if you hurt her, best friend or not, I will kick your ass."

"I don't want to hurt her. That's the last thing I want to do."

"Then you have to fix this."

Wright shook his head, not sure he heard Dev correctly.

"Don't look at me like that. I'm not going to forbid y'all being together. It's not the 1800s. It'll be weird for a while, but I want my sister to be happy. I want you to be happy. Right now, neither of you are happy because you screwed up and she's scared."

"I know. I did a top-notch job of ruining everything."

Dev gave him a hard stare. "Wright, I've seen you in the kitchen, taking a disaster and turning it into a delicacy."

Speaking of . . . he took a look inside the oven.

"Do you love my sister?" Dev asked from behind him.

Wright kept his eyes on the oven as he answered. "So much it hurts."

When he turned, Dev's smile was small, a fraction of what he was capable of, but joy still seeped through. "Then you better find her."

That was exactly what he intended to do.

Chapter 25

Sophie kept driving, no idea where she was going.

Down the mountain, around the turns too fast, her brakes squealing on one particularly sharp bend.

Her heart kicked, adrenaline rushing like live wires along her limbs.

She skidded to a stop on the side of the road and threw the car into park.

"No." With her fingers dug into her hair, she squeezed her eyes shut. She was not dying on some road. Not because she was upset, not for him, not for anything.

All she wanted was to get away, but if she didn't pull it together she'd be the cause of the disaster she feared so much.

"I'm not going let something awful happen," she told her parents.

No, their photograph wasn't anywhere near her, but she saw them in her mind as clearly as any picture.

"I . . . I don't know what to do."

She could avoid crashing her car, for a start.

She hadn't been able to do anything to save her folks, but she could at least look out for herself.

"I know." Sophie nodded, eyes still shut. Flying off the handle never ended well for her, no matter how often she tried. "I'll calm down. It's just . . ."

Wright was leaving her.

He swore he wasn't, but his argument was semantics. Tiny details. All of which he'd kept from her.

How could he keep that from her after what they'd shared?

Sophie opened her eyes. She needed to get farther away from him, but not at risk of life and limb.

The rest of the way down the mountain, she stayed under the limit. Once she reached the bottom, she headed east.

She drove until she ended up on the long driveway that led to Chateau Jolie.

Why she chose here was a muddied mixture of needing to be away from it all, but if she was honest, it was a call back to a time and place she'd been so certain and sure.

Here, she'd been content with Wright. That day, she let happiness in and there wasn't a sign of the outside world. He'd planned the whole afternoon for them

For her.

Because he knew they wouldn't have that time and opportunity otherwise.

Sophie's hands began to shake, her face and limbs going fiery hot, her ears ringing.

By the time she parked in the small lot, her stomach was in such knots, she opened the door, thinking she might get sick.

She and Wright had a good thing, and it'd not only all gone to hell in a handbasket, but it had done so *in front* of her entire family.

With a groan, she put her feet on the ground and lowered her head, rocking back and forth a bit.

Maybe it was all a dream.

She'd nurtured all these emotions and expectations, putting so much meaning into what she and Wright had, until she made herself believe it was real, even if it wasn't—maybe she'd made up the whole argument they'd had right in front of her family. Spilling the truth about what they'd been up to.

No sane person would really do that, blurting out that their chef and friend wasn't only walking out on them but had been sleeping with their sister for weeks now.

A wave of vertigo washed over her, and she sat back, pinching her eyes closed.

But she'd done exactly that. And then she ran.

Why not make a bad situation worse, right? Take something from horrible—like her mother showing up out of nowhere and finding out Wright might leave Honeywilde—and ramp the whole thing up to catastrophic by having their meltdown in front of everyone.

"Way to go." She scrubbed her hands over her face.

A cough made her jump.

"Sophie?" Brooke, manager and one of the owners of the Chateau, stood by her car, concern hardening her regal features.

"Yeah." Sophie tried to play it casual, though she probably looked a mess. "Hey. How's it going?"

"It's . . ." Brooke cocked her head to the side, her brow wrinkled. "It's going all right, I guess. I saw you pull in as I was walking up from the vineyard. Looked like you were about to—

Are you sick? Is there anything I can get you?"

"Oh . . . um, no. I'm fine." She swiped at her face, her lips trembling. "Just, y'know, getting some fresh air."

Brooke squinted harder. She wasn't buying it. "Maybe you should get out of that hot car then?"

If she stood up right now, her legs might not hold her.

Physically, she was fine. Her heart was the only thing hurting, but her legs were weak. Pretending she was okay was enough work while sitting down. Forget having to stand up and move around like her happiness wasn't blown to pieces.

"No, I'm okay. I . . ." *Need a place to hide from my life and losing the man I thought I loved.*

Brooke studied her, and she was not going away.

It dawned on Sophie that Brooke had sisters. Several sisters.

What were the chances she'd faced this scenario before? And knew Sophie was lying to save face.

They could stay here, like this, for who knew how long, or she could fess up and tell Brooke why she'd randomly shown up at her chateau.

Lies had not been her friend today, and she didn't want to participate in more.

Sophie lifted her face toward Brooke but closed her eyes with a sigh. "Family drama at Honeywilde. I had to get the hell out of there and have a moment alone. So here I am. At your place. At the competition's, because I couldn't stand to be around my family one more minute."

Brook laughed and Sophie opened her eyes.

"Sorry." Brooke covered her mouth, the laughter fading. "I'm not laughing at you. But I happen to know exactly what you mean. I know all too well."

Sophie let her shoulders slump.

"Why don't you come inside? It's cooler. I'll make some lemonade."

She plastered on a smile. "No. Thank you, though. I just need a moment."

Brooke frowned, and still didn't leave. "Is there someone I can call for you? If not family, then a friend?"

A friend was the reason she was in this state. "I don't want to talk to a friend right now."

She nodded with a hum of consideration. "Well . . ." Hands on her hips, Brooke studied the parking lot. "I'm not going to leave you out here, and that's final. You can come inside the competition's place and at least let me get you some lemonade or coffee or something."

"I don't—"

"It's not happenin', Red." Brooke cut her off. "You're not staying out here to wallow in this heat."

Sophie gaped at the sophisticated woman before her; all perfect hair and pearl earrings, and she'd called Sophie "Red" with a look like she was about to go find a hickory stick.

A laugh burst from Sophie's lips. "You do have sisters, huh?"

Brooke's stubborn stare wasn't budging. "Two of them. Younger. Now, are you coming inside or do I have to drag you?"

With a shake of her head, Sophie pushed herself from the driver's seat. "No ma'am. I'll come inside."

"Wonderful." And like that, the manager of Jolie morphed back into the picture of regal femininity. She led the way into the chateau's main floor. "I hope you understand. I can't, in good conscience, leave you out there, looking so upset."

"Don't sugarcoat it. I look awful."

"Okay, fine, you look a mess. Woman to woman, as someone who's been there, I'm not going to let you melt in this miserable heat, looking like hell."

The chateau was blissfully cool, the inside lit with only natural light and a couple of lamps near reception.

"Would you like lemonade or coffee? Or iced tea?"

Her throat was raw from crying the night before and all the arguing today. "Coffee sounds nice." She sat in one of the wingback chairs near a window while Brooke wandered away.

Eventually the scent of fresh brewed coffee, along with the sound of someone bustling in the kitchen, warmed her nerves.

Until she thought about kitchens and the person who worked in one.

"Coffee was a bad idea."

"What's that?" Brooke joined her with a serving tray and sat it on a small ottoman between them.

"Nothing."

Brooke studied her, but didn't push. "If you say so. Here, have some." The coffee at Jolie was served in elegant white cups with a saucer and French press. "I brought some pastries from this morning too. Pain au chocolat, in case you're hungry."

She couldn't even think of food, not even in the form of a plate of chocolate-filled pastry.

"Wow, things must be bad if you can resist these." Brooke plucked one from the tray.

"I'm really sorry about this. I don't mean to be a bother."

"Oh please. This is not a bother. A bother is the time I was woken up in the wee hours of the morning because my littlest sister, Reagan, found out her fiancé was running around with the new female bartender at the Tavern."

"The one who had the sleeve of tattoos?"

"That's the one."

"She hasn't worked there in months."

"Yeah well, you don't mess with my baby sister. Don't hear much about the ex-fiancé these days either." Brooke cocked an eyebrow as she sipped her coffee, and Sophie felt a tinge of hero worship already.

They sat quietly for a while, veritable strangers, sipping coffee as though they were in a café.

Finally, Brooke put her coffee down and reached for a napkin. "So. Do you want to talk about it, or are we going to sit here in silence until you check in or go home? I'm fine either way, but I have tons of paperwork waiting on me, and this might go faster if you tell me what's wrong."

Checking in would be easier than going back to face her family.

"I'll check in, but I don't want to talk."

"Fair enough." Brooke ate more of her croissant, but the silence didn't draw out for long this time. "You know, your Honeywilde might have the market on biscuits, but we make the best pastries. No offense to your chef."

Sophie cringed, putting her coffee down.

"Okay, so it *is* about the cute chef you rolled in here with the other day."

"We didn't *roll* in here."

Brooke's laugh was completely incongruous with her appearance. A great big boom of a laugh. "You totally rolled in here." Her smile was brilliant; perfect white teeth, even her red lipstick was still perfect. "And then you rolled upstairs," she muttered.

Sophie hid her face in her hands.

"Now, now. I'm not saying it to pick at you. I'm stating facts. You two were obviously . . . you know." Brooke lined her two pointer fingers up, side by side. "Do you even remember the cellar tour or the wine? I recall showing you some top-notch selections, while you only had eyes for each other."

"We weren't that obvious."

Brooke sat back and ate her pastry, one dark eyebrow arched again.

"Were we really that obvious?"

"Yep."

Sophie rolled her eyes. Of course they were. She was so smitten. Wright, the Prince Charming of her youth, had planned a special day for her. He'd meant what he said about doing something special for them.

Her lip trembled against her coffee cup, and she set the cup down before her hands did the same.

"We don't have to talk about him if it upsets you that much."

"No, no. It's not . . ." Not what? She didn't have another reasonable explanation for being here, for her reaction to talking about him.

Her heart was broken, and she could no longer deny it.

"Our chef—Wright, the guy I was here with—he's leaving."

Brooke's dark eyes went wide, her expressive eyebrows raised. "No way. He's been with you guys forever."

"He's been looking to leave Honeywilde for a while, and now he is. But he didn't tell me until today and we've been . . . you know." Losing him was a hit to the inn, but nothing compared to the damage to her heart.

Whether the depth of their connection was something she'd created in her mind or a very real and vital thing that he felt as much as her, he was leaving, and ripping her heart in two.

Even after that night he'd tried to kiss her and they hadn't spoken for weeks, she'd gone right back to believing the best of him. She thought he was different; needed him to be different.

She loved him, and when you loved someone, they could easily hurt you. Life had taught her that years ago, and still she'd let him in.

She'd allowed all of this to happen.

Wright's words came back to her, what he'd said about using his leaving as another reason to back away. Even before she knew he was leaving, she was backing away.

She began backing off as soon as her mother returned.

All it'd taken was one hint of a problem, and she was stepping back. Then, when the going really got tough, what had she done?

Sophie looked around the cozy lobby of her family's competition.

She ran away.

Wright was wrong for lying to her, but he wasn't wrong about her fear.

They'd been too close, happiness in her grasp, and she'd thrown it back at Wright and run.

She didn't hate Wright for wanting more. Hate wasn't something she did, and if he wanted to do something else with his life, that was his choice.

But she was furious with him for keeping this from her.

"Oh." Brooke's voice was solemn, her eyes filled with understanding. "It's like that."

Sophie swiped at her eyes. "Like what?"

"I've seen that look before. I've even worn that look. He broke your heart. We start talking about him, even mention the name Wright, and your whole face crumples. There it went again."

Sophie tried to shrug off her emotions, but it was too late. Brooke saw.

She scooted to the end of her seat and leaned forward. "Hey. Does he know how you feel? This chef of yours?"

"Yes. As does everyone else now. Including my brother, Wright's best friend. They didn't know until today. We kind of . . . hid it from them."

Brooke sucked a breath in between her teeth.

"Exactly." Sophie nodded. "And Sue Bradley showed up last night."

"*You're kidding?* You're not kidding."

Sophie shook her head.

"Damn. You really have had a rough go of it. Why were y'all

keeping the . . ." She lined her fingers up side by side again. "From your brothers."

"Because . . ." Because she'd wanted to.

Because even if her family accepted that she wanted to be with Dev's best friend, and even if they eventually got over the paradigm shift of who they were to each other and everyone else, it'd still be an issue at first.

There would be problems and disagreement, scrutiny, confrontation and heated discussions. And she hated all of that.

For years she'd fought the darker side of relationships, trying like hell to keep her pieced-together family in the light. Something as unexpected or even slightly controversial as her and Wright would push the Bradleys into the gray area, after they all finally had that elusive peace and prosperity they'd lacked forever.

So she'd hidden who she was and what she really wanted from her family. She'd lied to them because she didn't think they could deal with the truth.

Sophie let her head fall back on the fancy lobby chair.

"Shit." She borrowed Wright's favorite word when he was beating himself up.

What hurt her so much and made her so damn mad at Wright was the *exact* same thing she'd done to her family.

She'd been so certain she was doing the right thing. So sure of herself, insisting she was protecting her brothers by keeping the truth from them. But she was only protecting herself. Afraid to disturb the peace because *she* longed for it. Scared of losing the bit of happiness she'd finally found.

Wright claimed he hadn't told her about the job opportunities because he was afraid she couldn't handle it. Maybe that was partially true, but he was protecting himself too. He was afraid of losing her.

Sophie rolled her head to the side to find Brooke studying her. The woman's piercing gaze unnerved her, but she confessed anyway. "I think maybe I screwed up too."

Brooke sipped her coffee, quiet a moment before nodding. "Probably. When it comes to matters of the heart, in my ill-fated experience, it often takes two to screw things up."

With a shaky sigh, Sophie studied the ornate painted ceiling of the chateau's lobby. Tiny woodland creatures stared down, and a deer stood in judgment of her. She'd been harsh when it came to judging Wright.

He thought he was doing the right thing, not telling her about leaving Honeywilde, the same way she'd thought she was wise to keep their relationship a secret.

They were both wrong. But now what?

She wanted someone to hold her, tell her everything would be okay. That person for her was now Wright. He was back at Honeywilde, where she'd left him, telling him they were over.

Brooke stood and held out her hand. "That's enough. Stop rolling this around in your head or you'll drive yourself mad. Trust me. Let's get you checked in. You can stay here tonight, on the house. Wash up, take a nap. Whatever. And then come back down later and have dinner with me. Take some time away from Honeywilde to get your thoughts together."

Sophie nodded as she got to her feet.

"You never know. When the dust settles on all this, things might not be as bad as you think."

Chapter 26

For hours he drove around, looking for Sophie.

He checked the Tavern, the diner she loved, every yurt and empty cabin at Honeywilde—since hiding out in there was sometimes a thing.

By evening, he was desperate and checking all of the nearest lookout points along the Blue Ridge Parkway when his phone went off.

He scrambled, praying the call was from Sophie.

Instead, Dev's name showed up.

"I need you to call this number," Dev said before he could even get out the word "hello." "Ask for Brooke, the manager of Chateau Jolie. She said she'd only talk to you."

As soon as Dev mentioned Brooke, Wright knew. Sophie had gone to Jolie.

He repeated the number back to Dev and hung up, still repeating it in his mind as he dialed.

Brooke answered.

"This is Wright. Wright McAdams. Devlin Bradley told me to call you."

"I have something here. Call it a lost and found. Are you looking for someone?"

"Thank God." He rested his forehead against the steering wheel, the weight on his shoulders not gone but a few pounds lighter. "Is Sophie okay? I've looked everywhere."

"Good answer. Because if you haven't been searching for her, I was going to tell you to take a flying leap. She's a sweet girl."

"I know she is. Is she okay?"

"Physically, she's fine. But no, she is not okay. You lied to her."

Wright sat upright at Brooke's tone. "I know I did, and I'm sorry."

"Did you tell her that?"

He nibbled at his bottom lip. No, he hadn't. Because he'd been too busy trying to defend his behavior.

"Mmm-hmm."

"I want to tell her now. I want to see her and say I'm sorry. I will never do anything to hurt her again and—"

"That'll do, that'll do." Brooke stopped him. "And don't quote me on this, but I think she has some things she'd like to say to you too. You can come on over *if* you're going to make things right."

"I am," he promised. He even had gifts. "I'll be right there."

When he made it to the Chateau, he hurried down the hall, hands full, to their special room. He needed to apologize, beg forgiveness, whatever he had to do to keep Sophie in his life.

First, he'd give her his gift, then let her speak, apologize, and grovel if he needed to. Anything to make it right.

After setting his bag down, he knocked twice. Finally, the safety lock slid back, the door slowly opening.

Sophie stood in the doorway, rumpled and wrinkly, pillow lines on her face. She was beautiful. The most gorgeous sight he'd ever seen.

"I was wrong. I should've told you about the jobs in Charleston and Asheville." His plan from earlier went out the window; everything he wanted to say came spewing out instead. "I should've told you when we were here together. Or the next day. Or any day. I'm sorry I didn't. I don't want to go anywhere if it means losing you."

Sophie's mouth opened and closed, soundless. She stepped back and let him into the room.

Once inside, they hovered in the doorway.

"How did you know I was here?"

He wanted to reach for her so badly his fingers twitched with the need. "I should've known, but this time, I couldn't predict you. Brooke called the inn."

Sophie rubbed her eyes. "She did?"

"I think she's looking out for you. I've been trying to find you all day. Everyone is worried."

Her face fell. "How are my brothers?"

"Actually, they're better than you might expect."

The way her nose scrunched up tore at his heart. "Really?"

"Really. And I spoke with Dev."

Her eyes went round. "Oh."

Wright held his arm out toward the end of the bed. They could at least sit.

Wariness in her gaze, Sophie sat stiffly on the edge.

He eased down beside her. "He's mad that we lied, but he said . . . well, he wants us to be happy, and if that means being together, he'll be okay with that."

"But your happiness means leaving Honeywilde."

"Not if it means losing you. I can stay and be happy."

She was shaking her head before he could finish the sentence. "No more lying. I know that's not really what you want, and I don't want you to stay at Honeywilde if your dream is to try something new."

"What I want is you. I want both. Yes, I want to work somewhere else, somewhere new and challenging, but more than anything, I want to be with you. I want to find a way for us to be together, even if we aren't working side by side. And I should've told you exactly that."

She worried her bottom lip between her teeth.

"I want you, Sophie. There's no one else for me, and that's why I should've told you about New York and Charleston and Asheville. I shouldn't have tried to protect you or hide the fact I was leaving. I should've known you could handle the truth, because it's us."

She dropped her gaze, fidgeting with a thread on the comforter. "I didn't exactly give you cause to think I could handle it. Not with my track record. Wright, I . . . I'm sorry too."

He opened his mouth to stop her, but she didn't allow it. "No, I was wrong. And I'm sorry. You were right about the fight not only being about you leaving. With my mom back and you and me being so close, I got scared. The first hurdle we faced and I push you away. I thought, in the middle of all that going on . . . I don't know. I thought I'd lose you if we told my family right then. There was already so much hurt and anger, and it'd mean losing you."

"But that's just it." With his hands out, he turned toward her. "That's what I realized when I was talking to your mom."

Her chin jerked up. "You talked to my mom?"

"Yeah. And I realized as we were talking, I went through the last two weeks reminding myself, constantly telling myself that you and I would work because we were *different*. I know how things were with those other guys, but I also knew this was me and you. What we have is better than all that. We can weather the turmoil. We don't need everything to be perfect and peaceful in order to survive. Even though you're scared, even if everyone else is a mess, we can still be okay. I'm not going to lose you, you understand? Because what we have is different. It's—"

"Special." A sad smile curled her lips.

"Exactly." With a gruff sigh, he looked away. "And I ruined everything because I forgot that. Believing we couldn't survive me leaving Honeywilde or that you couldn't handle the truth instead of giving you the chance to decide. Giving us the chance to work it out. I should've trusted you."

Pushing herself up, she leaned into his field of vision, the same way he'd done to her, plenty of times. "You should've, but it's kind of understandable why you didn't. You know how I get, but yeah, I wish I'd known about you wanting to leave. I don't know for sure if I would've been able to handle that kind of information, or you wanting to talk about the future, but with you ..." She barely lifted one shoulder. "I feel like with you, I could. With you, sometimes I think anything is possible. Like I might even be able to hold on to happiness."

He knew the perfect opening when he saw it.

"There's only one way to find out." Wright took her hand in his. He didn't care if it was him shaking or her. Probably both of them. "Soph, I love you. I was wrong for not telling you days ago. I should've told you the last time we were here because that's when I felt it. I knew when I was in this room with you. You were getting dressed and looking at me like I was nuts for lying there, staring at you."

A laugh escaped her at the memory.

"I knew then, you're the one. I want to be with you more than I want anything else in this world. If I could go back in time, I would tell past me to get his head out of his ass because you're the best thing that will ever happen to me. I'd tell him to sit down with you, and even though it might scare you and even though you might run, I should talk about the future and how much I want you in mine. Let you decide. Trust you to be strong enough to make that decision."

Her bottom lip trembled as she smiled.

"But I'm doing that now because I can't time travel."

She bit her lip against the ghost of a smile.

"I want to do something beyond being head chef at Honeywilde *and* I want to be with you. For as long as we have left on this earth. I've wasted way too much time debating and fighting and keeping the truth from people, including you. So there it is. What happens next is up to you, but I love you, Sophie. I always have."

He'd known her forever, but Sophie still managed to shock the shit out of him on occasion.

When she threw her arms around him, almost knocking him back on the bed, she did exactly that.

Wright wrapped his arms around her and buried his face against her hair.

She wasn't saying anything, but this had to be a good sign.

Eventually, she let him go, her eyes shining, the tip of her nose a little red. "I love you too, Wright McAdams. You big dummy, I've loved you for years."

He kissed her, with enough force that this time they did fall back on the bed. He kissed her like he hadn't seen her in weeks.

Affectionate, seeking kisses, like long-lost lovers.

Then her tongue sought his, and the kisses quickly turned sensual, hungry.

Sophie slid her legs around him, wrapping them around his waist, holding him close.

Wright pushed himself up on one arm, brushing her hair back on the pillow with his free hand. "I want you so bad right now."

"I'm right here." She arched against him.

He kissed her, finding his favorite freckles again, following the trail of his kisses with his hands, stripping Sophie bare. She tugged at his clothes and there were no more words.

He loved her, and she loved him. And her family knew it. That was all he needed to know about his future. The rest, they'd find together.

"Please." Sophie writhed beneath him, grabbing his hand to touch her.

As soon as he brushed against her flesh, she moaned, ready and slick.

"God, Soph." He groaned and gripped the pillow.

"Now, Wright." With a surer touch and determination than she'd ever shown before, she shifted beneath him, stroking the length of his cock before hooking a leg around his hip.

Wright took her hips and sank into her, both of them shaking with the need.

They were wired and greedy, desperate kisses and loving touches, sweat trickling down his back within minutes.

She pushed at his shoulder and he got the hint, rolling over.

Sophie rose above him, hands planted on his chest, straddling his waist, and his cock deep inside her. She tossed her head, her hair falling over one shoulder, and he swore he could come from the sight alone.

Arching her lower back, she moved her hips, riding him. Wright thrust into her, committing every sensation to memory.

Even if he had this, for the rest of his life, he'd never have enough. He wanted to remember every detail, every noise of pleasure like he'd memorized Sophie's freckles.

Sophie leaned forward, pressing her lips to his, and when she eased away, she was smiling, her happiness unmistakable.

Wright came, and she came with him, crying out his name.

It wasn't until moments later, both of them lying in tumbled sheets, that Sophie spoke again. "In the spirit of trusting each other with the truth, there's something else you should know about me."

He rolled to face her, his hand on her hip.

"Sometimes, when I'm stressed out, I talk to my parents. My birth parents. It's weird, they're dead, I know, but it helps. I used to think I was a little nuts, but I don't even care anymore. I just wanted you to know."

He smiled, running his hand up her side. "Thank you. And that's not weird. It helps you. That's all that matters. *Weird* is talking to food, which I do sometimes. When I'm cooking. I get frustrated or stressed, and I cook and talk to the food. Or if a dish isn't turning out the way I want. That's mostly cursing."

Sophie's giggle was beautiful music.

"I raised hell at a soufflé one time. It'd already fallen, so I figured what could it hurt?" As soon as he mentioned the soufflé debacle, he remembered the other part of his apology for Sophie. "Oh shit." Wright half fell out of bed as he hurried to the hotel room door.

"Where are you going?" Sophie sat up, tugging a sheet free to wrap around her.

"Hang on."

He jerked a towel off the rod in the bathroom, wrapped it around his waist, and quickly checked the hall. Perfect. No people, only an insulated bag.

"Yes." He hurried back into the room.

"What is that?"

"The other half of my apology." He plopped the bag on the bed and crawled on as she unzipped it.

"Are you kidding me? Wright!" Sophie's face lit up as she covered her mouth, dissolving into giggles.

That reaction was precisely why he'd taken the time to bake another bourbon cherry pie.

He tugged two forks from the side compartment. "I was hoping if my words weren't enough, I could win you over with food."

"A pie a day until I forgive you?"

"Something like that." He passed her a fork. "Here. Dig in."

Sophie stayed his hand before he could dip in. "Okay, but wait. I want you to fill me in on everything Dev said. Whatever I missed because I was a chicken and ran away."

"Soph—"

"No. I did. I ran away. But I'm never running again. And . . . you have to decide on Charleston or Asheville?"

His stomach jumped. "Yeah."

Tapping the fork against her lips, she was quiet a moment. "Well . . . I'm okay with either. We'll make it work, no matter what. But Asheville is a *really* cute town."

Losing his battle, he broke out into a grin.

"I'm just saying. Not as cute as Windamere, but close."

He leaned over the pie and pressed his lips to her temple. "I know. And I would love to tell you all about the job offer and the restaurant there."

"Over pie?"

"Over pie." He nodded.

Sophie held her fork up. "Then an oath."

"A pie oath?"

She rolled her eyes. "I guess so. We have beer apologies and pie oaths. I don't know, put your fork up."

Wright put his fork up.

"From now on, no more hiding and no more lies. We'll trust each other with the truth."

"And our hearts," he added.

"Yes." She bit at her lip in thought. "And when it's only the two of us, we never use pie plates."

He smiled and tapped his fork against hers. "Ever."

Chapter 27

Her insides were knotted up like a pretzel, but she was doing this. Her grip on Wright's hand tight enough to probably cut off his circulation, she reached the door of Roark's office.

"All you have to do is listen," he reminded her.

Last night, he'd told her she should hear her mother out, but whether or not she and her brothers chose to forgive, move on, hold on to their anger—that was up to them. But for Wright, would she at least listen? He wanted this for her, for the pain of the past to start to heal.

"I know."

"Do you want me to go in with you?"

She did, but she needed to do this on her own. She was strong enough. "No. Thank you. Stay close, though. I'll find you right after."

With another reassuring squeeze, Wright kissed her, and she walked into the office.

Inside, Suzanne Bradley sat in one of the two guest chairs opposite Roark, and two other chairs were squeezed in around his desk, not quite making a circle.

She took the seat between Dev and Trevor, Trevor sitting closest to their mom.

"Thank you for talking with me." Sue spoke first. "I know the timing was awful, and I should've called first." Her gaze found Trevor. "But when I talked to Trev and he told me Devlin's news and about the inn . . . I guess I got ahead of myself. And I'm sorry for that." Sue dipped her chin, studying her hands in her lap. "It's not all I'm sorry for."

Everyone remained quiet. A stifling silence until she spoke again.

"That really is why I'm here. I can't imagine the stuff running through your minds, but I'm only here to say I'm proud of what you all have done here and...I'm sorry. For everything."

Trevor fidgeted, chewing on his lips until finally, he spoke up. "This didn't come out of nowhere, guys. We . . . it took a while to come to this. We've spoken a lot over the last few months and maybe I should've said something, but I didn't think y'all were ready. *I* wasn't ready. But when mom said her doctor thought making amends and setting things straight with her kids was important . . ." He shrugged. "I know it's the right thing to do."

"But popping up here and saying you're sorry doesn't magically make everything right." Dev didn't look at anyone; resentment shrouding his face.

Sophie wanted to reach for him, somehow make everything better, but she couldn't. This wasn't her wrong to set right. Maybe it couldn't be set right. Either way, now she knew she could be there for her brother, but the weight of peace wasn't hers to bear.

"I know that." Sue spoke to the floor. "And I know what's done is done."

"Damn right it is," Dev muttered.

"But I couldn't go the rest of my life not saying I'm sorry. I'm sorry I left. I shouldn't have, but I was weak. I'm better now. Well enough to know how badly I messed up. I can't go back and fix what I did wrong and I don't expect forgiveness. I struggled and this place . . ." She glanced around. "This wasn't for me. We did our best, but our best was nowhere near enough. I was sick, and not treating it. Your father drank and that didn't help his temper."

Dev cut his eyes over toward Roark.

"We thought about divorcing when all of you were younger. Then we thought about selling Honeywilde. Selling out, giving this up. But we didn't want to quit. Not on this place or on you kids. Selling off Honeywilde would've meant—We didn't want to rob you of what was rightfully yours. Roark loved this place. Your grandfather wanted it to be yours someday. Sophie, you loved it. We knew all of you could do so much more than we ever did, and this place . . ." she cleared her throat, quiet for a handful of seconds. "This place was all we had to give you. The inn kept you kids together. We couldn't give away what was yours."

Silence fell again, and Sophie realized she was trembling. No longer because of her nerves, but from shock. She had never imagined hearing an apology from her mother. She'd assumed they'd all go the rest of their lives with the weight of resentment dragging around behind them like a ball and chain.

Not that any of them were ready to forgive and forget, but to even have an apology to consider was more than she'd ever hoped for.

Their mother's voice was shaky when she spoke again. "And you've done so well with it. All of you. You're better than we were, always have been."

"We're not better than you." Roark finally spoke, drawing Sophie's attention. "Maybe we're more committed because this is something we actually want, but we're not better people. We've struggled too."

"But we didn't quit on each other." Dev glared at Roark.

"I know. You're exactly right." Roark gave him a firm nod. "We didn't quit, and we won't. We have each other to lean on. Maybe you guys didn't have anyone, but we do."

Sophie thought about where she'd be without her brothers. How alone she'd be without them. How isolated she would have become. She only had them because the Bradleys had agreed to take her in.

"You did do one thing right though." Sophie's voice cracked as she shifted in her seat. Dev scowled at her, but she smiled softly, looking at him and her brothers as she spoke. "You gave me a family, even though you didn't have to."

Dev swallowed hard.

"You took me in, and yeah, it was hard. Our childhood was okay and then it wasn't, but I wasn't alone. And if . . . you know, if for no other reason than that, I feel like I should try. I can try to forgive you."

Trevor shot her a hopeful glance.

"I can't promise anything and I can't forget the past. I don't think any of us can. I don't speak for my brothers, but I . . . I will try."

Trevor took her hand. "Our childhood wasn't ideal, but it wasn't all bad. We had one another. You gave us that at least."

Dev's face was still a blank mask. It would take more than one apology for him to forgive and move on. But maybe this was a start. "You gave us each other. I'm glad for that, but the rest . . ." He shook his head. "I can't suddenly get over everything else and move past it. Even if I wanted to."

Sue's voice was wobbly, her eyes wet. "I don't expect you to. I'm not asking for anything in return. I can't. That's part of what my doctor told me. All I wanted was a chance to talk to you."

Dev jerked his chin down in a nod.

All of them sat in silence. What else was there to say right now? There was plenty they could say, but Sophie was wrung out. She imagined her brothers felt the same.

Still, they couldn't sit there forever.

Roark was the one to finally speak up.

The act was so reassuring, it made Sophie smile.

"So...you've talked and we listened." His face remained stoic, but she could see the storm of emotion in his eyes. "And that's probably enough for now. Unless anyone has something else?"

No one spoke or made eye contact. Roark's tone and open-ended "for now" left the opportunity for more. Nothing was miraculously fixed, but this family meeting was light-years better than the disaster she'd expected.

This wasn't the end of the world, and her family hadn't fallen apart in the face of their past.

Her life was still in one piece. And she was still happy.

As everyone began to shift and move, she had to say it. One last thing before they didn't speak again until who knew when.

Something she needed to voice, for herself as much as anyone else. "I want to say, before you leave..." She turned to her mom. The woman who took her in, even though she could barely manage the children and life she already led. "I was shocked, the other night, and defensive, but I'm glad you came back to talk to us."

The rest, she didn't say directly to anyone. Maybe she spoke to her brothers or maybe to herself. A reminder for times she was sure to need it. "I don't know how we make peace with the past, and we might not ever get there. We may never get over the hurt, and maybe we'll always be a little frayed at the edges. But that's okay. We're doing okay exactly like we are. Everything doesn't have to be perfect in order for me to be happy."

Epilogue

A month later...

"You make the prettiest best man." Wright twirled a lock of her hair around his finger.

She smoothed the collar of his shirt. "I don't know, you're looking mighty pretty yourself."

"And I feel pretty." He winked as he scooped her closer, his hand at the small of her back. "When Dev told me we got to forgo tuxes in favor of khakis and a nice shirt, I think I hollered. Then I hugged him."

Though she would love to see Wright in a tux someday, the look Anna and Dev had chosen for their wedding was beautiful, and fitting. She and Madison and Anna's cousin wore dresses they'd chosen for themselves in shades of off-white, while Wright and Dev both wore dress khakis and crisp white shirts.

Enough seating for about forty people, tops, lined a semicircle near the edge of the lake, and Brenda, their florist, had arranged a few pieces with cascades of white and rich green.

For a casual, early fall wedding at sunset, it was perfect.

Knowing the two people getting married would make each other happy for the rest of their days was even better.

And they would definitely be happy. If they were lucky, maybe they'd be as happy as Sophie.

The thought no longer scared her the way it once did.

Occasionally, she'd get a wave of panic. Everything would go a little too well for a while—Wright keeping his apartment so when he was off work he was close, or having a nice phone chat with her mom, or Dev sitting with her in the restaurant at night as they finished up their work for the day and telling her how much it meant to see her and

Wright truly together, and how they fit each other so well—and she'd get scared. Convinced that somehow everything she had would be taken away.

But Wright was always there for her, and he'd remind her that though there would be bad days to balance out the good, letting herself be happy didn't mean she would chase it away.

"Okay, stop pawing each other. You're going to wrinkle, and Madison will chew our asses." Dev shoved at Wright's shoulder. "How do I look? Do I look okay? You guys look great."

Wright let himself be peeled away and checked Dev over. "You look like you're about to get hitched."

Her brother was nervous, and it was adorable.

Off and on for weeks now, he'd get bouts of giddiness and nerves, a rarity for Devlin Bradley. But it was proof of his feelings for Anna.

"You leaving for Asheville this weekend?" Dev shifted on his feet, incapable of being still.

Wright shot her a look. "Nah, I'm hanging around all week to make sure Marco is up to speed. Then I start at the flagship restaurant next weekend. New South cuisine, all garden to table, very high end."

"Hoity-toity." Dev grinned. "Do you get one of those tall white hats? Set shit on fire, but on purpose this time?"

"Ha ha. No on the hat. Yes to the flambé."

Dev glanced at Sophie with a small smile. "Asheville isn't so bad, I guess. You guys can make it work."

Yes, they could.

"We're definitely making it work." Wright gave words to how she felt.

Dev clapped him on the back a little harder than necessary in his enthusiasm. "I'm happy for you, man. I think someday . . . eventually, you'll be back, but whatever. I'm happy for you."

They shared a grin.

"Oh, I'll be back?" Wright asked.

"Not right away. I know you've got to go sow your wild food oats or whatever it is you chefs do, but someday." Dev shrugged. "Shit happens. You get married to my sister, have kids. You'll be back at Honeywilde."

Wright's mouth dropped open a millisecond before Sophie's.

"Dev." She shoved his arm.

"Don't give me those looks. You date my sister, your ass better marry her someday. Or if she doesn't want to get married, do whatever it is she wants. You make her happy, that's all I ask."

Wright saluted him, earning a choice curse word, but Dev was still smiling.

The truth struck Sophie, powerful.

Wright needed to go off and be his own man, work for people he hadn't known his entire life and learn more. *Do* more; be challenged and prove he was capable. But years from now . . .

Who knew what might happen?

And for the first time in her life, she wasn't scared of the future or the possibilities.

"Okay, everyone look at me. Let me see you." Madison appeared, snapping her fingers at them. "Good. Good. Wright, you have the rings?"

"Yes ma'am. In my pocket." He patted them and gave Sophie a wink that made her toes curl.

"Great, let's go ahead and take our places. Roark is with Anna. So beautiful, Dev, oh my god." She put her hand over her heart.

With her father gone and her mother barely willing to attend, Anna had asked Roark to walk her down the aisle.

He had agreed, stone-faced but with a tremor in his voice.

Sophie wondered if it hit him then the way it'd hit her: Their family was growing. Hopefully it would only continue to grow, which meant more people to love, and have their love in return.

The thought warmed her heart, with only a little bit of worry. Because loving people didn't mean losing them, and allowing them to love you in return was the key to finding—and keeping—happiness.

"Where is Trevor?" Madison searched for their brother, who was supposed to be in charge of cueing the music.

"I believe he's gotten distracted by Brooke." Sophie pointed to the front row.

Their mother sat on one side of him. Trevor miraculously convinced Dev to let her attend, and Dev's agreement shocked all of them, but then that's what Dev did best. Brooke sat on Trevor's other side.

Trev seemed mesmerized by the chateau's manager.

"Who?"

"Brooke. The manager at Jolie. You'll meet her at the reception. She's awesome." And out of Trevor's league.

As Madison went to cue Trev to cue the music, Sophie turned to Wright. "A kiss before we take our places?"

"I thought you'd never ask." He leaned down and pressed his mouth to hers, the tip of his tongue tickling the seam of her lips, a promise of things to come.

Desire and love, friendship, faithfulness, and so much more.

Not only tonight, but tomorrow and the day after that. Now she could look forward to the future rather than fear it, her arms open to welcome whatever the world brought her and cling tightly to those she loved most.

ABOUT THE AUTHOR

Heather McGovern writes contemporary romance in swoony Southern settings. While her love of travel and adventure takes her far, there is no place quite like home. She lives in South Carolina with her husband and son and a collection of Legos that's threatening to take over the house. When she isn't writing, she's working out or binging on books and Netflix.

She is a member of Romance Writers of America, as well as Carolina Romance Writers, and she's represented by Nicole Resciniti of the Seymour Agency.

Connect with Heather on her website, Facebook, Twitter, or her group blog. She'd love to hear from you!

heathermcgovernnovels.com
www.facebook.com/Heather.McGovern.Novels
https://twitter.com/heathermcgovern
https://badgirlzwrite.com

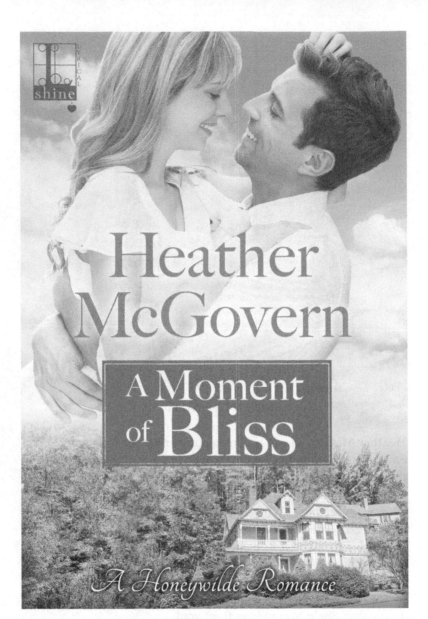

Heather McGovern

A Moment of Bliss

A Honeywilde Romance

Heather
McGovern

A Date with
Desire

A Honeywilde Romance